BLOOD PERFECT

A Joe Turner Mystery

T.L. BEQUETTE

Black Rose Writing | Texas

©2022 by T.L. Bequette
All rights reserved. No part of this book may be reproduced, stored in a retrieval system or transmitted in any form or by any means without the prior written permission of the publishers, except by a reviewer who may quote brief passages in a review to be printed in a newspaper, magazine or journal.

The author grants the final approval for this literary material.

First printing

This is a work of fiction. Names, characters, businesses, places, events, and incidents are either the products of the author's imagination or used in a fictitious manner. Any resemblance to actual persons, living or dead, or actual events is purely coincidental.

ISBN: 978-1-68433-996-9
PUBLISHED BY BLACK ROSE WRITING
www.blackrosewriting.com

Printed in the United States of America
Suggested Retail Price (SRP) $20.95

Blood Perfect is printed in Baskerville

*As a planet-friendly publisher, Black Rose Writing does its best to eliminate unnecessary waste to reduce paper usage and energy costs, while never compromising the reading experience. As a result, the final word count vs. page count may not meet common expectations.

Praise for
BLOOD PERFECT

"T. L. Bequette masterfully builds his series, creating growth in his characters through each novel. Combining supreme character building and a fast-paced mystery… readers won't be able to set the book down until the final page. In short, Joe Turner is well on the way to becoming a fixture in contemporary mystery fiction."
–Chanticleer Book Reviews

"After his rousing debut, *Good Lookin'* (2021), Bequette returns with a tale that solidifies Turner as a charmingly reliable champion of the innocent."
–Kirkus Reviews

"5/5 Stars. A fantastic read for fans of courtroom drama, light detective work, and endings with a twist… that will keep you interested from cover to cover."
–San Francisco Book Reviews

"Fascinating… entices the reader on the opening page to dive into a stunningly readable and exciting effort. I am waiting impatiently for the next book in what I hope is a long series."
–Mark Hewitt, award-winning author of the *Duncan Hunter Thriller* series

BLOOD PERFECT

BLOOD PERFECT

PROLOGUE

Closing argument had always been my favorite part of a jury trial. Some attorneys relished the cross examination of a hostile witness, but I found it unpleasantly confrontational. Direct examination of my client was fraught with disaster—like the time my client accused of drunk driving began slurring his words on the stand.

But closing arguments were just me, selling my case to the jury. The stifling rules about mischaracterizing evidence were put on hold in the closing, and it was always the most relaxing and enjoyable part of the trial.

All of this made what was happening to me at this very second quite unthinkable.

My closing had begun well enough. I'd spoken about the prosecution's burden of proof and was making good eye contact with some of the jurors. I was commenting on my client's upbringing in Oakland and his various means of employment when it happened.

Until that instant, so much of the case had baffled me and I'd had the distinct impression that there were forces at work unknown to me. But just then, my own words jostled the jigsaw puzzle in my brain, and a stray piece settled perfectly into place. The puzzle now complete, its image shook me to my core.

I stopped in mid-sentence and felt a wave of heat flush my face. Reaching for the railing of the jury box, the floor began to undulate under my feet. I turned toward the judge to request a recess, but all at once the courtroom's lights rapidly dimmed.

And now I lay face down in the courtroom. I feel hands patting my shoulders and taste blood on my bottom lip.

CHAPTER 1

Four Days Ago, August 25, 2021

"Who is Roger Moore?" Yellow teeth crunched an apple slice as he settled back into a cracked leather sofa. A brown tweed sweater sagged from his arms. "Who fucking knows," he sighed, loosening his belt a notch.

He stared at the shiny flat screen on the wall of his cramped apartment, the television a gift from his granddaughter. She acted like she had given him a rocket ship. He didn't like the glare.

At sixty-five, he had taken the job as caretaker of this crap hotel called the Islander. His brother-in-law had made it seem more like an ocean front resort than a seedy flophouse in west Oakland. He snorted at the absurdity.

"Who is Joe DiMaggio." He smiled at the memory, his bald spot cooled by the worn leather. "Joe D.," he sighed. "That wop could hit." A toe pried off one shoe, then the other, the leather loafers falling to an oval rug he had purchased on a reservation in Arizona.

"Who is, uh. . . Neil Armstrong. . .John Glenn. Okay Alex, so fucking smart with the answers in your hands."

He exhaled and shifted his shoulders, melding into his spot. Today had been the first day of the month and that made it his least favorite. Everyone had an excuse. I got laid off, I got robbed, my mom died. One tenant's mom died every three or four months.

But no matter how lame the excuse, he was the bad guy. If you can't pay the freight, just say so, or better yet, move out. But stop with the lying excuses. Try working a day in your miserable life. And no, I'm not going to lend you fifty bucks so you can buy dope, and no, you can't use the office phone.

He wouldn't be in this shithole much longer though, thanks to his brother's half-wit son, Denny. The kid couldn't be trusted behind the front desk, but damn if he couldn't play the ponies. It was like that retard in the movie who could count cards. Kid spent every waking hour down at the stables, shoveling shit, feeding them carrots and placing bets. Claims he conversates with the horses somehow. Loopy fucker can think what he wants if he keeps bringing in seven hundred a week. The kid don't even care that he keeps the winnings. Give him a twenty once in a while and keep him in carrots and he's happy as a pig in slop.

CHAPTER 2

—Joe,

Sorry I haven't been in touch in a while (if you consider a decade a while.) I know it's strange to email you out of the blue, but a family friend who lives in Oakland needs a good criminal defense attorney (some minor matter of an attempted murder), and the last I heard, you defended criminals, I mean, defended the rights of the accused. Anyway, I found your website and tracked you down. The accused is a gardener my mom knows. His girlfriend might call. If so, blame me.

How are you? Married? Children? Time in prison? I'd love to hear from you. I'm a real estate agent in LA and have a beautiful six-year old daughter, Isabella. We're currently arguing about the bath. Gotta go.

Amanda Kensey—

"Morning, Turner. So how can you possibly top your titanic jaywalking victory?"

"The Monert case, I guess." I gestured toward an accordion file on my desk.

"Oh wow. You're actually going to try that case?"

"That's what I do, Andy. I try cases. You know, in a courtroom. You've probably seen one on television?"

"Isn't this the guy who was found passed out at the wheel? Let me guess, it was prescription meds for his ailing back?" My partner,

Andrew Kopp, had strolled into our modest third-floor office on the outskirts of downtown Oakland to pick up his mail and offer his usual brand of encouragement. He was a personal injury lawyer, and we spent most of our time in the office denigrating each other's practices.

"He was sleeping, Andy. Can't a guy get some shut-eye on the side of the road without being arrested? And more importantly, he's a truck driver, so if he pleads out, he's fired."

"Then by all means, keep him on the streets behind the wheel of a giant truck. No wonder you drink so much," he said, eyeing empties overflowing our recycling bin. "You need it to live with yourself," a parting shot, as he headed for the elevator.

"Beats heavy lifting," I called after him.

Andy had interrupted my reply to Amanda's email, which had interrupted important fantasy baseball research, which had interrupted my preparation for a singularly boring drunk driving trial I had no chance to win.

Amanda was my one that got away. At least that's the way I saw it, my small mind conveniently disregarding the fact that we'd never dated. Not to mention she had been out of my league, both in appearance and college social standing. A late bloomer in every respect, pimples had dotted my boyish face throughout most of college. I was 6'2" like my dad, and while I had inherited his athletic frame and strong jaw, a lack of confidence made me slouch. At least, that's what my mom told me well into my twenties. I'd never even set foot in the leafy sorority neighborhood Amanda called home. My friends and I referred to it as "the land of the beautiful people."

I also saw no reason to believe that she knew how I felt. We'd been friends since meeting in our freshman seminar class at Cal, and I recalled times spent with her like yesterday. I remember the first moment I became smitten. We had made plans to hang out one afternoon. When I asked what she wanted to do, she'd shrugged her shoulders and deadpanned, "I don't know. Get drunk, throw rocks?" This was the girl for me.

We passed an entire Friday afternoon on the roof of my dorm, tormenting passersby and people watching. We'd kissed passionately once our senior year, both drunk on Sangria. When she fell asleep I quietly left her room. When she didn't mention it the next time I saw her, I wondered if she remembered it at all.

Exotic looking, with thick black hair and mocha skin, she came from a family that didn't fit the Cal mold—mixed race, a single mom, a brother in rehab. In a world of over-stressed students, I admired her impetuous free spirit. She once kidnapped me to go bowling during finals and it was probably the most fun I'd had in my life. Also, our senses of humor matched, making for immediate chemistry. (Our senses of humor had actually made us fast friends, but I preferred to focus on the chemistry.)

Chronically self-conscious, I admired her self-assuredness and respected her strength. Despite these fond memories, my feelings remained unspoken, fearing a version of the inevitable "let's-not-ruin-our-friendship" rejection.

—Amanda,
It was great to hear from you, although I'm somewhat embarrassed you found my lame website. Just what I always wanted to be known for: drugs, domestic violence, and sex crimes. I'd appreciate any ideas on the site. I'm contemplating a new slogan, "Setting America Free, One Felon at a Time."
I heard through the grapevine how your marriage turned out. Very sorry. So the guy actually left you while you were pregnant? Isn't that against some sort of marital code or something? Good God.
I'm sure you're stunned I'm still single, what with my job as defender of felons being such a babe magnet.
Thanks again for emailing me and sending along the referral. I'll keep you apprised of the fate of the gardener.
JT—

CHAPTER 3

It usually comes after I have wine with dinner or eat red meat. Sometimes when I sleep, or like today when I'm quiet and alone in my office. Generally, I sense it coming on, slowly gathering around the edges of my mind. I can keep it there a while by filling my brain with other thoughts. Lots of little realities work best. But that's tiring and I can still feel it looming there. It always comes in the end, so it's probably better to just let it happen.

I am following her inside, my view through the lens of a jerky home movie projector. Her heels tap a familiar cadence on cement, then hardwood, a comforting orange and green dress pattern in view above, tan shiny calves just below eye level.

Then all hell breaks loose.

The screen goes black for a moment as a soundtrack of deep, distorted groans pounds my ears. She screams my father's name, rushing to his side and the screen is lit again, her slender, flailing arms and panicked face framed by the warm yellow walls of my childhood kitchen. She moves as if on ice, slipping to the linoleum, confused and floundering. Jagged screams pierce my ears, then softer heaves of sorrow as the lens begins to streak. She slips to the floor again, then rises to meet my eyes, the projector frozen in a close-up of her terrified helplessness.

Then I am warm in her arms, her soft scented hands blocking my view, moving quickly down a hallway. My face burrows into her overcoat and its familiar smell. I press my face into its textured fabric and squeeze my eyes tight, tunneling away from the horror of the kitchen, clinging to my gently quivering mother.

I was twelve when my dad was murdered. I don't remember when I stopped trying to remember his death, but it was around the time the flashbacks began.

I remember missing my bed when we stayed in a hotel afterwards and the loneliness of moving into a smaller house across town. I recall hating the funeral and wondering how hearing stories about him while wearing uncomfortable clothes was supposed to be comforting. Mainly, I remember the gaping void in my life that followed. As for the murder, though, all that was left was the chaotic and cryptic home movie that showed details without perspective.

Still breathing heavily, I reclined at my desk, feeling the familiar nauseous regret. I wiped my clammy brow and gazed around the room, searching for my mind's escape.

My eyes fell on an empty beer bottle resting in its sweat ring on my white oak desk. I smiled, recalling the mock celebration with Andy following the morning's victory in a jaywalking case. I was certain the judge's sole concern was reaching a verdict before lunch time. I gathered myself for a walk to the office kitchen and another beer. I had hoped to work late, but knew I'd be worthless now.

After a time, I managed to refocus and complete some very important fantasy baseball research before heading for my train ride home. It was Friday, after all. My favorite sport was still on my mind as I waited for the elevator.

When I was eleven, I convinced my parents to send me away to baseball camp where I became friends with a boy named Ray Borges, who had the gift of spitting very accurately. This fascinated me to no end since I loved everything about baseball, not the least of all, spitting. Soon, I could place a soda bottle on the ground and spit into its narrow neck.

As I boarded the elevator for the ride to the lobby, I noticed its creaks and groans, even louder in the vacant building. As I descended, my thoughts turned to the baseball playoffs and spitting.

From years of use, I knew that when the elevator door slid open, a two-inch gap formed a little larger than the neck of a coke bottle. Feeling nostalgic, I lined up over my target, my head as close to the door of the elevator as possible and prepared for my window of opportunity. Channeling Ray, when the door opened I let loose an unusually long and drippy swath of saliva. Out of practice, the string of spit clung to my bottom lip and dropped in slow motion, bottoming out, then inching toward the floor.

I saw her first in my peripheral vision while my lip remained tied to the floor. My eyes strained upward, gradually and painfully aware that I had stopped short of the lobby and that I wasn't the only one working late.

Of course, it was her.

I had seen her twice before, each time in the elevator where we exchanged silent greetings and goodbyes, her smiling casually, me, gawking more than gazing into her green eyes, smelling something vaguely lime, wishing I could be witty.

I deduced that she worked for the Office of the Oakland Symphony, having eliminated the only other occupant on the second floor, the Meat Cutters Local 47. I had even thought of something to say next time we met. "You guys are pretty quiet for a symphony," I would quip, spontaneously. Not a terrible line, no risk to offend, easy to remember.

Glancing upward, lip still tied to the floor, I caught only glimpses: strawberry blonde waves, a flash of pearls, pointy shoes pausing briefly before leaping past me, retreating to the far corner of the elevator behind me. I decided to save my symphony line for another time.

CHAPTER 4

Four Days Ago, August 25, 2021

Twenty blocks away, Sergeant Thomas Simmons ducked under the police tape that marked the scene of an attempted murder. At least it wasn't a homicide. His case clearance rate needed a boost, and providing the victim cooperated, there would be at least one witness to the crime.

"Vans, give me some good news." The Sergeant and Officer Vanner had been classmates in the academy over a decade ago.

"Hey, Tom. You drew the long straw for once. Stabbing victim told me the perp's name and room number. It'll only cost you a beer."

"No shit? You got it."

"The vic said, and I quote, 'Allston Walker stabbed me. He lives in room 112.'"

CHAPTER 5

On my ride home, still reeling from the elevator fiasco, my cell phone rang.

"Hi, Mom," I answered, unenthusiastically. Non-weekend calls usually meant a family member needed legal advice. My family, being litigious and frugal, never hesitates in this regard.

"Hello, Joseph. Sorry to bother you, and I know you are so busy, and I wouldn't ask, but the poor man just seems so lost. . ."

"What's up, Mom?"

"Well, it's your great Uncle Gene. It seems he's drafted a will using one of those online services but now has forgotten what's in it. He's wondering if you could read it and sort of outline it for him?"

"Mom, I hate to sound rude, but this is the third time this month. And I know even less about wills than I do about your car insurance policy or Aunt Helen's landlord issue."

"I know, Joe, and you're so generous with your time. I'll just forward Gene's email and you can ignore it if you want."

"Truly, mom, it's not about the time." Truly, it was mostly about the time. "It's just that I'm a criminal defense attorney, and this family has me committing malpractice right and left."

"Okay, thanks. Love you. Talk to you Sunday."

"Love you. Bye, Mom." I grumbled to myself that if I owned a gas station, my family members would probably just pull up to the pump without paying.

My objection to my mother's request was rare. Having paid for my education, for her it was inconceivable I could know so little about so many aspects of the law. Not wanting to disappoint, I rendered opinions on everything from community property to the finer points of tax law, fashioning my counsel through vague recollections of law school concepts, common sense, and discussions with Andy, who seems to have paid more attention in law school.

The calls received at the office from criminal defendants who pay are more welcome and less mentally taxing. Immediate advice is usually some version of "Don't talk to the police," or "Don't lead the police to the place where you may have heard a body is buried."

Simple communication, however, can be difficult. The San Francisco Bay Area is one of the most ethnically diverse areas in the world, so language barriers are common.

But by far the biggest obstacle in speaking with my clients cuts across all nationalities. Whether it is attributable to the nerves that accompany being accused of a crime, their fear of leaving out an important detail or, as I suspect, a genetic trait linked to criminal behavior, a remarkable number of my clients find it utterly impossible to summarize anything. The criminal mind is linear.

"Mr. Blauman, how long after your last drink did you leave the bar?"

"Well, I arrived at the bar around four, mainly because of the traffic. My first drink was a whiskey sour. I had an argument with Fred about the Raiders—He's a Niners guy. That must have been around 5:30 p.m. and then we started doing shots. . ."

I've often wondered how many crimes are committed for lack of forethought and believe that linear thinking is likely the sociological key to aberrant behavior. At a minimum, it makes communication with my clients the most difficult part of my job.

A few days later, after poring over my uncle's indecipherable Last Will and Testament, I returned the phone call of one Stephanie Hartung. After enduring a fact-intensive account of her last forty-eight hours on earth and dispensing some cautionary advice about speaking to the police, I agreed to visit her boyfriend in the Alameda County Jail. His name was Allston Walker.

CHAPTER 6

On the fifteen-mile drive from Oakland to the Santa Rita Jail, I stole glances at Allston Walker's inmate profile. His bail was one million dollars. It would take one hundred thousand, secured by property, for him to walk out the front door of Santa Rita, the main jail serving Alameda County.

Some places are nice to visit, but you wouldn't want to live there. Jail is neither. Santa Rita is a cruel place in many respects. For starters, it's named for the Patron Saint of Lost, Impossible and Forgotten Causes. Why not just name the place the Dungeon of Hopelessness?

Also, the jail is surrounded by verdant rolling hills. While a lot of the jail is below ground and windowless, an inmate's occasional glimpse of the hills or whiff of the gentle breezes must seem tantalizingly close, yet completely unattainable.

The visiting conditions at the Santa Rita Jail discourage visitation. Both inmate and visitor sit in tiny, musty rooms that mirror each other, separated by soundproof glass. The rooms are five feet by four feet, just large enough for stainless steels stools, bolted to the floor on each side of the glass. Phones hang from the wall on stiff metal cords that stretch just short of the stools so that each party must lean uncomfortably toward the wall or stand while bent at the waist.

As the dread of the visit set in, as usual, I wondered why I had followed my father's footsteps in the law. I suppose, in some roundabout way, I chose my profession, but not really. What I chose was a very impractical major in college—history. I chose not to work for a museum, not to work after college at all, and not to enter the military or Peace Corps. I chose not to pursue an MBA out of fear of numbers, nor a graduate degree in history, satisfied with my vague overview of the subject. So law school it was.

Fresh out of Georgetown Law, I did a stint in the Bronx D.A.'s Office but was drawn back to the San Francisco Bay Area. It's where I grew up, the son of longtime District Attorney of Alameda County, Jack Turner.

I had enjoyed being a D.A. like my dad, but he had always spoken of defense as a noble pursuit. Besides, having my own private practice allowed for more freedom. That, and a few busybodies from the D.A.'s Human Resources Department needed to justify their jobs.

Their interview had been so transparent. Did I wish I drank less? The correct answer was yes. Every non-alcoholic who drank at all would say so for general health reasons, whereas an alcoholic would be in total denial. Did I have a rule about drinking before 5:00 p.m.? Of course not, because if you need to have a rule, there's a problem. So I had aced the test, but in the long run it had seemed prudent to leave.

Now I practiced criminal defense in Oakland, location being the key to both real estate and criminal defense, only in the inverse. You wouldn't want to live in most of Oakland, and that's why it's perfect for a criminal defense practice. Poet Gertrude Stein famously remarked about the city, "There's no there, there." That may be so, but there's plenty of violence there. Lately, there'd been a murder in the city roughly every other day.

As I waited for my prospective client in the damp room, chilled by my steel seat, I wondered about his explanation. Would it be the complete denial of everything? "Honestly, sir, I don't even know nothing about nothing. Why I'm here, who got shot, and why anyone would want to shoot Boogy."

Or would it be the unintentional admission? "It was self-defense. I saw him ball up his fist like he wanted to hit me, so I had no choice but to pump seven rounds into his chest."

Allston Walker took his place on the other side of the glass, our faces only a foot apart. Immediately, I knew his appearance would not help his cause. So distinctive was his face that it was difficult to imagine how anyone could have mistaken Walker for any other human on earth, let alone the man who tried to kill him with a knife. Pale brown skin stretched taut over small features. His closely shaved hairline was nearly invisible, faded brown meeting gray, giving the first impression of baldness. Pink eyes darted from a crevice.

Up close, his face appeared compressed from top to bottom. Pinched together like play dough, his features formed from a series of horizontal wrinkles. His face seemed wider than it was long, as if it had been removed and replaced sideways on his long, sinewy neck. His mouth was in permanent grimace, his eyes in constant squint. The face was not nice, I thought. In fact, it looked rather mean.

CHAPTER 7

Hi Joe,
Great to hear from you. Thanks for reassuring me that my ex (I've taken to calling him "the 'hole'") was a little out of bounds. Yes, your profession is a little icky, but I bet you've got some great stories. I can see how defending criminals may not be a babe magnet, but I'm a little biased when it comes to attorneys. I just ended a relationship with one and have sworn off them. Attached are pictures of Isabella. Write back.
P.S. Did you ever marry Laura from college?

Amanda,
Here's a quick summary of why never to date attorneys. First, they're hyper-competitive, argumentative pricks. They are attracted to the profession because of these very traits. Think about it. Their jobs are to wade into other's disagreements and argue for them. Not just small disagreements, mind you. Only the ones where either freedom or money is at stake and there's no hope for compromise.
Second, lawyers are obsessed with hierarchy and titles. In what other profession are they so important? Within the law firm itself, there are senior partners, equity partners, partners, associates, paralegals, assistants and receptionists, all referred to by title without fail. Last names are used only for the important. Full names only when referring to those of higher rank. (My paralegal will

research that issue. My Partner, Al Blauman and our Senior Partner, Colin Murray will make the final decision. I'll leave the file with our receptionist.)

Most importantly for someone creative like you, attorneys are the least creative people in the world. The job saps every ounce of creativity from you like a giant sapper thing. Creativity to a lawyer is finding an interesting way to interpret the Code of Bankruptcy. (Oh, cool, if you read subsection (d) in conjunction with the case notes, perhaps the entire section is inapplicable!)

So, don't date lawyers. I, of course, prefer to think of myself as more of a barrister.

Laura married an obscenely wealthy investment banker who, I suppose, is rather handsome, if you like the male model look. (I like to think his penis is the size of an earthworm.)

Joe

Amanda's comment about criminal law being the source of good stories had taken me back to my childhood. Dad had grown up dirt poor in Arkansas and had either inherited or learned a unique ability to spin a yarn. Growing up in the Ozarks, he had explained that without television or radio, his friends and relatives would pass the time sometimes with music, but mostly just talking on the porch.

At bedtime, he would tell me hilarious stories, often drawing on his twenty years in the courtrooms of Alameda County for material. Dad embellished the tales and often included a talking animal and some flatulence – the height of comedy for most boys.

My favorite stories centered on the rulings of an incompetent judge named Alister Nincompoop, whose rulings Dad delivered with a haughty English accent. Nincompoop was renowned for being unable to make any difficult decision. I heard myself chuckle out loud recalling Dad's rambling rendition of the judge's interminable considerations of every aspect of a decision. "On the one hand..." the judge would say, seemingly nearing a decision, "but on the other..." as I laughed until my side hurt.

I pictured my dad, sitting on my bed, telling me about Everett Buttinski, who appeared before the judge for his forty-third violation of excessive public flatulence. Everyone wondered whether Buttinski would finally be jailed. On one hand, the offense was minor, but on the other, Buttinski's loud farts were a menace. It would be a tough decision for Judge Nincompoop in a packed and smelly courtroom.

True to form, the judge passed the buck, rescheduling Buttinski's case in another department. At least for that day, Buttinski avoided incarceration. No one knew, however, that vowing to never be taken alive, Buttinski had strapped enough dynamite to his body to blow the roof off the courthouse. This all became apparent when, on the way home, Buttinski let loose a particularly powerful fart and hence became the first man ever—I would mouth the words with my dad—"to fart himself to death."

CHAPTER 8

After introducing myself, I expressed my hope that the arrest had been a big misunderstanding. Perhaps the victim had mistaken Walker for another man who lived in room 112. Wishfully, I asked, "Do you know who lives in 112?"

"I live in 112," came a gravelly response from one of the horizontal crevasses, "but I didn't stab the man."

"Okay," I replied, reassuring myself, poorly disguising my disappointment. "Well, is there, I mean, uh, any reason anyone would think you wanted to stab him?" Other than your face, of course, I thought to myself. "I mean, there's usually a motive for a violent crime like this. Will the victim be able to point to a disagreement that you had with him?"

"Yeah," he replied in three syllables of exaggerated disgust. "But I ain't gonna stab nobody over no seventy dollars."

I refrained from asking if he had stabbed the victim for any other reason. "Of course not, Mr. Walker. Did anyone see you arguing with the victim?"

"I'm not sure. Maybe Denny, his nephew, but he's usually at the track. Nice kid, but he's, you know, touched in the head. And I don't know, I think maybe Paul, the custodian, was there."

"Does Paul know you?"

"Yeah. Lives two doors down."

"Is this an apartment complex?"

"The Islander Hotel. In west Oakland. The victim is the caretaker there. Name's Devaney."

"So your argument was about rent?"

"Yeah, but I told you I ain't stabbing nobody…"

"Over no seventy dollars. I got that."

Since Walker seemed intent on testing my powers of optimism, I decided to switch gears and collect some harmless information about names and ages of various members of his family. Allston was never married, had a son and daughter about my age, and a girlfriend, presumably Ms. Hartung.

As I filled out my pre-printed form, I assessed: The victim had told the police that Allston Walker, who lived in room 112 of the Islander, had stabbed him within an inch of his life over a dispute about late rent money. The mean-looking man on the other side of the glass was named Allston Walker, lived in room 112, and had argued with the victim about the rent. At least, I thought, sarcastically, I had Walker's unequivocal denial that he would ever stab someone over an argument about seventy dollars.

I told Walker that Ms. Hartung had agreed to retain my services.

"That'd be her inheritance money. Hope you're worth it."

"Mr. Walker, I'll do my best for you, but it's up to you," I said, failing to hide my exasperation. "If you'd like for me to represent you, I will. If not, that's fine, too." Given his attitude and what little I knew about the case, I was half-rooting for a "no thanks."

"I guess anything's better than the public pretender," he shrugged, smiling at his hackneyed insult to the Alameda Public Defenders Office. Some of the most dedicated lawyers I knew worked in that office, but as with most free services their attorneys were vastly underappreciated by their clients.

With that ringing endorsement, I promised to see Walker in court in two days and turned away from him to push a button, signaling the end of my interview. "Is there anything you wanted to tell me before I leave, Mr. Walker?" I asked, apologizing for facing the opposite direction.

"Yeah. I just want you to know that I'm just…" The voice trailed off, then resumed, after a long sigh. "I'm just at a loss, man. I didn't do this. I didn't fucking stab that man. He must have thought it was me, but if you show him a picture of me, he's got to know it wasn't me." He paused and breathed deeply. "It ain't in me to stab nobody for no argument about money." Facing away from the scowl, the gravelly voice was deep, calm and unwavering.

Over the years, I have become proficient in reading people, particularly their truthfulness. This comes from listening to clients lie to my face through the bars of custody. There are unsophisticated liars, who will tell you they didn't do it, and even if they did, they didn't do it very much. Then there are the more sophisticated, obsequious, and upbeat combination car salesmen/game show hosts. Ultimately, they are usually revealed by trying too hard, betrayed both by the desperation brought on by their custody status and an enthusiasm for their craft.

The people behind bars who are telling the truth have no enthusiasm. If guilty, they are disappointed in themselves and resigned to their grim futures. If actually innocent, they are too devastated, too utterly despondent to pretend to be happy to see me, even if they think I will help. The damage has been done. Some of their life has been taken away, never to be returned, and you can taste their bitterness through the bars.

The innocent are first apoplectic, then disbelieving, then bitter, then depressed. As I drove away from the jail, I reflected on Allston Walker's visage, tinted yellow through the glass. Staring past the permanent grimace, I could see all these emotions close to the surface, peering through close-set eyes, seeping through the creases of his hardened face.

If my first impression of Allston Walker was mean, the next was innocent.

CHAPTER 9

My first appearance in court for my newest client was uneventful. I entered the case formally as Mr. Walker's attorney of record, pleaded not guilty on his behalf, and set the date for the preliminary hearing.

Walker, in no mood to "fart around," asserted his right to a speedy trial, so the preliminary hearing was set three weeks away, which gave me very little time to investigate the case and prepare for the hearing. More importantly, it probably would mean that Devaney would not recover in time to testify at the hearing, which was more of a concern for the defense than the prosecution.

In lieu of the victim, the prosecution would call police officers to testify as to Devaney's identification of the defendant. So one of the main benefits of a preliminary hearing for the defense—an opportunity to cross examine the victim—would not happen with Walker's no-farting schedule.

I walked to Ratto's Deli after court for a roast beef and Swiss and headed back to my office. Andy joined me in the elevator. "So, what's the defense to your new attempted murder? Let me guess. Your guy just got caught up?"

Andy's was a good guess. Getting "caught up" was by far my clients' most popular explanation for their arrests. The first time a suspect told me he got caught up, I assumed he committed the crime because he was caught up in the emotion of the moment. As in, "Everyone was shooting at everyone else, and I just got caught up and started shooting, too." This interpretation of "getting caught up" is incorrect.

As has since been made clear, the phrase is shorthand for being wrongfully arrested when "getting caught up" in the backwash of arrests that accompany any crime scene. To hear them tell it, police arrive and immediately begin arresting everyone in sight, without regard to their culpability. Truly innocent people, then, are caught up in the wave of arrests. It is remarkable how many law-abiding citizens get caught up like dolphins in a tuna net.

A review of the police reports in any given case usually paints a slightly different picture. Drafted by police who are motivated to justify the arrest and persuade the prosecutor to prosecute, arrest reports are not exactly an unbiased version of the facts. Anyway, I was relieved that "getting caught up" had never passed Walker's lips.

Between bites of my sandwich, I reviewed the mail, checked my phone—I was doing that more frequently lately—then cleared a space on my desk for the forty-six page police report documenting the attempted murder of Jefferson Beauregard Devaney by Allston Walker.

My phone buzzed, a text from Amanda.

—*A model and an investment banker? Obviously, she's married a psychopath. What really happened with you and Laura? You guys seemed very happy.*—

—*Amanda, please allow me to refer to myself in the third person, as does my current client Bernard Thibideaux. Joe lets life happen to him. In order to be with someone, you eventually have to act. Joe doesn't act. Joe reacts.*—

—*Thanks for writing about your feelings, albeit in the third person. You really poured your heart out.*—

CHAPTER 10

I was about to respond when Carolyn, our long-time assistant, poked her head in the door. "There's a Stephanie Hartung here to see you." I had heard the knock on the door, but had assumed it was one of Andy's appointments, as my appointment with Walker's girlfriend wasn't scheduled for another forty-five minutes. Carolyn mentioned that she had asked for the bathroom key twice already and mouthed the word "wacky."

"At least she showed," I thought, always mildly surprised by the arrival of a scheduled appointment. Ms. Hartung sat in the lobby of my office like a sparrow about to take flight on an instant's notice. Knees together, elbows out, she hunched behind oversized sunglasses, her tiny nose seeming to sniff the air for danger. I introduced myself, shook a tiny, clammy hand and escorted her into my office. After resuming her furtive perch on a chair across from my desk, the silence was broken.

"Don't get me wrong," she began, which I thought was an odd place to begin. "Do I want to be here? Not particularly. Am I more than a little confused? Of course, I am. And while I may be way off base, my relationship with Allston notwithstanding, this has really thrown me for a loop." She spoke rapidly.

No, auctioneers spoke rapidly. Hers was a torrent of words, spilling over a waterfall on top of each other. Her speech pattern of caveats and rhetorical questions was dizzying. "And you're probably thinking, 'Oh, my lord no, I mean, are you kidding me?' I mean, it's not like I haven't been a total stranger to drama. Quite the opposite, in fact."

While I tried to understand the opposite of not being a stranger to something, she prattled on incessantly, in a stream of double negatives and prefaces that went on forever, leaving me flailing for her intent. It was one of the hundreds of times in my career when I wished someone else was in my office to share my experience. Someone I could turn to now and ask, "Are you getting any of this?"

Instead, I sat alone, feeling underwater dull, hopeless to keep up with her fire hose of words. Did I lack the mental acumen to understand her dizzying intellect? Perhaps. Or, quite the opposite, as I was beginning to surmise, was her pretzel logic the result of some combination of drugs and psychoses?

I waited for her to breathe in order to quickly interject, but was much too slow. About four minutes and three missed breath opportunities later, my timing was perfect.

"Wait!" I blurted, sounding louder and more desperate than I had planned. She froze, the sparrow attempting a motionless disguise, her eyes bulging. But I hesitated too long, and she was off, speaking even more rapidly, apparently making up for seconds lost.

"I'm so incredibly sorry, I mean, you must think, well, who knows what anyone's thinking, really. I mean, I'm here just to offer assistance, whatever that would be. I don't know, except to say to that to the extent that, as you may know, Alls—I call him Alls but in court they refer to him as Allston V. Walker—and I had no idea, as you may or may not know, that he has ever used his middle name as he was named after an aunt that he probably didn't mention to you..."

"Ms. Hartung!" I butted in, not waiting for a breath, and deciding to capitalize on her fear. "We're going to proceed in a question-and-answer fashion. What is your full name and date of birth?"

She paused, surprised, and answered, "Stephanie Louise Hartung, 11-29-68."

"What is your relationship to Allston Walker?"

"I mean, things have been better, which is no surprise. In some ways…"

"Girlfriend or wife?"

"Girlfriend."

"Allston tells me you live at 1115 Gilstrap Avenue in Oakland."

"Yes."

"And Allston stayed at your place a few nights a week?"

"Yes. We've been on again off again for years, but lately, he's been spending the night from Friday through Sunday." She kept talking about her relationship with Allston as I digested her answer, which was not good for the home team.

Walker had told me that he had gone to Stephanie's after work on the night of the attack on Devaney, which was a Tuesday. As Hartung continued, now moving from Allston's annoying habit of leaving the lights on in her home to his appetite for pasta, my thoughts turned to the upcoming trial. I pictured a scowling Allston on the witness stand bumbling through a confused explanation of how it was that, while normally on Tuesdays he would have every opportunity to try to kill Devaney, on this particular Tuesday, he just happened to deviate from his routine, conveniently creating his alibi.

The sudden silence was deafening as she sat motionless, her face fixed in a question, awaiting my response to what I assumed was a question about Allston's ultimate fate.

"Allston is in a tough spot," I began in my well-practiced tone for families of the accused. The goal was to set low expectations and be vague without crushing their souls. "The caretaker of this hotel has accused Allston of trying to kill him with a knife after an argument about rent money. He…"

"Oh my God, I know. Can you imagine? I mean, Lord knows Allston has his faults."

I tried in vain to interrupt, my traffic cop hand signal having a better chance of stopping a bull at full charge. Now, however, she was cutting into my designated fantasy baseball time. I grabbed my Black's Law Dictionary off the shelf behind me. I hadn't cracked it open since law school graduation. It had been a gift from a well-meaning relative, but it was big and impressive, so I kept it behind my desk.

The crash on my oak desk made my guest jump, and more importantly, stop talking. "Ms. Hartung," I said firmly. "I'd like you to listen. Just calm down and listen. You can help Allston, but only if you listen." I paused, almost hoping she would give me cause for another dramatic moment with the book. She pantomimed zipping her lips, so I continued.

"Allston told me he was at your house on the evening of the attempted murder. Is this true?"

"Yes."

"Were you there with him around nine?"

"No, I worked late. Got home about eleven."

"Then how do you know Allston was there?"

"It's true, Allston gets off work early on Tuesdays, and since I have a home care job that night, he sometimes crashes at my place so my daughter won't have to spend the night by herself."

I was so elated by her focus and brevity, it took me a while to grasp the content. "So, it seems your daughter can verify Allston's alibi—that he was present in your apartment on the night of the attack."

"No, she spent the night at a friend's house." Of course she did.

"So, Ms. Hartung, can anyone verify that Allston was at your place?"

"Well, Julia, my daughter Alana's friend, can verify that she called my house looking for Alana, and that Allston answered the phone."

"At least a man answered the phone."

"Well, yes."

It was something, I supposed. "Also, because the jury will expect this, I will ask you at the trial whether you believe that Allston was capable of such a violent act."

"No. Not Allston. He would never try to kill a man for seventy bucks."

I made a mental note to work with Hartung on fine-tuning this answer. I made another mental note that it was the second time someone on the defense side had felt the need to qualify the answer to that question.

CHAPTER 11

August 25, 2021

The caretaker had started the day in a foul mood. He'd been soaking up the last of his egg yolks with his toast when Denny came in to pick up his uncle's wagering money. As usual, it was fifty dollars, plus five for Denny's lunch and carrots for the horses.

"Morning Uncle Jeff," Denny said with a smile.

"You only won ten yesterday," grumbled Devaney, ignoring the greeting. "That dog won't hunt." He was dreading his collection rounds.

Denny's smile widened. "What does that mean? Uncle J…"

"Do better at the track, Denny," Devaney cut in, without looking up from his plate. "Make your uncle more money. If that horse Beau is runnin', bet on him."

"You ain't got to worry today, Uncle Jeff. Beau's hurt but this horse Bridges has been telling me how good he feels."

"If Beau is runnin', bet on him. He's been a winner for us. And Denny, how many times do I have to tell you? Horses can't talk. You make yourself sound like even more of a half-wit than you are."

Denny stuffed the carrot money in one pocket and the betting money in the other, then quietly left. He wished his uncle wouldn't call him that. And he knew horses couldn't actually talk, but they could tell him things all the same.

CHAPTER 12

After Walker's girlfriend had darted away, I returned to the Walker binder. Like most books I read, I skipped to the photos. I opened the binder to find Devaney's face, covered in blood, grimacing back at me. My first conclusion was that my lunch was over. My second was that the attempted murder had nearly succeeded.

If Devaney's assailant was a mystery, the gravity and desperation of the struggle was plainly revealed. Green buckling linoleum peaked through puddles of crimson, the hotel manager's cramped home smeared and streaked from sliding shoes. An old rotary phone rested on the edge of a table, its bloody handle dangling to the floor on a spiral cord.

Angry black gashes on his forehead, cartoon-like eyebrows raised in shock. A naked torso, pale and bulky, two eye-shaped wounds on his stomach.

Devaney on a stretcher, eyes nearly shut, tubes coiling from his arms. A rigid duct emerging from his throat, an oxygen mask thoughtfully concealing his private agony. I slid my unfinished sandwich into the trash.

Wider angles revealed all the tiny living space, the walls streaked with blood. With Devaney up on his feet, the two men would have filled up the apartment without much room to spare, neither having the space to retreat.

I thought for a moment. The alleged motive suggested a more premeditated, planned attack. After all, Walker would have had time to think about the best way to assassinate his victim; however, the photos showed that the assault was a crime of passion, more likely the result of a lover's quarrel or a spontaneous and inflammatory insult. I closed the binder and fished my sandwich out of the trash. It was still mostly wrapped, after all.

I worked up my nerve and texted Amanda.

— *Thanks again for the referral. I met with his girlfriend today.*

— *Is there a good defense?—*

— *There's a defense. Classic SOMDI.—*

—*Okay, Joe. I'll bite. What's the SOMDI defense?—*

— *Some other mother did it.—*

— *Of course. So how was the girlfriend?—*

— *Wacky. Was it wrong not to mention I've never won an attempted murder case?—*

— *Seriously???—*

—*Kidding. My record is one acquittal, three convictions and one hung jury, which, given the conviction rate, is hall of fame material.—*

—*Which, I'm sure, is of great comfort to the three on death row.—*

—*Smartass. Nice ass, but smartass.—*

—*Oh, JT, it HAS been a long time. I'll be in your neck of the woods this weekend. We should get together.—*

—*Great!—*

That last line had taken me about thirty-five minutes to draft. I was beyond excited to see her and spent the drive home convincing myself to tell her I was interested in her beyond friendship. I would tell her. Probably.

Home was a two-bedroom bungalow on a quiet street in the Glenview section of Oakland. The neighborhood was safely out of the war zone, but only a ten-minute drive to the courthouse and convenient to the BART train.

I had managed the down payment with a timely inheritance check from my favorite uncle, who spoiled me even in his death. While the home's exterior fit nicely in the hilly neighborhood of narrow streets and tidy homes, my interior décor remained a half-step above a college dorm room.

A hideous mustard recliner, left in the garage by the previous owner, now proudly dominated the living quarters. It sat in the middle of the room, covering too much hardwood floor, but the perfect distance from a flat screen, my only furnishing purchase of note. The kitchen was outdated, but the microwave worked, and there was a small patio for barbecuing.

I popped open a beer and settled in my recliner with a copy of the Walker reports.

CHAPTER 13

August 25, 2021

Shortly after noon, Devaney set off to knock on the doors of those who hadn't made their payment, steeling himself for the ordeal. If the rent remained unpaid today, he'd tape an eviction notice to their doors early tomorrow morning, while the slackers slept.

Devaney wasn't looking forward to the stop at Room 116 so he figured he'd get it over with. Before he could knock, the door swung open, the doorway filled by a sneering, muscular Latino in his early twenties with a shaved head. He wore a sleeveless undershirt and black sweatpants. "I told you never to come around my place," the young man said hatefully.

"Look, Camacho, I don't know what you think happened, but I would never touch…"

"Get the fuck out of here!" he growled, thrusting the heels of both hands into Devaney's chest.

The caretaker staggered backwards into the hotel courtyard. "Rent's due," he said meekly and continued on with his rounds, muttering obscenities under his breath.

CHAPTER 14

Officer Lawrence Vanner, Badge No. 323:
On August 25, at 20:08 hours, I was dispatched to the Islander Hotel at 641 West Grand Avenue in the City of Oakland for a reported stabbing. Arriving with lights and sirens deployed, Officer Percy and I exited our patrol vehicle and proceeded inside the lobby of the hotel, a three-story multi-unit structure.

The Walker police reports were typical in many respects. Most are written by sleep-deprived officers who, with rare exception, are men and women of action, not words. Documenting observations in excruciating detail, the reports are drafted with full knowledge that someday some sleazy criminal defense attorney will pick them apart. So not surprisingly, the Walker reports told a simple story that led to one inevitable conclusion.

Upon entering the hotel Officer Lawrence Vanner found Devaney lying in a pool of blood. The officer leaned down near Devaney, who said in a faint voice that Allston Walker had stabbed him, informing the officer that Walker lived in Room #112. Devaney said his assailant was a Black male, light complexion, five foot, eight inches, 170 pounds.

Officer Harvey Percy, Vanner's partner that night, called the ambulance and waited as the victim faded in and out of consciousness. Aaron Souza and Cameron Peters, paramedics with Patriot Emergency, stabilized Devaney and loaded him into their ambulance. Ten minutes later, Devaney was at County Hospital, which serves as a triage unit for many of the city's wounded.

I flipped through the voluminous medical records. Devaney was suffering from multiple stab wounds to his left chest, back and abdomen. He was bleeding internally and underwent emergency surgery to repair his severely lacerated liver and stomach lining. He was on life support until noon the next day. A laceration to his forehead would require twelve staples.

After surgery, Oakland Police Officer Erik Johnson interviewed Devaney. According to the officer, although unable to speak, he was conscious and coherent. Officer Johnson documented his conversation with the patient in his police report as follows: (V1 stands for victim, even though there was only one victim. The questions are also numbered, because police officers number everything.)

1. Are you Jefferson Devaney? V1 Devaney nodded yes. 2. Do you work at 641 W. Grand? V1 Devaney nodded yes. 3. Is the person who stabbed you a Black male named Allston Walker? V1 Devaney nodded yes. 4. Does Allston Walker live at 641 W. Grand in room 112? V1 Devaney again nodded yes.

To cement the identification, Oakland Police Sergeant Cruz showed the victim a single photograph of Allston Walker, asking if this was the man who had attacked him. Devaney asked for his glasses before examining the photograph. The sergeant drove the victim's daughter, Janice, to the hotel, where she retrieved them. Devaney looked at the photograph of Walker and immediately nodded, scribbling "That's him" on a notepad. This was the face of his attacker.

Back at the Islander, Walker's room was searched and processed for blood, hair and fibers. No such evidence was found. There's some good news, I thought to myself. At least Devaney's blood wasn't all over my client's room.

I had yet to see a statement by Walker. If he had managed to keep his mouth shut, it would be the best news yet. The criminal defense attorney's most common advice to suspects is to refrain from speaking to the police. "But won't they think I have something to hide?" is the most common client objection. My most common reply is "Yes" followed by an awkward silence in which I attempt, unsuccessfully, to will my client to know what I'm thinking, which is, "because you *do* have something to hide!"

Police interrogations of my clients usually go something like this: "Mr. Suspect, I know you say you were on the other side of town, but these cell phone records seem to indicate otherwise. What's that? You forgot that you had to go across town to get gas at the station near the murder scene? By the way, we lied about the phone records, but I'm sure your credit card statement will back that up. Oh, you paid cash? No problem, I know that gas station has a great surveillance camera. Do you know your partner in crime snitched on you this morning? Oh, it was all his idea? We actually lied about the snitching. Who's your partner?"

As I leafed through the police report in the Walker case, although ever hopeful, I knew I would find it eventually. And I did. A very lengthy statement signed by my client laying out, in great detail, his whereabouts and activity on the night of the attack on Devaney. Walker told of his argument with the caretaker, telling the police it happened around 1:30 p.m. He worked until 6:30 p.m. then drove straight to his girlfriend's house afterwards, arriving about 6:45 p.m. Walker confirmed that he paid his rent to Assistant Manager Richard Erickson the following morning, a few minutes prior to his arrest.

I called Chuck Argenal, a private detective I used for most of my cases. Chuck is an ageing hippie who wears flip-flops and cargo shorts ten months a year and sports a gray ponytail.

He isn't exactly a highly motivated self-starter, but the pool of reasonably priced private investigators is shallow. Besides, Chuck is a walking encyclopedia of movie lines and southern idioms, so his entertainment value is high.

"Hi, Chuck, I sent you the Walker police reports. Are you in?"

"You had me at 'hello'. What do you need?"

"For starters, interview Devaney, if he'll talk to us, and the ambulance drivers. Also, subpoena the girl's phone records to prove the alibi call, and check our guy's prior theft charges for allegations of violence. I don't want to find out in trial."

"Yippie-ki-yay, motherfucker!"

CHAPTER 15

On Saturday I woke up nervous about seeing Amanda. Two Bloody Marys helped, and I was off, driving east from Oakland through the Caldecott Tunnel to pick her up for lunch. She was staying with her mother in the tony suburb of Orinda during her real estate conference.

"Mrs. Kensey?" The fit and tan woman in her late sixties looked up from a rosebush.

"Hello, please call me Rose," she said, smiling her daughter's smile. "You must be the lawyer friend," she said, peeling off a canvas glove to take my hand.

"Yes. Joe Turner. Sorry for sneaking up on you. The gate was open." The gate was large and wrought iron and guarded a lengthy paved private driveway that led to a Spanish style home of stucco and terracotta bordered by an immaculate flower garden.

"Not at all. I was in my own world. It's such a beautiful day."

"It is. And your flowers are beautiful."

"You're sweet. For years we hired a gardener, but now I wouldn't dream of it."

I looked up at the sound of a screen door. "Hi, Joe." Motherhood had somehow enhanced Amanda's beauty. Her body, while no longer petite and perky, now possessed womanly curves. She moved gracefully toward me and more confidently than I recalled. Her eyes, though, were the same. Smiling deep brown eyes that windowed a carefree and honest soul. We embraced. It seemed longer than normal, but I wasn't sure.

I drove her to Berkeley, the site of her conference, and we got slices and talked about our careers and her daughter.

"Where is Isabella staying while you're here?"

"She's currently being spoiled by my sister. What are aunts for, I guess. And I know it's only been one day, but I miss her so much." Boy was her smile beautiful.

Conversation came easy, as it always had, and as we walked around the Cal campus, our conversation turned to my most recent case.

"How's it going?" she asked.

I turned to her and smiled. "Really?" I asked, genuinely questioning her interest.

"Yes, why?"

"I don't know. Usually, women tend to find my job a bit, what's the word... icky."

Amanda laughed. "So, try me."

I shrugged. "Well, it's an attempted murder case, which makes it more difficult than your average murder case."

"Yeah? Why?"

"Because there's no victim to deal with in a murder case," I answered with a grimace, bracing for her reaction.

Amanda groaned. "Okay, a little icky. But I see your point. What else makes it a tough case?"

Wow, she was really interested. "The facts. Facts are an underrated aspect of any case."

"That seems obvious, right?" she asked.

"It should be, but a lot of attorneys, because we have egos the size of Texas..."

"Men tend to exaggerate about size," she cut in.

"Funny. Can we stick to the topic, Ms. Kensey?"

"Sorry, Counselor, carry on."

"Anyway, most trial attorneys will tell you the key to the case is their unique ability to connect with the jury, or their superior cross examination skills, or their ability to create a theme of the case."

"And here I thought all you needed to do was come up with a catchy phrase, like 'If the glove doesn't fit, you must acquit.'"

"Any ideas in that regard?"

"How about, "It wasn't Walker. He's no stalker.""

"First, I didn't know you knew his name. And second, that's the worst catch phrase I've ever heard."

"I'll work on it."

"Anyway, if you gave lawyers truth serums, they'd admit that by far the single most important aspect of any trial is the facts. Lawyers don't decide cases. Facts do."

"So that's it, you're stuck with the facts and helpless? Attorneys must make some difference."

"Only this attorney."

"Really? Oh, I knew I had chosen the right one." Her brown eyes were wide with mock admiration.

"I haven't been given the truth serum. And my enormously gigantic, um, what were we talking about?"

"Your ego, I assume," she giggled.

"Yes, my ego allows me to believe that I can make a difference, even for clients like Mr. Walker."

"How? Oh, tell me how, you genius man. I'll do my best to understand."

"I'll go slowly. The key to trial success centers on the defense attorney's ability to provide to the jury an explanation of the facts alternative to the prosecution's. I call this a TACT."

"A what?"

"A TACT. A Turner Alternate Crime Theory. The brilliance of the TACT is that it invariably has as its unshakable premise my clients' complete and total innocence."

"Joseph Wingate Turner! Your intellect is simply stunning."

"Thank you, and if I could remember your equally hideous middle name, I'd tease you about it. What was it, Vaneece? Viola?" I was secretly happy she had remembered mine.

"Oh no," she smiled. "Never to be repeated."

"Okay, I digress. I've been working on Walker's TACT. Tell me what you think."

"Okay."

"Whoever attempted to kill Devaney committed a crime of passion. These crimes are generally thought to have at their root human emotion; catching a lover in bed with another or reacting to harm or insult to a family member."

"I don't think Walker and Devaney were lovers."

"Ignoring the wholly inappropriate comment from the jury, crimes of passion are often identifiable by the weapon and number and location of wounds. The most common weapons of crimes of passion are kitchen knives. They are the most prevalent weapon in the place where such crimes are most often committed. The weapon used by the perpetrator in this case was—I paused for dramatic effect—one kitchen knife."

"I'm with you so far," she said as we settled on a bench.

"The many wounds suffered by the victim in our case are also consistent with a crime of passion. Rather than acting with the goal of death in mind, the crime is more about the perpetrator, each blow an act of anger. The locations of the blows in a crime of passion are also instructive. They tend to be in varied locations, as opposed to a surgical strike. So, Ms. Kensey, the attempted murder of Devaney, in many ways, then, was a textbook crime of passion. He was stabbed with a kitchen knife left on the shelf of his putative home. He was stabbed numerous times all over his body."

"Oh, 'putative.' He's showing off that Georgetown education."

"However," I continued, undaunted, trying a British accent, "in this particular case, the passionate nature of the attack is very much at odds with the original location of the weapon." I rose, and began pacing with one hand behind my back. Amanda was laughing, but also listening. She could be the perfect woman.

"Devaney was stabbed with a knife that he left lying on a shelf. As the victim dozed in his apartment, the knife was not visible from the lobby. Therefore, whoever entered Devaney's office did so unarmed, yet carrying enough rage to commit the blood-thirsty attack, which, as my kin in Arkansas might say, don't sit right."

"That's actually a good point."

"Thank you, my dear woman. And, Watson, is it not unreasonable to think that the villain, with murderous intentions, sneaked behind the counter and entered the office unarmed, but sincerely hopeful that a weapon would avail itself?"

"Clearly absurd," she said.

"And is it not of equal absurdity to posit that the attacker entered the office uninvited but with no evil intentions—perhaps to borrow a cup of sugar—and then somehow acquired the uncontrollable rage after a few moments of watching the victim doze?"

"Indeed."

"It is, of course, much more satisfying and probable that the victim committed the crime in a fit of rage. For this to have occurred, the victim must have been in the presence of the attacker and done something or said something to inspire the passion. More importantly, the villain must have been near the knife when the fit of passion took hold. Passion, my dear Ms. Kensey, most inspired, (another pause, and then crescendo), by a woman!"

"Was it not odd," I asked, wishing I smoked a pipe, "that Mr. Devaney, although married, spent nearly seven nights every week at the hotel? And would it be inconceivable that Devaney might, on occasion, invite behind the counter one of the many women of the evening who populate his neighborhood and ply their trade at the Islander Hotel? And would not this, more so than any petty argument about late rent, provide the makings for a true crime of passion?"

"Wow, that's…"

"Also," I interrupted, "while adrenaline can be a very powerful source of strength, Mr. Devaney's account of his heroics was not the easiest to swallow. Could a sixty-seven-year-old man, not in the best of shape, go from having a knife plunged into his chest while he slept to wrestling his attacker to the floor? Whether or not Devaney was overstating his heroics, a female attacker would make things more plausible." I plopped down next to Amanda, my performance complete.

"It's not bad," Amanda said, her tone serious after several minutes of thought. "Do you think that's what happened?"

"I don't know," I answered after some consideration. "The theory does rely on Devaney outright lying, rather than just being mistaken. That's not ideal."

"Especially if the jury likes him," she put in. "Are there really a lot of prostitutes in the area?"

"Yeah, the Islander is on the blade." She looked at me sideways. "It means a strip where prostitutes walk."

"Could you forward me the police reports?" she asked. "Now you've got me interested in this."

"Really? Okay, sure."

Our weekend had been everything I had hoped. We had connected again for drinks after her afternoon conference. Sunday found me on my couch, sitting next to her. I was certain she could hear my heart, a bass drum vibrating my lips as I prepared to speak.

CHAPTER 16

August 25, 2021

Two more stops. Room 67, the Dormans. Devaney sighed in disgust. No more dishonest passel of crooks ever walked the earth. They'd steal anything that wasn't tied down, so paying their rent was sort of contrary to their whole outlook on life. They usually weren't mean about it. Just constantly lying. I paid you last week, my mom said we wouldn't have to pay this month, or whatever excuse popped into their heads.

"What the fuck do you want?" One of the brothers answered the door. They all looked the same to Devaney. Black as night, in and out of jail.

"Rent's due."

"Yeah, cracker, don't suppose you're here to fix the goddamn lock on my door that I told you about six weeks ago."

"I've told maintenance. Meantime, the rent is due." Devaney felt the frustration about to boil over. There was only so much abuse a man could take. Even though he knew a lie was coming, he felt the switch about to flip.

"My brother already paid the rent this morning," the young man said calmly.

"To hell he did!" Devaney heard himself shout, his red face contorted in anger. Immediately, he knew that he'd gone too far.

The young man stood in the doorway glaring hatred into Devaney's eyes until the caretaker was forced to look away, then moved to within inches of his face. "You disrespect me in my home," he whispered, with a hateful smile. "You best watch yourself, cracker." Devaney slinked away with a pit in his stomach.

CHAPTER 17

My time with Amanda was a rocket ship and a hammock in the shade, all in one. She spoke plainly but with meaning, and I could tell her outlook was clear and warm, a view east before sunset, when the sun is soft and bright. Her full lips and tan shoulders, a beckon to the hammock.

We had been so comfortable with each other as friends, the progression seemed obvious. On the other hand, we had known each other so long without romance, I was afraid our status as friends was entrenched. Mortified, rather than afraid.

But I had waited long enough. The random case referral had brought us together again, and I was not going to let another opportunity pass. We sat on my couch, idly talking before I would give her a ride to the airport. "Tell her how you feel!" my mind screamed at myself. It was now or never. Or worse, later, with a cowardly text. What, was I going to spend the rest of my life snuggled up to my phone, entertaining myself with my stupid jokes?

Amanda said something about calling for a ride to the airport. "Don't be silly," I heard myself say over the booming bass drum in my chest. "I'll drive you." Then my mouth got dry, and I felt weak. But I did it.

"I've developed quite a crush on you, Amanda," I whispered. There was no response. Apparently, it had been well below a whisper. Turns out I had just mouthed the words. Then Amanda turned her beautiful face toward mine and looked into my eyes. "I'm glad I'm here," she said, touching my arm.

"Me, too," I heard myself say while feeling myself abruptly rise from the couch. "It's been great. And I'm glad you liked the conference."

The brief remainder of her stay was somewhat of a blur. Empty small talk on the way to the airport, then a hug. As she turned to go, my hand stayed on her back until she moved away. I desperately hoped she noticed.

On the drive back from the airport, tormented, I retreated to my warm womb of daydreams. I was back, sitting next to Amanda on my couch. Only this time, I lean closer to her, our eyes meeting, as I gently tuck a stray lock of her hair behind her ear. Amanda's gorgeous, full lips part in a half-smile as she leans closer—close enough to whisper in my ear, "I want you, Joe Turner."

Then she is in my arms, her lush breasts pressed into my chest. I lift her vanilla fragrant hair from her neck and kiss it, her skin beneath my lips as warm and soft as it looks. I continue nibbling and tasting her neck as she moans softly with pleasure. Then she turns and places her lips on mine, opening up for an eager kiss as her arms pull me tightly to her. Our breathing quickens together and all I can think about is undressing her and exploring all those luscious curves with my tongue and hands.

But I take my time, trailing a line of gentle searching kisses down her neck to her collarbone, hearing Amanda say, breathlessly, "Don't stop, Joe." She pulls my shirt over my head and begins to slowly unbutton her blouse and slips off her bra. Her nipples are hard as I graze my lips over them. Then her hands are at my belt. She pushes me back on the couch and gives me a mischievous grin, taking me into her mouth. I gasp with pleasure. "I'm not going to last long if you keep doing that," I murmur.

When she looks up at me, I see my own longing matched in her eyes. I pull her to me, rotating her body until she is lying on the couch. I slip her skirt and panties off and work my way down her body, my mouth on soft skin. Her legs part for me, and I use my tongue to gently coax her legs further apart, teasing her as she moans with pleasure. Her fingers are at my hair now, pulling my mouth deep into her, until her hips thrust up in climax. "Counselor," she whispers in a throaty voice, "come here now." She pulls me in for a deep kiss while taking me in her hand. Those brown eyes glaze over with passion as she moves her hips toward me and takes me inside her.

A car ahead of me stopped abruptly for a yellow light and I slammed the brakes, jolting me out of my daydream. I'd been so lost in my Amanda fantasy, I'd been driving on autopilot. "You suck, Joe," I told myself as I pulled into my parking spot.

Inside, the bright blue bottle of gin glistened on the counter. The color reminded me of a bike I got for Christmas when I was seven. Such a happy color.

I put on sweatpants so I wouldn't wake up in my jeans. Human Resources should have asked me that question, I laughed to myself. "Do you have drinking clothes?"

I tossed a lime in the air and caught it behind my back, a happy dance before a boozy evening watching old movies. I rolled the plump fruit on my cutting board, teasing my mouth for a drink. "My pathetic version of foreplay," I chided myself.

I sliced several wedges, then put the knife safely away. The ice clinked, the tonic bottle hissed, and I slowly raised the glass, the fizz tickling my nose before the first sip. It never disappointed.

CHAPTER 18

On Monday morning, with Walker's preliminary hearing just two days away, I picked up an audio recording of my client's statement to the police. I checked for the Miranda warning, then listened to the actual statement later on my commute home.

The Miranda warning is, perhaps, the least understood rule of law in the history of jurisprudence. Most people have heard the rights recited on television. While cinching the cuffs on the bad guy in the penultimate scene, the heroic officer announces in a voice dripping with self-satisfaction, "Mr. Scumbag, you have the right to remain silent. You have the right to an attorney…"

The voice is gradually drowned out by the crescendo of theme music as the camera slowly zooms out from above, revealing an aerial view of the destruction wrought by the chase scene as the bad guy is guided into the back seat of a patrol vehicle.

The Supreme Court ruled, in Miranda v. Arizona, that the well-known advisement is mandatory before a suspect can be interrogated while in custody. If the suspect is not told of his right to remain silent in very specific language, the suspect's statement, or even confession, can be kept from the jury.

Many criminal defendants have come to view the Miranda rule as some sort of impenetrable shield from prosecution. ("I understand that the surveillance video shows me robbing the liquor store, Mr. Turner. Perhaps you didn't hear me the first time. No one read me my rights!")

Unfortunately for Walker, not only did Sergeant Simmons read him his Miranda warnings, Allston signed a form indicating that he understood those rights before he made his statement. At least he had not confessed.

Devaney's 911 call and another police report arrived via email the following morning and with them, the first rays of hope for the defense. Amid groans of agony, the victim had told the 911 operator he'd been stabbed. Doing her best to keep him awake and alive, the operator asked if he knew the person who had stabbed him. "No," he replied, the word escaping through clenched teeth. It was true that moments later, he would name his attacker. Still, it was something.

More intriguing was the report filed by Officer Vanner. He recounted that while on the way to the Islander Hotel, responding with lights and sirens, about two blocks from his destination, the officer noticed a young man running down the sidewalk in the opposite direction.

The officer screeched his patrol car to a stop and spoke to the man. Apparently satisfied that he was not a suspect, and with the stabbing victim in mind, the officer returned to his car and sped to the crime scene. While Vanner certainly could not be faulted for leaving the potential suspect to tend to the victim, given the current status of the defense, the running man was gold.

The report left many questions unanswered about the running man. Was he asked where he was going? What did he look like? Were his hands checked for cuts? Was his clothing examined for blood splatter? Did he make an attempt to evade the police? Unfortunately, as the police would soon "have their man," all of these questions would go unanswered, at least until the trial.

I opened the file labeled "Walker Statement" and my client's raspy voice filled my office. Absent his face, he sounded somewhat more pleasant, but only just. He told the police that after working a landscaping job at a bank in Berkeley from 3:00 p.m. until 6:30 p.m., he drove to Hartung's home in north Oakland. He didn't return to the hotel that evening, didn't go out, and didn't see anyone while he was there. He didn't buy gas on the way home or use his cell phone that night, as it wasn't charged.

I dialed the jail to schedule another visit with Walker. I was hoping my reticent client could provide a scintilla of evidence to support his story. Perhaps he had ordered pizza or watched pay-per-view? Maybe a neighbor came over to borrow a cup of flour. Then again, maybe his story couldn't be verified because he was busy trying to kill Devaney.

CHAPTER 19

August 25, 2021

"Hi there, Jeff, c'mon in. I was just about to make some tea." The smallish man in his sixties was one of the Islander's few white residents and the hotel's longest tenured guest.

"Arnie, I'm just making the rounds. Listen, the rent's due and I really can't keep giving you breaks."

"Oh, I know, Jeff. I can get it to you in a week. My tax check should be here soon."

"Look, Arnie. I hate to be this way but management is very clear. One day late means an eviction notice. I've been floating you for going on three months now."

"I know, and I surely appreciate it but I just…"

"Sorry, Arnie," Devaney cut in. "My hands are tied."

"So, what is it you're sayin', Jeff? You wouldn't evict your old poker buddy, would you? Hell, I'm the only resident here who isn't a drain on society. You said it yourself."

Devaney stood silently with his palms up until the door slammed in his face.

CHAPTER 20

In theory, the preliminary hearing is designed to filter out the cases for which there is not enough evidence to have a trial. In practice, only an infinitesimal percentage of cases are dismissed at this stage. Commenting on the ease of prosecutors getting over this pretrial hurdle, New York State Chief Judge Sol Wachtler is famous for opining that "You can indict a ham sandwich."

Walker's preliminary hearing was set in Department 609, the fiefdom of noted ball buster, Judge Richard Headley. Yes, that's really his name, and yes, that's his nickname, likely since age twelve. It did nothing to help matters that Judge Headley was in a perpetual state of irritation. He wore a look on his face like he'd left medicine on his tongue for too long and seemed to despise attorneys.

The District Attorney assigned to the case at this juncture was Harrison Quinn, a young go-getter who enthusiastically greeted me and appeared positively thrilled with his role as a prosecutor. It was the custom of the D.A.'s Office to assign relatively young attorneys to preliminary hearings. It was a perfect forum in which to practice direct examination, and there was no jury to worry about. Also, even if things went horribly wrong, clearing the preliminary hearing bar was a virtual certainty.

I took my place opposite him at the counsel table and in due course Walker was ushered out into the courtroom, shuffling to the counsel table in ankle irons. He wore his familiar yellow inmate sweats, squinting under the bright florescent courtroom lights.

Judge Headley took the bench and did not disappoint. "Greetings, gentlemen. Calling the case of Allston Walker. We're here, I can only presume, because you two failed to settle this case. This failure necessitates a preliminary hearing. Does Mr. Walker waive a formal reading of the complaint?" The judge looked at me. He never addressed an attorney by his name.

"Yes, Your Honor."

"Mr. Prosecutor, call your first witness."

"Your Honor, my first witness is just downstairs in our office," the young D.A. said weakly. "I will get him."

I cringed.

"Counsel, why isn't he here, ready to testify? Did this hearing come as a surprise to you?"

"No, Your Honor."

"Don't ever come to my courtroom again not prepared to proceed!" boomed Judge Dickhead.

"No, Your Honor. I will not. I just thought..."

"Do me a favor and try not to think! Now go and get your witness!"

Five uncomfortable minutes followed. The scowling judge remained on the bench, sitting motionless. To my right, Walker, confirmed member of the scowling hall of fame, sat chained to his chair. The courtroom was silent, devoid of the polite chatter among the court staff, all taking their cues from their dictator.

Finally, the prosecutor entered the courtroom with his witness in tow. Predictably, it was Officer Vanner. The officer testified that he had been dispatched to the scene, had found Devaney in a pool of blood, and had initiated life-saving measures until the paramedics arrived.

"Did you ask Mr. Devaney who had attacked him," Quinn asked.

"Yes."

"And what was Mr. Devaney's answer?"

"May I refer to my notes?"

"No, you may not." interrupted the judge. "Would your notes refresh your recollection?"

"Yes," said the officer, undoubtedly thinking, "Why else would I want to refer to my notes."

"Then," continued the judge, "refer to your notes and let us know when your recollection has been refreshed."

Technically, the judge was correct. The officer's report was hearsay and not admissible as a document. This meant the officer was not allowed to read it into the record. Most judges would have trusted the D.A. to know the rules.

"Yes, my recollection has been refreshed," said the officer. "Devaney said, 'Allston Walker stabbed me. He lives in room 112.'"

"And did you later confirm who lived in room 112 of the Islander Hotel on the date of the attack on Mr. Devaney?"

"Yes. Allston Walker did."

After Officer Vanner had identified Mr. Walker for the judge, I began a brief cross examination. I elicited Devaney's grave condition and blood loss, doing what I could to call into question the victim's mental acuity at the time of the identification of my client.

Predictably, the officer stood up for his victim, indicating that he seemed to know where he was and was able, while in obvious pain, to answer questions appropriately, including providing the officer with his name and age.

All of this was bad news for the defense, but at least I had learned this for the first time at the preliminary hearing and not in front of the jury. In short order, Walker was formally "held to answer" for the charge of attempted murder, and court was adjourned.

CHAPTER 21

In the weeks that followed, supplemental reports trickled in. I pored over the transcript of the preliminary hearing, hoping for a crack to appear in the prosecution's case. My contact with Amanda became far less frequent since the fiasco on the couch, so I was relieved to see her name on my phone.

—Hi Joe. It was good to see you.—
—Yes. Sorry, I guess I was more nervous than I expected.—
—You were a wreck. Haha. But still tall and handsome.—
—Funny you mention height. I am six foot two inches tall. I appear taller, but only because most men overstate their own height by at least an inch, thereby skewing the world's perception. —
—So, you're the only honest guy when it comes to height?—
—I never exaggerate my height but am contemplating doing so in the future to bring it in line with the general perception and to avoid this tiresome explanation each time I report my height and am met with skepticism that I must be taller, "because my husband is six foot, three and you're taller than him."—
—My, you've put a lot of thought into this. I have to go feed my child.—
—No wait, I have so much more to say on the subject......—

Andy poked his head in my office. "Can you give me a ride to Court? I have to file a motion."

"Sorry, I take the train on Thursdays."

"Why?"

"Uh, I'm leasing so I need to cut down on my mileage."

"Yeah, but why Thursdays?"

"Huh?" I pretended to be distracted by a text.

"Never mind. Later."

I took the train on Thursdays so I could drink with strangers. Every other Thursday, wine and cheese would appear in the lobby of the building next door. It was some sort of Chamber of Commerce mixer. I could never keep track of the weeks, so I swung by every Thursday just in case.

Drinking with friends was fine, but they could be judgmental about how much I drank. Not to mention that they didn't drink enough for my taste. So, I'd slap on a nametag and engage in just enough small talk to appear social while I sucked down the free Chardonnay and Sauvignon Blanc preferred by the mostly female mixers.

"So, a criminal defense attorney. Wow. So, how do you...like when you know they're guilty. I mean, I know everyone deserves a defense, but I just could never do that. But I know it's a necessary job, but if I knew my client was guilty, I'd just be like ahhhhh." She mimicked a crazy face and shook her head as if insane. I'm no wordsmith, but her gesture was one of my pet peeves—people who were so inarticulate they had to act out what they meant.

Her nametag read, "Andrea Loper, Executive Coach." She wore a green pantsuit, her hair tamed into submission by enough hairspray to deplete the ozone.

It had been a while since I'd been asked the question, and while Andrea Loper's fumbling effort was hardly accusatory, as with the countless times before, I found it insulting. "Gee, you must be a real dirt bag," Andrea was really saying. "I mean, defending scum like that, I know it's a necessary job, but morally I could never stoop to that level."

I wanted to ask, "Andrea, how long have you been a feckless lackey? Did you major in pointless doublespeak? Tell me, Andrea, how in God's name can you bring yourself to undertake such a meaningless job as executive coach? Reminding self-important people to ask about a client's spouse's name, choosing the color of a suit, reserving a vegetarian meal on a flight. I, for one, could never cope with such an utterly hollow existence. But I know it's a necessary job."

Thankfully, though, I was only three glasses of wine in, so I didn't rant. "Because everyone deserves their best defense."

"But if you know they are guilty, then what's the point."

"It's not for me to say if they're guilty."

"But usually, you know if they're guilty, right?"

"Sometimes strongly suspect, but it's hard to know for sure." She rolled her eyes. "Look," I continued, pausing for a cool gulp of Chardonnay, "Since 1970, seventy-five people have been released from death row after being proven innocent by DNA tests." It was close to that number, anyway. "One hundred percent of these people were convicted of murder at trial by a unanimous jury. You do the math."

"But that's an extreme case. I'm sure sometimes you know for sure."

"Andrea, do you have children?"

"Yes, two."

"Okay, what if, heaven forbid, one of them were accused of a crime they did not commit. You wouldn't just want me to assume their guilt and mail it in."

"No."

"And the police don't arrest the wrong people on purpose. They do so because there is evidence of guilt. Either a well-meaning but false identification or something else."

"Okay." She wanted me to shut up now, so she just kept agreeing.

"And believe me. Everyone, and I mean everyone—your most depraved, evil and sociopathic criminals—all of them have someone who loves their child as much as you love yours. So why should Andrea Loper's child get special treatment?"

She still looked skeptical. "I think I'll stick to being an executive coach."

"That's probably for the best."

CHAPTER 22

Contrary to an East Coaster's view of the West, there exist distinct seasons in California. Much less distinct, of course, than in the East. California seasons do not announce their arrival like a shovel full of snow so much as gently nuzzle the senses awake with fragrance and feel.

As a child, associating the seasons with sports, I would swear to my mom I could smell baseball and football. Now, as I walked up the long cement path that led to the lobby of the Santa Rita Jail, leaves from the scrub oaks crunching underfoot, a breeze that had shooed away summer helped me along.

The green expanse was fresh cut, stretching out from the great complex like a major league ballpark before a three-tiered stadium. As I made my way to the door of Mr. Walker's modern-day dungeon, I caught a whiff of football and wondered how many people smelled sports. The late day shadows cast by the jail would reach a pitcher's mound as they do in September, during the playoffs.

Inside the jail, stale warmth smothers my senses with the smell of a mop bucket, filth stewing in disinfectant. The lobby is sparsely furnished, with a few metal benches usually occupied by an attorney or bail bondsman. Behind thick glass, deputies scurry about silently in the jail's state of the art hub and swivel in elevated chairs that face a fifteen-foot-high wall of video screens.

I exchanged my state bar card for a clip-on red badge that read "Maximum" in black letters, and was directed to a heavy metal door that led to one of the several quarter-mile long hallways that extend from the hub like giant tentacles. Six feet in width with an eight-foot ceiling and white tile floors, the hallways must be among the longest in the world.

The view to the end is an artist's lesson in perspective, shrinking until gone. Absurd windows, not four inches in height, adorn the very top of one wall in relentless intervals. The medieval slits are too high for use, too narrow to allow any perspective, and for good measure, fitted with opaque glass that filters all but the faintest of sunlight.

As my footsteps tapped against the tiles and echoed off an unseen wall at the tunnel's end, I planned my time with my client. While I had gone over my client's defense generally, Mr. Walker had been reluctant to practice his direct examination testimony. The adage that an attorney should never ask a question he didn't know the answer to was true enough for cross examination. I certainly was not going to violate the principle with my own client because he didn't feel like talking.

After a ten-minute walk, with still no end of the hallway in sight, I arrived at Unit 21, so designated by its stenciled number spray painted on its gray door. The door clicked and unlocked as I reached for its handle. I entered to find no change to the dismal amenities. Allston nodded to me through the glass and grabbed his phone as I wedged myself into position.

"Allston, I'd like to begin to review trial testimony. The impression that you make with the jury is critical. Also, it's a good way for me to learn about the case."

"I'm gonna tell you the truth. Don't worry about it," he said defensively.

I explained that while I was sure he would tell the truth it was very important that we plan his testimony so that I would remember what questions to ask and so that he wouldn't say anything that might hurt his case.

A grunt seemed to say, "You're an idiot, but go ahead. I got nowhere else to be."

"Okay, Allston, after introducing yourself to the jury, I'll ask, 'Mr. Walker, do you have a good memory of your activities on August 25, 2021?'"

Allston exhaled, "Yes," sounding like a child responding to a parent's question about whether or not he washed his hands before dinner.

"And how did that day begin?"

"We've been over this. I told you I couldn't have stabbed him because I was at work."

"The jurors won't know anything about you, Allston, so please, let's get through this. Mr. Walker, please tell the jury how your day started on..."

"You got to be kidding."

"Mr. Walker," I said sternly, doing my best to control my temper, "if you don't mind, I'd like to practice our direct examination."

"Why do we got to practice telling the truth?"

"Because I don't like to lose!" I yelled, no longer trying to control my temper. "Because you, if you hadn't noticed, are in jail!" I yelled some more. "And at your trial, a very old and sympathetic man will say he is one hundred percent certain that you tried to kill him!"

"I told you I..."

"I know, you didn't try to kill him. Well, our defense isn't going to be 'but I didn't try to kill him,'" I yelled louder. "This is not a fucking parking ticket and right now I actually don't give a shit if you spend the rest of your miserable life in prison, but in case I change my mind someday, I don't want it to be on my conscience!"

Yelling felt good, so I kept it up. "So, if you want to be crusty and stubborn, you'll probably have a good reason to for the next fifty years, but for now, humor me and prepare for this trial." I slammed down the phone and stretched my legs.

After a few minutes, I picked up the receiver, still facing away from my client. "Ain't got to be perfect," he said, as calm as ever.

"That's true," I said, returning his tone.

"In fact, if it's practiced, ain't nobody will believe it."

"Also true," I agreed. "But on the other hand, I need you to include some details so the jury will believe you."

"It just ain't got to be perfect. It's the truth," he said firmly.

And with that, Allston Walker presented his defense. He told me about his argument with Devaney, his day at work, and the call from a girl asking for Hartung's daughter around 8:20 p.m. Since the attack occurred at 8:10 p.m., the phone call was by no means an airtight alibi. Walker may have had time to attack Devaney, then retreat to his girlfriend's house to take the call. I made a note to have Chuck drive and time the route.

Walker wasn't exactly a chatterbox, but he cooperated and even provided a few details. True to his word, it wasn't perfect, but it was something.

"Allston, do you have any idea who could have committed the crime?" I didn't expect an answer, even if he had a theory. The snitch culture in Oakland was entrenched, and by naming someone else, he'd be endangering himself and his family.

"No," he said shaking his head and smiling at the question.

As I waited for the deputy to arrive to let me out, I was surprised by my client's attempt at small talk. "Today's Monday, right? You gonna watch some football tonight?"

"I'll probably catch some of the game. You like football?"

"Yeah," he said, looking toward the ceiling, obviously recalling something very specific. "I used to watch with my uncle. My aunt would bake an apple pie. You talk about perfect," he said, reclining against the wall and closing his eyes. "Now that was perfect," he said softly.

Walker was indulging in a moment of calm, freeing himself through the cement walls of the jail, out of the cold dampness, into the sunshine, to somewhere very familiar, where I could see him taste the comfort and sweetness of warm apple pie. It was the only time I saw him smile.

As Walker became more relaxed with me, something about him seemed vaguely familiar. I had noticed it during our first jail visit. He had a way of cocking his head to one side when he smiled. I had a weird sensation we'd met before.

CHAPTER 23

As I drove back to my office, although happy to make a breakthrough of sorts, missing the opportunity to examine Devaney at the preliminary hearing loomed as an important setback. Although I had seen lots of gory photos of the victim, I shuddered at the thought of heading into a trial having never spoken to the man. While Devaney seemed one hundred percent certain of his identification of my client, his credibility as a witness was still an open question. He had been, after all, nearing a state of shock when he told the police the name of his attacker.

The matter of his glasses was also a potential point of inquiry. I knew he needed them to identify Walker's photo at the hospital, but was he near or far-sighted? And Devaney had told the police his glasses had been knocked off in the struggle, but I hadn't seen any glasses on the floor in the crime scene photos.

Devaney's account of the disagreement with Walker about the rent payment was also curious. He told the police that it had occurred at 7:30 p.m., only forty-five minutes before he was attacked. But according to Walker, the argument happened around 1:30 p.m., when he returned to the Islander on his lunch break. If, in Devaney's mind, the dispute with Walker had taken place much closer in time to the attack, perhaps that had influenced his memory. Walker said Devaney's assistant was present at the argument, so I texted Chuck to check it out.

Also, Devaney's initial exchange with the 911 operator was interesting. When asked, "Do you know the name of the person who did this to you?" Devaney had replied, "No." While I presumed Devaney would tell me he knew it was Walker but had momentarily forgotten his name, it would be nice to hear him explain it.

I dialed the D.A.'s Office from my car. "Matt Eisner, please." Matt had been my dad's right-hand man in the office and was still a close friend of our family. He held considerable sway in the office, and made the pre-trial plea offers—the defendant's last chance to settle the case before rolling the dice with the jury. While Matt would never compromise a prosecution, he was nothing if not fair.

The senior prosecutor would also recognize that both the defense and the prosecution would be hamstrung by Devaney's non-appearance at the preliminary hearing. In order to make an appropriate plea offer prior to trial, assessing the victim's credibility as a witness was essential.

"You know, your dad would tell you to piss off," he said fondly, his raspy bass reminding me of John Wayne. It seemed Matt couldn't speak to me about a case without mentioning my father, and I had gotten used to it.

"I thought he was the fairest man you've ever met?"

"He was! He was also tough as a one-eyed alley cat. And don't talk back to your elders."

"All I want is..."

"All you want is to cross examine his ass," he laughed. "I'll give you fifteen minutes. In my office. I'll ask the questions. You sit there and comb your ponytail."

"Perfect. Thanks."

"You know, I haven't given up yet. We'll find him, Joey."

"I know, Matt. Thanks."

"Give my best to your mom."

"I will."

After my dad was murdered in our home nearly three decades ago, Matt had monitored the investigation and kept our family apprised. Even though the murder had been officially classified as a cold case, Matt still ended every conversation the same, vowing not to give up until he, personally, prosecuted the murderer.

When I switched from prosecution to defense, Matt was devastated. "Might as well grow a fucking ponytail, then," he had said. The fact that I never had grown a ponytail did not deter his endless jibes about my imaginary ponytail.

The veteran D.A. provided a welcome link to my father. While I was dead set on making my own way as a litigator, I had been surprised to find my pleasure and pride when judges and attorneys remembered his career.

I recalled snapshots of my dad. A crackling laugh, whiskers against my cheek, and walking to the barbershop. I leaped to match his stride, swinging on a thick and calloused hand. I remember serious talks, when he'd speak to me like an adult. "Joseph, lying is a very serious matter."

This case had been dredging up memories, long buried. It could have been Walker himself, soft-spoken yet plain-speaking, like my dad. And were my father alive, he would have been about Walker's age. Or perhaps it was the similarity of the two crimes—the assault on Devaney and my dad's murder—each savage knife attacks. Deep down, I knew the answer lie somewhere deep in the recesses of my mind, buried under layers of scar tissue that shrouded my childhood memory.

CHAPTER 24

I walked into the office to find Chuck sifting through police reports and photographs. He spoke without looking up. "First, what's our defense again? Second, do we really want to go to trial on this case, and third, what's our defense again? And please don't spin your prostitute angle. Andy told me about it."

"Not impressed?"

"He's even older than I am, and it takes me all night to do what I used to do all night."

"If he's young enough to fight off someone who stuck a knife in his chest, he's young enough to hire a prostitute."

"Maybe. But unless the jury won't like him for some reason, it will be a tough sell."

"Yeah," I admitted. "I was just throwing it out there. It's not like defenses are leaping into our lap."

"Again, why are we going to trial?"

"Innocent client, Chuck. He says so. How's the investigation progressing?"

"So far, slower than molasses in January but I'm just backing up for a running start. Devaney wouldn't talk to me. No surprise. I spoke to the paramedic who wrote the report. He had nothing to add. The other paramedic—Peters—has moved twice. Still looking for him. I subpoenaed Devaney's medical records. Also, I got police reports on Walker's prior auto theft cases. No allegations of violence."

"So, no prior vicious knife attacks over seventy dollars. I guess that's something."

"Yeah, apparently, he was just a friendly, neighborhood car burglar. Case closed. Call in the jury."

"On the plus side, I just spoke to Erickson, Devaney's fill-in. He confirms your client's statement about the timing of the argument about the rent. Devaney was way off about the time. I'll subpoena him."

As my venerable investigator gathered his notes to leave, I asked him to time the drive from Walker's landscaping site to Ms. Hartung's house, and to come with me to my meeting with Devaney.

"Wouldn't miss it."

"Any other ideas, Chuck?"

"You're gonna need a bigger boat."

"Ever helpful. Thanks."

I checked my email and found a discovery disclosure from the District Attorney, subject heading *People v. Walker, Surveillance Tape*. I swallowed hard.

I had been surprised that at least a part of the crime hadn't been caught on tape. With the proliferation of security cameras in both businesses and residences, sometimes it seemed as if the entire city of Oakland was under constant video surveillance. Police cruisers were equipped with mounted cameras, as were police officers themselves. If there was a gap in the coverage, it was usually filled with someone with a phone, eager to capture any event of remote consequence.

The trend had been a game-changer in the courtroom. For the most part, the videos had benefited the cause of justice. More crimes were being solved, perhaps even discouraged, and the police were being kept more honest.

I opened the file labeled, "Islander, Surveillance," and felt my body tense as it loaded. The video was shot from one fixed camera focused on the front door of the hotel from a position outside the building. The video was anything but high definition, the Islander having installed the system years ago. The footage provided covered August 25, from 1:00 a.m. to midnight. I fast forwarded to the time of the stabbing, 20:08 military time. I stopped the video seconds later, as a figure wearing a black hoodie backed out of the door, and disappeared from view to the left of the frame.

I watched the same 3 seconds of footage a dozen times, craning my neck as if it would somehow help see past the hoodie. Finally, I gave up, convinced the video provided almost nothing of evidentiary value. Even assuming the person caught on video was the attacker, which seemed a safe bet, an identification on any level was impossible. The hoodie shrouded the suspect's face completely. It was also very loose-fitting, making it impossible to gauge his body type. Even his height was a mystery, for while he appeared to be crouching, his legs disappeared beneath the frame. I wondered if the attacker backed out of the front door because he was aware of the camera.

Pushing myself back from my desk, I exhaled deeply. While the video couldn't eliminate Walker as the suspect, it certainly wasn't evidence of his guilt. I wondered if my relief revealed how I actually felt about Walker's innocence. Alone with my thoughts, on some level, I knew what was coming.

The projector in my head clicks on. My mother's warm scent is no longer with me, and the awful smell is back. It reminds me of a homeless camp I pass on the way to court. My view down the hall is blocked from above. I must be under something, hiding. Darkness covers all but a chaotic stripe at the bottom of the screen. Amid writhing forms, glints of steel flash down from above. I try to make my legs move but they are shaking in spasm. The soundtrack is low and muffled grunts, pierced now and again by the higher pitch shrieks of pain that ring in my head like microphone feedback.

After a time, mom is holding me again. The pain noises subside, but now echo off the walls of my mind. The crackle of a police radio interrupts the groans from time to time, but the nauseating smell lingers. My legs have stopped quivering and now the regret washes over me in a lukewarm wave of nausea. As I crane forward to see down the hallway, a warm, familiar hand gently presses my forehead away. The noise fades and my eyes relax into darkness.

CHAPTER 25

I came to know that my dad's murder was horrific, in part from the way the subject was scrupulously avoided by my mother and other relatives. Were the subject even mentioned by my family, it was usually as a marker in time, and invariably referred to as "Dad's death." ("I'm not sure when they purchased the store. It was some time after 'Dad's death.'") Whenever someone referred to the actual murder in my presence, it was met by a long and awkward silence.

The thing about silence is it allows plenty of time and space for wondering about the reason for the silence. Was it the natural repression of a traumatic event, or specifically designed to keep my memory buried? Was there something my mother wanted kept from me? Had I left a door unlocked for the attackers? I was just a kid, but still the silence was haunting.

I was in high school when my mother spoke about it with me. I got the short version and that was fine, and my flashbacks began to make sense. My dad, the local District Attorney, had been surprised in his home by a burglar and then killed. No arrest had been made.

I was home over Christmas break, sophomore year in college, when I first saw the binder in a bedroom closet while looking for wrapping paper. It was labeled simply, "Jack's Investigation" on its spine in my mother's neat printing. I had known immediately what it was but had left it alone.

Now, visiting my mother on Labor Day weekend in my second childhood home, something drew me back. The dreams had become more frequent lately, and details of his murder were beginning to seep into my consciousness. Perhaps the amateur psychologist in me thought that bringing the horror out of my subconscious would help. After dinner, I wandered into a guest bedroom. As I slid open the pocket door of the closet, memories of hide-and-seek flooded back—sitting on uncomfortable shoes, my knees folded at impossible angles, peering out a slit in the closet door.

I cleared a place to sit now on the closet's floor, moving away ridiculous looking shoes from a bygone era, and sat down. I slid the binder from its place on the closet's back wall, shrouded in hanging clothes last worn during the Nixon administration. As I cracked it, the book's musty pages were cool to the touch. Yellow newspaper clippings, neatly arranged in plastic sleeves, had to be peeled apart. I reclined against the comfort of the soft dresses and read about my father's death.

It was immediately apparent that my mother had done her best to help find my father's killer. A letter thanking Garrick Lew Investigations for taking the case, written on turquoise notepaper, was signed in her best kindergarten teacher cursive and neatly tucked in a pocket of the first binder.

In addition to the news articles, I found 247 type-written pages of police reports. As I perused the material, I was impressed with the content as well as the volume. My childhood hometown was the relatively crime-free suburb of Lafayette. The police, however, were experienced and thorough. They had collected trace evidence at the scene, canvassed the neighborhood, and developed leads.

The theory developed by the police, and generally accepted by the private investigator, was on page 89 of a summary by Sergeant Dave Severns:

Two thieves entered into the Turner residence at 971 Victoria Avenue at approximately 3:45 p.m. on Wednesday, March 3, 1996, gaining access through an open window on the east side of the property. The victim, Robert Jack Turner, arrived home early and surprised the thieves, who attacked him and after a prolonged struggle in the kitchen, stabbed him to death. The victim's wife, Diane Turner and their twelve-year-old son, Joseph, arrived home during the attack, but were not harmed. The suspects escaped with a jar full of coins and some jewelry.

I let the binder fall open on my legs as I reclined further into the clothing, and stared into space. This horrible, life-changing event, this calamity—the source of so much mental anguish and suffering that had taken a life and fractured a family—could be summarized in four sentences.

That was it. Two idiots chose one of hundreds of thousands of houses. My dad, by all accounts a hard-working man, happened to come home early. The police reports concluded that the suspects spent less than ten minutes in our home. Two dirt bags, ten minutes, for a jar of coins.

I cradled the binder and slowly leafed through it. The police found my mother smeared with my dad's blood and in shock. Later, she would tell them she arrived home to find her husband on the dining room floor trying to fight off his attackers. She ran to try to help him, but both men had knives. Slipping to the floor—probably in his blood—she was nearly stabbed herself. She rushed Joey to his bedroom and told him to get under the bed, then ran to her bedroom and called 911. After the attackers left, she ran to her husband and held him until the police arrived, and then went to comfort her son.

The investigation had been thorough. Descriptions were given by my mother, who had looked through police mug shots, to no avail. Our middle-class cul-de-sac neighborhood was canvassed and fingerprints were taken from the window at the point of entry.

Crime scene photos showed blood splatter in the kitchen and dining room. Crimson shoe prints traced my mom's frantic sprints down the hallway and blood smeared my Oakland Raiders bedspread where she held me afterwards. The police techs had collected nine different vials of blood from different locations in the kitchen and dining room. Knife attacks often result in cuts to the hands of the attackers, but DNA tests showed all the blood samples were my dad's.

My mind strayed to the photos of Jefferson Devaney's blood-streaked body, and then back to my father. I pictured his warm smile, and then saw it twisted in agony as he slipped helplessly in his own blood. I heard his calm voice teaching me to keep a baseball scorebook, and then imagined his panicked screams as he fought for his life. I felt his strong hands under my arms and the thrill as he tossed me over his head and caught me again. Then I saw his powerful form punctured and lifeless on linoleum.

The rest of the binder included supplemental reports, mostly following up on dead-end leads. I skimmed quickly, flipping through the slippery mimeograph pages, until I stopped cold.

It was a sketch artist's rendering of one of the suspects, obviously drawn under the instruction of my mother, the only adult witness in the case. The sketched image was of a young man. He was a light-skinned Black man, with close-set eyes, a pug nose and small mouth. I blinked away the image, moving the drawing this way and that, desperately studying the face from all angles. The spitting image of a young Allston Walker seemed to follow my gaze.

CHAPTER 26

Back in my office on Monday, I collected my thoughts, which until then, had been dominated by "Holy shit, I may be defending my father's killer!" There was a chance Walker had been in prison at the time of my dad's murder. His rap sheet showed he'd been incarcerated off and on from 1990 to 1996, but I couldn't determine if he'd been free from custody by the time my dad was killed. I called Chuck and asked him to subpoena his prison records to determine his release date.

It was really a lose-lose proposition, or such was my current mindset. I now had the opportunity to receive the very bad news that my father's murder was still unsolved, or the horrific news that I was defending his murderer.

But was this even possible? What were the odds, after all? I had to admit the discovery of my dad's crime scene details had addled my brain. Perhaps I wasn't thinking clearly. Suddenly, the idea that Walker had killed him seemed absurdly far-fetched. I needed a drink. Who was I kidding? I needed a vodka IV.

Back home, I wandered next door to visit with my neighbor, Bill Beltramo, an entertaining Bostonian and a Red Sox fanatic. As I had hoped, he offered me the first of more than a few Dark and Stormies and we talked baseball on his back patio until well after dark.

The next morning, I awakened to find myself naked, confused and wrapped in my comforter on my ugly recliner. I spotted what I hoped was water on the hardwood near my chair and followed more drops to the back door, where my soaked jeans, t-shirt and boxers lay wadded in a puddle.

After several moments, my memory of the evening slowly took shape. I recalled awakening to a hissing sound and the gradual feeling of lying in water. It wasn't until the sprinkler had sprayed my face at close range that I realized I had passed out on my back lawn on the walk home from my neighbor's. I must have stumbled, then been too drunk to get up.

My phone buzzed and I fished it out of the comforter. At least it was dry.

—Hey there, Counselor. You free next weekend? I want to see you.—

—Yes.—

After a very long and hot shower and a fried egg sandwich at Big Al's Cafe, I boarded the courthouse elevator bound for the D.A.'s Office and our meeting with the victim, Devaney. Chuck and I made room in the elevator for an elderly man with a cane. I had seen him at the information desk on the first floor, clearly having difficulty getting his bearings.

"What floor, sir?" I asked, feeling virtuous.

"Oh, thank you," he creaked, peering up from his stoop. "Ninth floor."

I stole a sideways glance at Chuck, who looked straight ahead, a wry smile forming on his weathered face. We both knew that the District Attorney's office was the sole occupant on the ninth floor.

He had shaved since the attack, but I now recalled his deep set brown dark eyes and buzz cut from the bloody photos. He wore a white dress shirt and khaki pants. A well-worn seersucker jacket fit loosely on his spindly frame, and almost obscured leather suspenders.

"Houston, we have a problem," said Chuck, after Devaney had been ushered into the office, no doubt to chat with Matt prior to our meeting.

"A Few Good Men?"

"Apollo 13. Commander Jim Lovell."

"Here's a line," I groused, "We're fucked. Lots of people on the Titanic played by lots of actors."

Our meeting with Devaney, under the watchful eye of Deputy District Attorney Eisner, confirmed our impression. Within thirty seconds, I had officially abandoned my prostitute theory.

Devaney was a friendly, nice old man, who would engender enormous sympathy with the jury. He had the demeanor of a southern gentleman and spoke with a drawl, sprinkling his speech with adorable southern sayings. He was decrepit and slow moving, clearly still recovering from his injuries.

After introductions, he leaned forward, resting forearms on the conference table, locking eyes with me, then Chuck.

"You folks seem very decent, and I know you're just doing your job, but let me be as clear as crystal. Your client is the man who tried to kill me. I have a pretty good memory for an old timer and I'm as certain now as when he did it."

"Well, thank you for taking the time to meet with us, Mr. Devaney. Chuck and I were just hoping to ask you a few specific questions about your identification, and…"

"I don't mean to be rude, but if you're hoping to trip me up, you're barking up the wrong tree."

"Sir, I certainly don't want to try to trick you at all. It's just that since we didn't have a chance to speak to you at the preliminary hearing, I was hoping…."

"Nah, I believe I've said what I needed to say," he said abruptly, staring me down. For the first time, I observed a departure from his polite and gracious persona and wondered about the real Devaney.

He was quick to recover his composure. "Look," he said, pausing to rub his smiling face, his scars still fresh, "the last thing I would want on my conscience is to railroad an innocent man." He paused again and smiled at me pleasantly. "Your client is guilty." He almost seemed apologetic, and I almost believed he meant it.

On my way out of the courthouse, I stopped by the master calendar court to see the likely courtroom destination for the Walker trial—the Walker ordeal, as I had taken to thinking of it. The trial would be heard by Judge Philip Arnadon. He was known to be a gentleman, fair to both sides, and not afraid to make a decision.

Back at my office, I was relieved to find that Walker's prison disciplinary file had arrived in the mail just in time for the trial. I had no reason to believe the D.A. had subpoenaed the files, but just in case, if Walker had stabbed someone in prison, I wanted to be the first to know.

I ripped open the manila envelope on the way out of the office. "Shit," I said out loud, handing the documents to Chuck, who was preparing subpoenas. Apparently, during his last stint in prison, Walker had spent two weeks in solitary confinement for possession of a shank.

"At least he didn't stab an inmate twice his age over a pack of cigarettes," said Chuck, walking out of the office.

"Not that we know of. See you, Chuck."

My phone buzzed. It was Andy, calling on his way home.

"Hey, did you have an appointment with a prostitute named Sierra Belton scheduled for this morning?"

"Never prostitutes on Fridays. Their rates are higher on weekdays. Why?"

"Well, one stopped by today. She said she had information on the Walker case. I'll text you her number."

"Wow, my prostitute theory won't go away. Thanks."

Well, this was interesting, to say the least. I forwarded her number to Chuck and asked him to schedule an appointment for

Monday morning before court. I wanted Chuck there in case she said something helpful but decided to change her tune at trial.

I worked late, got a burrito for dinner, and limited my drinking to four or five beers. Amanda was supposed to be in town tomorrow, so I fell asleep with happy thoughts.

CHAPTER 27

Saturday morning meant college football, but I found myself checking my phone every ten minutes. Finally.

—*Hey, my mom's away for the weekend. Come here!*—
—*See you in thirty!*—

Under normal circumstances, faced with an impending first-time sexual encounter, I would be a wreck. I attribute it to all the Woody Allen movies I had watched as a child. For no logical reason, I always wondered if I would be able to perform. Never mind that my track record was nearly perfect, except for the occasional issue if I had to take time to put on a condom. (I couldn't cover a bowl with plastic wrap, let alone under pressure.) Still, I worried.

Would she orgasm? Would I know if she faked it? And would she know that I knew and feel bad? Also, I worried about talking too much during sex. I wanted to be considerate, but not an optometrist in bed (Better here, or here? Here or here?)

And there was the awkward transition from making out clothed to the cumbersome and practical act of disrobing. If we took off our own clothes, the cocoon of intimacy took an abrupt hiatus. If we helped each other, the bra hooks or skinny jeans added another layer of stress. Not to mention what had become the minefield of manscaping expectations.

But deep down, I knew my second chance with Amanda would be different. From the moment I saw her words on my phone, I was at ease. Maybe it was the assertiveness of her message. It felt good to be wanted, after all. Whatever the reason, I floated to her carefree, thinking less, sensing and feeling everything.

A note on the front door read, "I'm in the shower. Made you a drink. It's on the counter." She was right, of course. I was relaxed, but a drink couldn't hurt. I sipped it and stood in the kitchen thinking of her in the shower.

She came in wearing a silky black robe, tied loosely below her ample breasts, olive, then milky white as they reached the fabric. We held each other as we spoke, intoxicated by relief and clarity, then began touching each other as we shared our thoughts, both without inhibition.

"I'm so glad I'm here," she said for the second time in two months, smiling at her joke.

"I'm so glad to hear you say that. I feel like such an idiot for last time," I heard myself saying, hearing the familiar panic in my voice that usually preceded nervous nonsense. "Obviously, I don't do a lot of dating, and not to imply that you do. That is, not that I think you date a lot. And not to, um, I mean, even if you did date a lot, not that it's bad." Fully aware that I was yammering like a fool, I was powerless to stop myself.

"I just think for so long you were just this sort of unattainable thing in my life. Not that I think I could ever attain you, whatever that means. ('For God's sake, Joe, stop talking.') It's just that when you sort of touched me. Not that you touched me in that way, it's just that when you touched my arm, I was like holy crap." Still unable to stop myself, even though I heard myself doing the crazy-face scream that I despised.

Thankfully, Amanda, who had been grinning sympathetically, interrupted. "Joseph Wingate Turner?"

"Yes, Amanda-absurd-middle-name-I've-forgotten Kensey?"

"Shut up and kiss me."

Then her lips were on mine before I could respond, her body pressing into me, my hands on her back, sliding to her hips. There were no unintentional brushes of a sweater, no calculated rests of a forearm. I touched her neck as she spoke, feeling her soft skin and the chords within, and traced over her robe down to her breasts. She moved forward until our faces nearly touched, each tasting the other's breath.

She led me down a hallway to a bedroom and shut the door behind us. She tugged at my belt and I undressed. We moved in slow motion, my every sense heightened—her vanilla scent, black satin curves, our slippery gin and tonic tongues.

For once, my focus was guiltless pleasure—her gentle moans, black curls still damp from the shower, tickling my chest. We gazed patiently, our smiles inches apart, as our bodies found each other. Whispering, heaving, gasping, then carelessly collapsing together.

CHAPTER 28

Later, we went for a walk in the foothills behind her mother's house. We talked about friends from college and our careers. While she spoke easily even as the incline increased, my words escaped in heavy breaths and gasps. Finally, she stopped, pretending to take in a view for my benefit.

"Doing okay there, Counselor?" she teased.

"Yeah," I said between breaths, "my standard ten-mile run really took it out of me this morning."

"Well, something took it out of you," she smirked, patting my butt.

"You crack yourself up, don't you, Kensey?"

"C'mon," she said, pulling me by the hand. "I promised to let you work on the trial, and I need to call my mom. She's braving an amusement park with Isabella."

"Wow. She's grandmother of the year. I'm sure Isabella is over the moon."

"Yeah, her mom's pretty darn happy, too," she said, squeezing my hand. I squeezed back.

After a shower, Amanda made BLTs. (She was the perfect woman.) I brought my laptop to her mom's office and settled in to the boring task of clipping and formatting the crime scene photos and surveillance tape for use at trial. I wasn't sure the image of the person in a black hoodie would be of any evidentiary value, but I had to be ready.

The evening found us on the patio with pizza and beer. Conscious of avoiding the impression of a lush and fairly certain I'd be naked again later, I made an effort to limit my intake of both.

"You're meeting with a what?" she asked with wide eyes, when I told her about my appointment with a prostitute.

"A prostitute. That's a woman who gets paid to ...."

"Thanks, smartass. And I'm not sure how I feel about this," she said smiling.

"I promise to use protection."

"You're incorrigible. How's the trial prep going? Any luck finding the real attacker?"

"No, if it wasn't Walker, the guy is a ghost."

"The *guy* is a ghost? Does this mean you've given up on your beloved TACT?"

"Sadly, yes. Devaney is the last person to cheat on his wife. Or at least that's the impression he gives."

"So, I guess the surveillance tape was of no use?"

"Not really. It shows a person leaving the hotel right after the attack, but you can't see his face." I stared into the distance.

"What are you thinking?" she asked reaching to hold my hand.

"Just thinking about the surveillance tape. If the camera were angled just a fraction differently, it would change everything."

"Yeah, funny how life turns on the slightest things." We kissed, each sure we were thinking the same thing. "Those legs have any energy left after the strenuous hike?"

"You mean the ten-mile run and the hike? Remarkably, yes."

Halfway through a peaceful sleep after more lovemaking, I got up quietly for water, parched from the salty pizza. As I passed by her mother's office on my way back to bed, the light of my laptop screen caught my eye. I peeked in to find Amanda, wrapped in a blanket on a couch, studying the fuzzy surveillance footage.

"Hey there," I said softly settling down beside her. "I thought you were still in bed."

"Hey. Sorry, I've had trouble sleeping lately. I came in here to read and saw your laptop on. I hope it's okay for me to take a look. I've never seen a surveillance video."

"Of course. Have you solved the case yet?"

"No, like you said, it's basically worthless," she said shutting the laptop, and leaning against me. C'mon, don't let me ruin your night's sleep." She followed me back to bed.

"Nice bed head, by the way," she murmured, her head settling on my chest.

"Normally, Ms. Amanda, I would cover my head in horror. But having just participated in sex of an Olympic quality, nothing can shake my confidence."

"I thought you were going to say 'professional quality,' but I guess that's on Monday."

"Good one, Kensey."

She tousled my hair and kissed me goodnight.

CHAPTER 29

Back at home on Sunday, I prepared for the trial, or more accurately failed to stay focused on the task. On one hand, the relationship with Amanda seemed completely natural and long overdue. We had always made each other laugh and shared a slightly jaded outlook on life. We had both grown up without fathers and had trusted each other with similar demons from our childhood.

On the other hand, since I had spent so much time wanting to be with her, part of me wondered if this was real. I imagined texting my old college friends who had chided me for spending time with her, torturing myself while she dated football stars and fraternity boys.

"So, what changed?" I asked myself as I peeled off my shirt in front of the bathroom mirror. My hairline was holding firm but beginning to gray. Owing completely to my mom's metabolism, I had remained thin. I had let my gym membership lapse a few years ago, and my muscle tone had followed suit. I flexed in the mirror, squinting to see a vague outline of my biceps.

I walked into the living room, chiding myself for my predictability. At the start of just about all my relationships, I pledged a renewed commitment to fitness. It usually lasted a few months, less time if the relationship ended before the pledge ran its course.

If the relationship was serious, then I may even vow to adjust my diet or alcohol intake, but these promises rarely made it past the idea phase. I was a professional in convincing myself it was unnecessary or even a bad idea. Stop eating brats from the cart outside the courthouse? Why torture myself, when carbs were the real evil? Cut down on hard liquor? It helped me sleep, which was important, especially during trials. Beer? But it provided the essential carbs for all the exercising.

The difficulty with maintaining a fitness routine was I disliked exercise in all forms. A swimmer in high school, I had swum my last lap. There was nothing more boring than the monotony of staring at the lines on the bottom of the pool.

Running was, frankly, too difficult. I wasn't overweight, and the cardiovascular benefit seemed a small payoff from the daily agony. Sure, it would be nice to be less out of breath when I took the stairs, but there was usually an elevator around.

Sometimes at the gym, I'd pedal the stationary bike while listening to music watching a ball game. Usually though, a few minutes in I would find that I had stopped pedaling, and once I lost the momentum the workout was over.

Lately, though, I had noticed a disturbing trend that needed addressing. There was a small but noticeable roll gaining a foothold around my midsection. On a husky guy the tiny bulge would look quite normal, but the pudge stood out against my thin frame.

It had first become apparent after a shower. When I straightened up after drying my legs, water escaped from the folds near my midsection and trickled to the floor. Also, I had noticed recently that when I sat up in bed without assistance of my arms—essentially performing a single sit-up, my stomach quivered.

With a ridiculously ambitious plan—also a hallmark of my forays into fitness—I set out to do one hundred sit-ups a night. Before I made it down to the floor, I had added one hundred pushups to the routine, never mind that fourteen was my lifetime best. After all, I didn't want to look ridiculous with a six-pack but no arm definition.

I lay on my back on the rug in front of the television and clicked to highlights of a golf tournament. A lot of those guys made me feel okay about my body. I bent my knees and tucked the toes of my sneakers under the bottom shelf of a low bookcase for leverage. Then, with my traditional deep breath and solemn pause worthy of embarking on a journey of life-changing magnitude, I began.

After twelve sit-ups, I had slightly adjusted my daily goal. I didn't want to fall victim to burnout, after all. I would rest a while, then resume with a goal of twenty. Also, I realized around number four that whoever decided it was better to do sit-ups with your hands behind your head was an idiot. It made the exercise significantly more difficult.

I found it was much more efficient for me to do the exercise with my hands near my sides, thrusting them forwards to create momentum. It was funny how certain ways of doing things just caught on and never changed. My way allowed me to accomplish at least twice as many sit-ups than the old way. I made it to seventeen using this method before I needed another rest.

After accomplishing my goal of twenty, I fell back to the floor, gasping for breath. Sit-ups were truly awful. Working your "core" was all the rage, but was it really worth it? I figured "core work" probably originated with one of those fitness videos made by muscle heads with an online degree in physical education.

I rolled to my side and took inventory. My tail bone was sore from the bumpy carpet and I feared my legs may never straighten again. Also, the rapid back and forth head movement had me feeling a little nauseous. With one hundred sit-ups still to do, I thought I'd had enough for one night. Also, the prospect of repeating the sit-up fiasco again tomorrow night was too much to bear, so I further revised my plan to do sit-ups and push-ups on alternating nights. I'd heard muscle heads at the gym talk about "core day" and "bicep day," so I thought this made sense.

"Tonight is beer night," I said aloud, while grabbing a beer from the fridge and heading for the recliner to watch a ballgame.

CHAPTER 30

Early on Monday morning I was alone in my quiet office, organizing my trial binder and thinking the case through. The best defense—the only defense, given Devaney's sympathetic jury appeal, was that the poor man had suffered such a traumatic event, his recognition of the event had been altered. I had to persuade at least one juror that when Devaney was essentially stabbed from his nap into consciousness, his mind never fully met the present and focused on his attacker. Instead, with the argument with Walker in his thoughts when he dozed off, he awoke struggling with someone he assumed was Allston Walker.

The theory was short on proof, but not wholly unsupported by the evidence. "Allston Walker stabbed me. He lives in room 112," Devaney had told Officer Vanner. However, Vanner's partner, Officer Percy, wrote that Devaney had "drifted in and out of consciousness."

And there was the 911 tape. "Do you know who stabbed you?" the dispatcher had asked Devaney. "No," he had replied. The prosecution might argue that while Devaney knew the identity of his attacker, he couldn't think of his name, an understandable mistake under the circumstances.

Paramedic Souza's report was bare bones, documenting Devaney's multiple stab wounds and his transportation to Highland Hospital with lights and sirens. The author of the report noted that he intubated the patient—med-speak for shoving a tube down his throat so he could breathe.

I forced myself to sort through the 87 crime scene photos. The theme of the montage was gore. Inevitably, my thoughts drifted to my father's murder, which stopped my trial preparation in its tracks.

Was I jumping to a wild conclusion? After all, on what was my suspicion based? An artist's rendering of mom's description? She could not have seen the killer for more than five seconds of panicked hysteria. Or was my paranoia based on more than that? Was there something in my own sub-conscious, something I might have seen that awful day as I peeked from behind my mother's green overcoat?

I should have Walker's prison records any day now. I reminded myself to gather Friday's mail on the way out of the office. If Walker had been out of custody at the time my dad died, I would declare a conflict of interest, relieving myself as his attorney.

Or would I? I wondered in a very dark recess of my mind. After all, I would be in the unique position to prosecute my father's killer, albeit for a different crime. While I didn't always know how to win a case, I was pretty certain I could find a way to lose.

"Twenty-two minutes." Chuck's baritone startled me as he walked in, unannounced, as usual.

"Chuck, you know I could have a woman in here. Speaking of which, the prostitute is a no-show."

"Shocker," he said sarcastically. "Picked up your mail downstairs," he said, and tossed some envelopes on my desk. "So, twenty-two minutes. I did the route on Saturday at the same time of night. That's roughly how long it would have taken Walker to get from the hotel to the Hartung's to answer Julia's call. Phone records show the call was made at 8:23 p.m."

"Okay, and the 911 call was placed at 8:10 p.m. So, I guess so long as the murderer would not have done something crazy like speeding away from the crime scene, it's an airtight alibi. And what other less than awesome news do you bring?"

"Still haven't found the other paramedic. And Hartung and Julia are subpoenaed and available."

It was a while before I saw the envelope from Solano State Prison among the mail on the edge of my desk. I was reaching for it when Chuck promptly sat on it while staring at his phone. "Ms. Belton just cancelled."

"Oh, great," I said sarcastically. Nothing about this case was going to be easy.

"Have you thought about your juror preferences?" Chuck asked, finally standing.

I shrugged, thinking about prison records. "What are your thoughts?"

"Anyone who might be sympathetic to the cause, I suppose. You know, like someone with no parents?"

"Hilarious."

"I got a hold of Julia, the daughter's friend. She verifies the phone call. Says some guy answered. Sounded older."

"Right." I was paying attention but kept glancing at the envelope.

"The drive is bad news. If Walker had sped away from the scene, he could probably make it to get the phone call."

"But if he's guilty, would he answer the phone?" I asked, now staring at the envelope. "Wouldn't he have been busy washing the blood off his clothing?"

"He might if he wanted an alibi."

I did not respond, and Chuck took the cue, moving toward the door. "I'll let you get busy. Good luck. I'll get you those subpoenas tomorrow. I'll try to reschedule with Ms. Belton." He paused in the door. "And, Joe?"

"Yes, Chuck?"

"Thank goodness he didn't kill your father." I sat, staring at him, mouth agape. "How in the fuck did you…"

"Elementary, my dear Watson," he said with a wink, and shut the door behind him.

I knew the result, but as I saw it in black and white, I felt relief wash over me again. On March 3, 1996, the worst day of my life, Allston Walker had been safely tucked away in prison.

I exhaled, whispering softly to myself. "SOMDI."

CHAPTER 31

Among courthouses in California, there is nothing resembling architectural uniformity. In once bankrupt Butte County, a large mobile home served as the Hall of Justice. Complete with stick-on wood paneling and an impossibly steep two-step entry, the courtroom did not lend gravitas to the presiding judge, who would have looked less out of place if he had shed the robe in favor of a white, sleeveless undershirt.

Other courthouses in the state are true architectural treasures. In Santa Barbara, an 18th century stucco and terracotta cathedral houses the Superior Court. In well-heeled Marin County, a Frank Lloyd Wright designed edifice blends with the rolling hills and the self-styled free spirits of the residents.

The Alameda County Courthouse, built in 1938 and financed by Roosevelt's New Deal, got it just right. Hard by Lake Merritt near downtown Oakland, even from a distance, the building is easily recognizable as a courthouse. The stout, four-sided, structure gleams in painted white stone, with columns in the front and a green steeple roof atop its eleven stories.

The courtrooms themselves are extravagant by today's government-building standards. The bench, counsel table, and clerk's station are all appointed in carved mahogany, the wood extending two-thirds up to the twenty-foot ceilings.

The grandeur of the courtrooms recalls a time when courtroom life meant theater, before the sheer number of criminal prosecutions made clearinghouses of courtrooms and an attorney's creativity and eloquence were crushed by the caseloads. Centered behind the bench in every courtroom, where the judges sit high above the proceedings, an enormous American flag is draped from the ceiling.

To the right of the bench is the witness stand, lower but still two steps above the floor of the courtroom, perfectly positioned so that its occupants look up to the judge, down to the lawyers, and can't hide from the jury. The jury box is encircled by an old railing, the chairs at fairly close quarters, anchored to the floor well before anyone had heard of business class.

Just like in the movies, a swinging gate separates the well of the court from the gallery, which is appointed with fifteen rows of flip-down wooden seats. From the gate, a wide center hallway leads to huge oaken double doors that guard, quite literally, the courtroom's exits.

Once in the early eighties, a defendant made a break for the exit during a lull in the courtroom proceedings. The Honorable Alfred Delucchi, a legal giant in the county who would later preside over the Scott Peterson trial, calmly flicked a switch somewhere within arm's reach. The defendant, who had reached top speed in his flight down the aisle, hit the double doors on a dead run. Locked tight by the judge's secret switch, the doors may as well have been an oak tree. The defendant was knocked to his back faster than he arrived and carried back into custody on a stretcher, groggy with a broken nose.

The Deputy District Attorney who would prosecute Allston Walker was waiting in Department 10 when I arrived. He was new to the office, a transfer from Los Angeles County, and we had never met.

"Arn Kotkin," he said, a bit too loud as we shook hands. "So, you've drawn this short straw. Nice to meet you, Joe," he said staring somewhere above my head. I wondered if the smirk was permanent.

Unlike some defense attorneys who prefer to demonize their opponents, I usually tried to play nice. Personal animosity was draining, and I was competitive enough without hating my opponent. Also, the Alameda County District Attorney's Office enjoys one of the best reputations in the country, boasting as alums former Supreme Court Chief Justice Earl Warren, vice-president Kamala Harris, and congressman Eric Swallwell. Clearly, though, they were not immune from regrettable hiring decisions.

"Mr. Turner, Mr. Kotkin, the judge will see you in chambers." With those words of the judge's long-time clerk, Charlotte Kingston, the trial of Allston Walker began as all felony trials begin in Judge Arnadon's courtroom, with an informal discussion of the case in the judge's comfortable, well-appointed chambers. Unfailingly polite, Judge Arnadon greeted us both and gestured toward a comfortable leather sofa and high-backed chair stationed in front of his desk.

As my adversary chose the chair, I scanned the wood-paneled walls, half-searching for content to support a smarmy remark, customary for such occasions. Photos and plaques made clear that the judge was a golfer and a family man. An antique persimmon driver leaned casually in a corner, and the box of cigars on his desk and a burgundy Persian underfoot gave the impression of a smoking room at a men's club.

I sank low into the sofa, its cushions soft from years of use by defense attorneys—a group not known for their physical fitness. The judge spun his chair slightly to face the D.A. "Attempted 187? What's this case about?" he asked, referring to the California Penal Code section which defines murder. The number has become common parlance for lawyers, judges and gangster rappers.

"It's a fairly simple case, Judge," Kotkin began, in an annoying game show host voice that I would soon learn to loathe. "The defendant and the victim argue about unpaid rent at the Islander

Hotel. Defendant comes back later and attacks the victim while he dozes in his apartment. Defendant plunges a knife into his chest. Incredibly, the victim, who's in his late sixties, is able to fight him off after being stabbed several times. He identifies the defendant to the police by name. He knows him. That's it. Pretty simple."

Apart from implying that someone in his late 60's was nearly feeble, which elicited a narrowing of the judge's bushy gray brow, it was a good prosecutorial summary of the case. Simple, direct, and not far off, I judged, from the prosecution's case itself.

The judge swiveled toward me and peered down over his reading glasses. "Mr. Turner?" There was an uncomfortable silence while I decided what to say, or more accurately, how much I had to say. Being quick on my feet is not my strong suit, which is odd, given my profession. Also, I very much wanted to say nothing.

While Kotkin knew the defense was misidentification, there were specific questions I preferred to leave unanswered for as long as possible. Would my client testify, would there be an alibi, and to what extent I would blame the attack on the man running away from the scene were all aspects of the case I preferred to keep under my hat for now.

Experience had taught me to share nothing with my opponent, just on the off chance I might reveal something they didn't know. That can probably be traced to a high school football coach who refused to let our team ever help an opponent up off the football field just in case that same player used that minute reserve of energy to make a game saving shoestring tackle later in the game.

While this was good strategy, being too circumspect with a judge is a different matter. "For God's sakes Joe, say something!" I told myself as the pregnant pause became uncomfortable. "My client has no history of violence, Judge, and he says he didn't do it." I shrugged, palms raised, the international sign among defense attorneys of 'Don't shoot the messenger, sorry to waste everyone's time, what can I say, just doing my job.' Judge Arnadon's smile probably meant that he knew I wanted to keep my cards face down, and he didn't press me for details.

"I assume no chance of settlement?" asked the judge.

Kotkin smiled at me, savoring his position of power. I was really starting to dislike this guy. "Mr. Walker can plead guilty to attempted murder for fifteen to life," he said.

"No sale," I answered, addressing the judge.

"Pretrial motions?" asked the judge.

"I might move to exclude my client's statement on Miranda grounds, Judge. I will let you know for sure tomorrow." I saw Kotkin's eyebrows raise and his eyes begin to lose focus as he searched his brain for the specifics of Walker's Miranda warning.

"Fine, we can take that up just prior to jury selection."

After a brief discussion of the trial's schedule, the judge took the bench to introduce himself to Walker, who would see the trial courtroom for the first time. I was anxious to see him, hoping that somehow my memory of his hard and compressed face may have been exaggerated in my mind's eye, perhaps accentuated by the unlit jail's cement motif.

Walker shuffled into the courtroom, shackled at the ankles, moving awkwardly and peering furtively around the massive room like a small animal overwhelmed by new surroundings. Squinting under the glare of the lights after a day in the courthouse's windowless holding tank, his face was more pinched together than ever, the grimace ever-present. He grunted a greeting and sat next to me at the counsel table.

Judge Arnadon welcomed Mr. Walker to his department and explained that the trial would proceed Monday through Thursday from 9:00 a.m. to 4:30 p.m., with a break for lunch, until its conclusion.

"We'll begin tomorrow morning with your motion to exclude your client's statement, Mr. Turner, and then roll into jury selection. Both parties should file your witness lists with Charlotte before you leave today. We're adjourned." The judge was out of his robe and off the bench before his last sentence was complete.

"A Miranda motion?" asked Kotkin, trying to sound casual. "I don't recall any basis for that."

"Yes," I replied, matter-of-factly. "I can't very well claim self-defense if my client's statement is in evidence." I gathered my file and left the prosecutor standing at the counsel table, hoping he wondered whether I was joking.

I had no intention of attempting to exclude Walker's statement. Not only was there no basis for the motion, but in telling the police he didn't commit the crime, his statement actually helped his case.

I just felt like fucking with Kotkin.

CHAPTER 32

I made a conscious effort to cut back on my alcohol intake during trials, more because it felt like I should than for any particular benefit. In fact, like this morning, my sobriety made me restless. Up at 5:00 a.m. and unable to sleep, I drove to the office to organize my trial binder for the tenth time.

I found a parking spot out front just before dawn and took the elevator to the fourth floor. I nearly put my key into the office front door before seeing the jagged hole in the glass next to the doorknob. Another break-in. Dammit! It was the second time this year. It wasn't as if Andy and I had anything to steal. We'd long since learned not to leave our laptops in the office and the burglars had deemed Carolyn's desktop too heavy for their trouble.

But there was the annoying clean-up, door repair and Andy's incessant jibes about my clients being responsible. Once, a foul stench had been left behind by someone who raided our office fridge and spent the night.

I pushed the door open and stepped over the broken glass, bracing myself for a stench. Thankfully, none came. I was about to open my office door when something moved inside. "Shit," I whispered to myself. They were still there.

I froze, my mind racing. I scanned the room for a weapon. I scooped a letter opener off Carolyn's desk. Who was I kidding? I had trouble killing flies. I couldn't stab anyone, and what if he had a gun? Think, Joe!

Then it came to me. I would trap the burglar inside, leave and call the police. I quietly grabbed a chair from our lobby and crept toward my office door. I'd seen this a thousand times on television. It must work. I leaned the chair silently against the door and wedged it under the doorknob.

I turned to leave and was a step inside our lobby when I heard footsteps behind me. Before I could turn around, I was shoved from behind and tumbled forward into a potted fern as the burglar ran out of the office.

Regaining my faculties, my first thought was so much for cutting back on alcohol. The resulting inability to sleep was the reason why I was currently face down in my office with a face full of potting soil.

I rose and made my way back to my office, shaking my head at my stupidity. Apparently, the old chair-under-the-doorknob trick only works if the door pushes open from the inside. The burglar had simply pulled the door open and stepped over the fallen chair.

I entered my office. Deep down, I wasn't surprised what I found. There, next to my desk on the floor were the two banker's boxes that comprised the Walker file. Their contents had been dumped on the desk and pilfered through.

It was still early in my representation of Allston Walker, but I had the distinct impression that there was much more than met the eye.

CHAPTER 33

Still reeling from the office fiasco, I walked into Department 10, dreading jury selection, the most tedious part of the trial. Voir dire, commonly known as jury selection, is as difficult to undertake as it is to pronounce. Hundreds of prospective jurors are summoned to Court with the chance of having their lives disrupted for the next several weeks. They are lectured about their civic duty, questioned about their biases and personal tragedies for the world to hear, and told they may be subjected to graphic photos. Most everyone, including the attorneys, is in a foul mood.

For Walker's jury, I would be leery of older jurors who had been victims of violence or lived alone and harbored those fears. I wouldn't be thrilled with senior citizens in general, who may be reticent to accept the contention that Mr. Devaney was ultimately mistaken. I wanted jurors who were liberal, anti-government, anti-police, and if available, jurors who harbor an unexplained hatred of hotel managers.

Given that the evidence against Walker seemed strong, I would follow the advice of Judge Alan Hymer. While an attorney with the Public Defender's Office, he had once disclosed to me his strategy for jury selection in hopeless cases.

"You want jurors who are stupid," he had told me with a gleam in his eye, "but who think they are smart." In the pursuit of a single holdout, the strategy was Machiavellian genius. While the majority of the jury saw the obvious truth borne out by the overwhelming evidence, the ideal juror could see the "real" truth, even in the face of a vocal majority who obviously did not have the benefit of his superior intellect.

Finally, given that a hung jury seemed like the only realistic goal, I wanted disagreeable jurors who might be apt to contradict popular sentiment and strong personalities who could resist caving into the popular opinion. Basically, I wanted jurors with whom I would least like to spend an unlimited time in a small room, attempting to form a consensus so that we could leave the small room.

Sitting next to Walker in Department 10 before the arrival of the venire, or prospective jurors, I noticed a young Hispanic man with a shaved head take a seat in the back row of the gallery before the judge took the bench. Concerned about another witness buried on Kotkin's list, I asked Walker if he knew him. Walker swiveled in his seat and nodded toward the young man, who barely acknowledged the greeting.

"That's just Paul Camacho, the custodian at the Islander. Good kid. Takes care of his younger sister. They live in 116. Good of him to come," he whispered, as the jury filed in.

Something about Walker's unusually chatty answer piqued my curiosity. Recalling that he had told me that the custodian saw him argue with Devaney, I had wondered why Camacho's name didn't appear in the police reports. Something was up. I stared hard at my client, holding my pensive smile for several seconds after he had turned to face the judge. Finally, Walker turned to look at me and gestured with his palms up, his face betraying nothing.

"All rise, Department 10 of the Superior Court of California, County of Alameda is in session." Walker rose, standing next to me. An unidentifiable thought caused the tiniest of ripples on my brain, barely noticeable as I listened to the idle chatter of the courtroom staff.

Judge Arnadon fairly burst through the door of his chambers and strode purposefully toward the bench, robe flowing behind him. His bailiff, a weathered man in his late fifties shot ramrod straight from his nail-clipping slouch as if spring loaded, his calls of "All rise, all rise" the perfect accompaniment as the judge ascended his perch.

His Honor looked nothing like the man talking golf with his feet up in chambers. His visage, although friendly and warm, bespoke a man with nothing but important business on his plate. Good afternoon, ladies and gentleman, flashing the smile that must have helped him during his career as a prosecutor.

"Calling the case of the People of the State of California versus Allston Walker. The record will reflect Mr. Kotkin is present as is Mr. Walker and his counsel, Mr. Turner. Mr. Kotkin, are you ready for trial?"

"The People are ready, Your Honor."

"Mr. Turner. Are you ready?"

"Defense is ready, Your Honor."

I glanced at Walker, seated directly to my left. As instructed, he was wearing a button-down shirt and khaki pants. Nothing too formal. Hopefully, something that said, "I manage a clothing store. How could I have possibly stabbed someone to death?"

The next few moments would be, as I had told Walker, in some ways, some of the worst of the trial. Walker acknowledged me with a nod of reassurance as the judge began. "Welcome to Department 10. You have been summoned to this department as prospective jurors in a criminal jury trial. This case is The People of the State of California v. Allston Walker. This is a criminal trial." I felt the most minute of air currents on the back of my neck, caused by 110 pairs of eyes shifting their gaze to the man sitting next to me.

"The District Attorney of Alameda County representing the People of the State of California, has accused Allston Vayne Walker of attempted murder." The courtroom fell silent—a complete silence that can only be achieved in a packed courtroom when everyone inhales at once.

This was the one time the prospective jurors were predictable: first, thinking "I have to get off this jury;" then wanting a glimpse of someone who had probably tried to kill someone; then curious to see what kind of slimy attorney was representing him. "Mr. Walker has denied these charges," the judge continued, "and must be presumed innocent until proven guilty."

"I'd like to introduce the participants in the trial. Representing the People is Deputy District Attorney Arnold Kotkin." The prosecutor rose, turned deliberately toward the jury, flashing a toothy grin. "Good morning, ladies and gentlemen," he said, managing to sound earnest and gracious, all in five words.

"The defendant is represented by Joe Turner," continued the judge. "Mr. Turner, please introduce your client."

I rose and turned to face the gallery. "Good morning. This is my client, Allston Walker." Mr. Walker rose, and so too did the bailiff, seated directly behind him. Hand on his holster, the bailiff may as well have held a sign over Mr. Walker that read "Dangerous Prisoner." Walker managed to smooth away the scowl long enough to say good morning to the prospective jurors.

After introductions of the courtroom staff, Ms. Kingston, the clerk, she of the beehive hair and sensible shoes, sing-songed her way through the first twelve unlucky jurors to be seated in the jury box. Charlotte had been a fixture in Judge Arnadon's department for as long as anyone could remember, had never lost her Wisconsin accent, and sounded as if she was perpetually teaching a group of kindergartners.

After the judge had questioned the first twelve unlucky patrons as to their place of residence in the county, marital status and the like, he turned to the prosecutor. "Mr. Kotkin. Thirty minutes." Judge Arnadon had taken to mumbling "Mr." and then belting "Kot" out of the side of his mouth, the last syllable of the name trailing off so much that it was inaudible. The effect was that of a bark from the bench at my opponent, which I enjoyed immensely.

Kotkin strolled to the podium, dragging his heels on the hardwood floor with every step, and greeted them with a syrupy smile. "I'd first like to thank you all for being here. You are fulfilling a most important civic duty, and you have my deepest gratitude."

"Ladies and gentlemen, how many people watch the television show CSI?" After six hands went up, Kotkin recited a familiar D.A. spiel, aimed at lowering jury expectations by pointing out that solving crime through hair fibers, DNA evidence, and soil samples is not realistic. I smiled at the predictability of my opponent and made a note to myself to reveal Kotkin to be the obsequious, condescending sycophant that he was. I used shorthand.

The monotony of voir dire was broken temporarily by juror number one, Dr. Cisneros, an obese pediatrician who had tried in vain to be excused because he was speaking at a conference in Los Angeles the following day. His excuse having been politely rejected by the judge, the doctor had stuffed himself and his oversized ego into juror seat number one, and sat seething, his arms crossed atop his belly.

Kotkin had asked the doctor individually, as he did every juror, whether he would vote to convict if he proved that Allston Walker was guilty beyond a reasonable doubt. Kotkin asked the obvious question to show the jury that he was confident in his ability to prove the case, and that the only thing that could go wrong was if the jury defied the law. All of which made Dr. Cisneros' response all the more surprising.

"No, I can't be fair," he said.

Kotkin was flustered. "Is there, um, a reason, sir, why, uh..."

"Why not?" interrupted Judge Arnadon, who had moved closer to the microphone. It was not the first time the judge had seen someone attempt to avoid jury service, but the doctor's brazen disrespect for the Court had offended him.

"I just don't think I can be fair, given the case," came the response from blubbering jowls.

"You mean given the timing of your conference."

The jowls were silent. The doctor was not an idiot. He knew that the trial could not proceed with him on the jury after his pronouncement, and there was a hint of a smile through the folds of skin.

"Counsel, approach," said the judge. "Stipulation for cause?" he asked when we reached the bench, a legal shorthand inquiry whether both lawyers would agree to excuse the doctor because he could not be fair.

"Yes, Your Honor," came the whispered response, in unison.

"Good. I'll excuse him after the jury is selected. Until then, consider him an alternate." And with that, Judge Arnadon had won. The pompous physician would remain through jury selection, precisely long enough for him to miss his conference.

The doctor had gathered his Times and leather satchel, and jostled his girth to the edge of his seat. He rose as the judge spoke, fully expecting to be excused.

"Mr. Kotkin, you may resume questioning." The doctor looked confused and remained standing.

"Am I excused?"

The judge ignored him. "Mr. Kotkin, proceed." Then, pretending to notice the doctor for the first time, "Dr. Cisneros, take your seat please. We have lots of work to do." The doctor lowered himself dejectedly into his chair, his Times and satchel sliding to the floor.

CHAPTER 34

August 25, 2021

The caretaker finished his rounds by 1:30 p.m. and was headed back to his apartment behind the front desk when another resident approached him.

"Hey, Sir, I just wanted to let you know my rent will be in your office tomorrow."

"Yeah, well, the problem is —you're 112, right?"

"Yes sir, Allston Walker in 112."

Devaney sighed wearily, his frustration building again. "The problem, Allston Walker in 112, is that your rent isn't due tomorrow. It was due yesterday."

"Look, I've been here for…"

"And I don't give a shit how long you've lived here. You're gonna get an eviction notice."

"Look! It's one damn day!" pleaded Walker, his index finger in the caretaker's face.

"Well then you'd better pack your shit." Devaney found Walker's name on his ledger and made a note, then brushed past him, intentionally shouldering him out of the way.

"What the fuck was that?" Walker called after him, seething.

Devaney waived a hand behind him in disgust. What was it with these people, thinking the world owed them a favor. Plenty of money to buy their precious weed, but none for their rent.

Devaney would deposit the checks and money orders at the bank and return to finish up the paperwork, which included six eviction notices—about average. It was 7:30 p.m. before he collapsed into his leather chair with an apple, kicked off his loafers, and clicked on the television.

CHAPTER 35

"Mrs. Edison," Kotkin resumed, his smile directed at a well-dressed African American woman in her sixties in seat number four. "You indicated that you are a devout Christian. Some people believe that they cannot sit in judgment of another. Would your religious beliefs hinder your ability to sit as a juror in this case?"

"No."

"Juror number six, Professor Liebowitz," Kotkin consulted his notes. "You will hear from the judge that one witness, if believed, is sufficient for me to prove my case. Do you have a problem with that law?"

"I would have a problem with that, yes. I would think that if he was guilty, you would see some sort of corroboration. I don't think I would base the entire verdict on one witness."

"Mr. Liebowitz, the law recognizes that sometimes crimes are committed against people with no one else around. Sometimes the only witness is the victim. This is obviously most often the case in sex offenses. This rule of law protects those victims by stating that it is possible to prove a case with the victim's testimony alone."

"Yes, I understand the rule. I just dispute the premise," said the professor. "Given what I know about eyewitness testimony, I wouldn't believe an eyewitness beyond a reasonable doubt if there was absolutely no other evidence." Much to my glee, Kotkin had picked a fight with the wrong juror.

Realizing that he could not afford to have Liebowitz serve on the jury, Kotkin now set about attempting to reveal to the judge that the juror could not be objectively fair. This would force the Court to excuse him. Otherwise, Kotkin would have to use one of his 20 challenges to get rid of the sociologist.

"So, Mr. Liebowitz, even in the face of overwhelming evidence, you would not convict if there was only one witness to the offense."

"I can't imagine a scenario in which I would do so."

"So, there's no way I could prove my case in your eyes if I had one eyewitness?"

"Correct."

"Your Honor, may we approach?" asked Kotkin, sensing victory.

The judge waved us up. "Do you want to try to save him?" he deadpanned, leaning over the microphone so the jury wouldn't hear, looking at me over his reading glasses.

"Sure."

"Don't take all day."

Now it would be my turn to convince the judge that Liebowitz was fit to serve. I approached the jury box.

"The law to which Mr. Kotkin refers, Mr. Liebowitz, doesn't say that you would have to convict with one believable witness. It just says that there is no rule that indicates more than one witness is required."

"Okay."

"I understand that your concern is the potential that eyewitnesses can be mistaken."

"Yes, given the research."

"Okay, and as you are aware, there are various circumstances that bear on a particular witness's ability to accurately perceive and remember."

"Yes."

"Whether a witness is under stress at the time of the event is one such circumstance. Also, the witness' ability to perceive, whether the witness and the suspect are of the same race, the length of time the witness viewed the suspect and so on, correct?"

"Yes."

"If, in the trial, you had access to all that information, then presumably you would be able to evaluate the identification, correct?"

"Yes."

"For example, say a nun with perfect vision sees someone she knows committing a crime in broad daylight. Surely in that scenario, you could rely on the one witness, right?"

"In that particular scenario, then yes I would."

"So, in some scenarios, you would agree that one witness could prove guilt?"

"Yes."

Mission accomplished, or so I thought. As I took my seat back at the counsel table, I noticed a Post-It on my legal pad. It read, in the careful printing of my client, "Not #6." I looked up again to confirm that juror six was Mr. Liebowitz.

Incredulous, I turned to my client, turning off the microphone on our table. "Are you sure?" I whispered, speaking out of the side of my mouth.

My brief acquaintance with Walker had taught me that while not the most articulate man, he was, nonetheless, a very effective communicator. He turned and stared straight at me, his face blank. Our eyes still locked, he tapped the Post-It note firmly with an index finger once, trapping it against the note pad for several seconds.

I exhaled and lifted my fingers off the table briefly, signaling surrender. While excusing Liebowitz looked for all the world like a terrible decision, Walker obviously felt strongly that the liberal Berkeley resident who didn't seem to like the prosecutor, who did an inordinate amount of smiling at me, and who distrusted eyewitness identifications—the very linchpin of the prosecution's case—was entirely the wrong person to serve on the jury.

Although technically, jury selection was the province of the attorney, I usually yielded to the requests of my clients. Besides, it seemed wrong to ignore the only strategic input Walker had given me to date. And it was, after all, his life that was on the line.

"Yes. And ladies and gentlemen, we've been at it now for a while. Let's take our morning break. We'll reconvene at 10:45 a.m." The jury pool filed out. Liebowitz flashed a polite smile in my direction as he left. I shot a glance at Walker, who stared straight ahead, ignoring me.

"The record should reflect that the jury has left the courtroom. Mr. Kotkin?"

"I move to excuse Mr. Liebowitz for cause," said the prosecutor. "He's biased against all eyewitness testimony."

"I'm not inclined to excuse. Mr. Turner, your position?"

I breathed deeply. "The defense has no opposition to excusing for cause, Your Honor."

The judge stared through me, digesting my comment. He started in hushed to calm tones and ended in a crescendo of intimidation. "In the future, Mr. Turner, I would greatly appreciate if you would refrain from wasting the Court's valuable time attempting to sharpen your dull courtroom skills. Understood?"

"Yes, Your Honor." Dull. Ouch.

Kotkin was apparently too intimidated to even smirk, for fear of the judge shifting his aim.

"What gives, Allston?" I whispered to my client. "That guy would have been great for us."

"Look," he said, "I don't need no one saying I'm innocent because of no study. I didn't stab that man. Period."

I wanted to ask him what difference it made why a juror found him not guilty, but there was no point in debating the issue.

"Sorry about getting you in trouble with the judge, though," he said.

"Don't worry about it." I appreciated the apology, but as His Honor descended the bench, no doubt headed for some long drags on a Cuban, I thought I noticed the hint of a grin forming on the hard and deeply lined face of my client.

I walked to my office at lunch to find Chuck at my desk. "By all means, Chuck, make yourself at home."

"Thanks," he responded, ignoring my jibe. He leaned back in my chair wearing a knowing smile. "Well, you're back on with the prostitute, Ms. Belton."

"I've heard that before. Does she seem, you know, wacky?"

"You mean is her cornbread done in the middle? Only spoke to her on the phone, but she seemed coherent. Besides, as you pointed out, we don't exactly have the luxury of being selective when it comes to witnesses."

"True."

"And get this," Chuck continued, unable to suppress a laugh, "she wants to meet you in the city library tomorrow after court."

"What?"

"That's what she said. I'll only meet with Mr. Turner and I'll do it in the library."

"Well, hopefully she didn't actually use the words, 'I'll do it in the library.'"

"You can't make this stuff up," he said, still laughing. "She said she'd meet you in one of the conference rooms. As I remember, they're windowless. Probably saves on hotel rooms."

"Yeah, only downside is you have to be really quiet. No moaning allowed." We both laughed like school children hearing a dirty joke.

"How's the jury?" Chuck asked, regaining his composure.

"Who knows? Typically, not exactly a jury of Walker's peers."

"Anyone who might be sympathetic to the cause? You know, like someone with no parents?"

"Hilarious."

CHAPTER 36

Back at the courthouse, jury selection carried on throughout the afternoon. Finally, at 4:15 p.m., the issue was settled. Seven women and five men would decide Walker's fate. Most were professional, and three were retired. I'd seen worse juries. But then, what did I know?

After the jury had left the courtroom, Kotkin plopped a six-page witness list down in front of me before filing it with the clerk.

"I assume you took a look at the surveillance video?" the prosecutor asked, sporting a wicked smile.

"Yeah, why?" I didn't look up from my laptop.

"Just wondered how you were going to deal with it. Pretty devastating evidence, right?" He was playing mind games and I was having none of it.

"Whatever." This guy was one colossal d-bag.

Judge Arnadon was still on the bench. "Mr. Kotkin, since the defense has abandoned its motion to suppress, we'll start with your opening statement tomorrow morning. What witnesses do you have scheduled for tomorrow?"

The order of witnesses called in a trial is often the source of strategic concern. While not required by any rule of law, it is generally thought courteous to disclose the order of witnesses during a trial, to allow the opponent to prepare his or her cross examination. Advantages gained in not sharing that information are negligible, usually only existing in the minds of inexperienced trial attorneys who tend to miss the forest for the trees. Predictably, when I had asked about the witness order, Kotkin said smugly, "We'll see."

The D.A.'s witness list was no help, as it included every person even remotely related to the case, from police officers who monitored radio traffic to nurses who wheeled Devaney's gurney. Kotkin's absurd 74-name list was a transparent ploy to keep me in the dark.

Judge Arnadon, however, was not about to let such petty antics invade his courtroom. Besides, if the Court knew the witness order in advance, it could plan ahead and chart the trial's course, not to mention schedule an occasional tee time in the late afternoon.

"I should have plenty of witnesses to fill the day, Your Honor," Kotkin responded, avoiding the judge's question as he shuffled papers at his table.

"Mr. Kotkin, I would like your list of witnesses now, and so, presumably would Mr. Turner."

Kotkin didn't look up from his work. "Your Honor, I have yet to decide..."

"Names!" shouted the judge suddenly. If His Honor had intended to get Mr. Kotkin's attention, it was accomplished. The smug prosecutor was instantly reduced to a stammering milquetoast. A flurry of papers rose from the prosecutor's table, and Kotkin stood slowly, stopping his ascent in a bow, his hands in a death grip on the table.

"Your Honor, sir, er, I didn't, uh. I'll absolutely, to, uh, be happy to, uh. I've got my witness list here somewhere. If I could just, Your Honor...."

"Give the list of actual witnesses to Mr. Turner and my clerk," the judge said calmly. Mr. Turner, do the same before you call your first witness. We're in recess. See you in the morning."

For the first time, it crossed my mind to call Walker as my first witness. Kotkin wouldn't expect it, and production of my actual witness list on the first day of defense testimony would not give him any extra time to prepare. Kotkin was clearly dragging me down to his level.

As I turned down the center aisle to leave, I was surprised to see the menacing young man with the shaved head—Walker's neighbor, Camacho—still sitting in the back row of the courtroom. I had seen Walker stealing glances behind us throughout jury selection and now I knew why. Sitting through the jury selection, Camacho was clearly sending a message of some kind. As I walked past him, his eyes remained locked on Walker. For a supportive friend, this guy was doing a remarkable imitation of a mortal enemy.

I checked my messages on my way to the elevator.

—*Hey Counselor, has the prosecution given up yet?*—
—*No, but another few weeks with Kotkin and we'll have another homicide on our hands.*—
—*Ooooh, I love it when you talk tough, cowboy. Call me later?*—
—*You bet your boots, little darlin'.*—

I looked up from my phone to find that Camacho had boarded the elevator. He was the sole occupant and still wore a menacing scowl. After a few tentative steps, I stopped and decided to catch the next one. Just before the elevator doors began to close, his dark eyes locked on mine. "Y'all best back off or get hurt," he said sneering as the doors moved toward the center framing his angry face. Then, three more words escaped just before the door met, slipping through the gap and piercing my soul. "You and Amanda."

CHAPTER 37

I staggered backwards, the threat to Amanda echoing in my ears. Then I felt myself running to the stairwell and bounding down, taking the steps three and four at a time as my left hand slid down the guard rail. Seven stories later I burst through double doors, scanning the courthouse lobby. But he was gone.

I collapsed on a bench, wondering what I would have done if I had caught up with Camacho. I sat there for several minutes, struggling to comprehend. I was sure I had heard him say it—I could still feel the words, jolting me like a concussion grenade—but had he actually threatened Amanda?

I needed to call her, but I had to collect myself. That, and I needed a drink. I walked to my car on wobbly legs and tried to make sense of it on the way home. Clearly, this Camacho guy was involved in the Devaney attack—either he'd done it himself or was protecting the perpetrator. Whatever the reason, he was desperate to keep his secret safe. I wondered if he'd been the burglar. It seemed a good bet.

Also, it seemed obvious that Walker knew something and was unwilling to share it, even if it meant spending the rest of his life in prison.

I could understand Camacho threatening me if he thought I was planning to blame him for the crime. What I could not fathom was how he knew about Amanda? She had only visited from LA twice.

It seemed impossible that this guy had gone to such lengths. Did he know where I lived? I supposed that he could have seen us together on a chance encounter, but he knew her name! One thing was certain. He knew how to rattle me.

After a gin and tonic, I called Amanda.

"He said what?" she said after a few seconds of silence. "I don't understand. Meaning me?"

"I assume so. I don't understand…"

"Joe, you're scaring me. What are you talking about?" I heard the panic rise in her voice. "He said I had better watch it?"

"I'm sorry, Amanda. It completely freaked me out, too."

"Who is this guy? I'm not understanding any of this."

"Walker isn't saying, but I assume either this guy attacked Devaney or he knows who did. Those were his words, though. 'You best back off or get hurt. You and Amanda.'"

"Jesus, Joe. It gives me chills knowing that he somehow knows who I am."

"I'm so sorry. I had no idea anything like this would happen. Look, I know he was probably just talking, but you should probably not visit me any time soon."

"Yeah, Izzy and I were planning a trip to San Diego to visit her cousins later this week. We might just leave a day or two early."

"Yeah, I'd feel better if you did."

Eventually, we managed to calm each other down. Camacho probably had been at the courthouse tracking Walker's case, where he could have overheard me say Amanda's name while I spoke to her on the phone. And since Walker hadn't told me anything, Camacho would soon learn that he was in no danger of being blamed for anything. Even so, I promised to call Matt Eisner. He could have the patrols increased in my neighborhood.

"I wish I was in your arms," she said.

"Yes," I sighed into the phone. "That would be perfect."

CHAPTER 38

The next morning, as I got organized at the counsel table, Kotkin sat in some sort of trance as the jury filed in. Judge Arnadon welcomed the jury and then turned to the prosecutor. "Mr. Kotkin, your opening statement."

Kotkin sat silently on the edge of his seat, head bowed, eyes closed for dramatic effect. His hands were flat against the counsel table, elbows out, a praying mantis, stoic and angular. The prosecutor, who by now only annoyed me when he exhaled, was not so subtly telling the jury, "I am deep in thought, combing the far reaches of my legal genius to fashion the most persuasive and eloquent argument in the history of jurisprudence." Five seconds passed.

"What a jackass," I whispered under my breath. Judge Arnadon leaned forward to peer over his reading glasses at the stock-still prosecutor. Then he turned his eyes slightly toward the ceiling, the gesture a subtle, yet unmistakable echo of my thoughts.

Finally, the Deputy District Attorney began a slow rise to his feet, pressing himself up from the table as if hoisting a boulder on his back, his gangly limbs unfolding like a recliner. He straightened, still in apparent concentration so deep he hoped to bend a spoon. Searching desperately for the precise words, which, of course, he had already chosen, he strolled to the well of the Court.

Taking strides too short for his legs, Kotkin dragged his heels on every step, clicking his soles against the worn tiles with every stride. It was remarkable, I thought. It was as if this guy had gotten a list of my pet peeves.

It was all I could do not to tackle him before he reached the podium. Finally there, he turned to the Judge and said, "Thank you, Your Honor," speaking solemnly and deliberately, as if he had just been knighted.

If I was hoping that Kotkin's opening statement would meander like his strides and irritate the jury, I was sorely disappointed. He was concise, direct and although confident, not as cocky as I had hoped. The D.A. started by introducing the victim to the jury and reviewing Devaney's activities on the day he was attacked.

The evidence would show, he told the jury confidently, that "this man,"—he paused and pointed to Walker—had committed this "heinous and cowardly crime." They always pointed, the gesture apparently drummed into the skulls of prosecutors on the first day of prosecutor school, sometime between being fitted with the black and white vision contacts and the insertion of metal rods up their backsides.

The prosecutor told the jury that they would hear from the victim, who would tell them the same thing he told the police on the night he had been attacked; that his attacker was Allston Walker. Another point with the index finger, belated and awkward.

"The evidence will be simple and precise and overwhelming," Kotkin concluded, "and at the conclusion of the evidence," I mouthed along with him, "I am confident that you will return a verdict of guilty."

The opening was a typically dry, understated, matter-of-fact prosecutor's opening statement. For all my petty criticisms, at its conclusion, I had no doubt that it had had its desired effect. The jury wondered why they were there. Faced with this clearly overwhelming evidence, why hadn't Walker just admitted guilt?

"Mr. Turner, does the defense wish to make an opening statement at this time?" The defense has the option of reserving its opening statement until after the prosecution's case-in-chief. Most right-minded defense attorneys realize that if you fail to respond to the prosecution's charges promptly in a strong denial, the prosecutor tends to carry the momentum throughout the trial, never to be regained. Being right-minded myself, I always make an opening statement.

I rose, then knelt to my client's ear and whispered, "Do you have any ideas? I have no clue what to say." The remark was a playful attempt to elicit a smile from my stone-faced client in hopes of humanizing him in the minds of the jury. Allston returned my jocular grin with the menacing sneer of a stone-cold killer. Perhaps later for the humanizing.

I strode purposefully to the podium.

"Good morning," I said, lifting my eyes to thirteen poker faces and juror number 8, who, to my relief, continued to smile pleasantly. "The first thing I'd like to point out is that what you just heard in the prosecutor's very eloquent and confident opening statement was nothing more than a prediction."

Kotkin sprang from his seat. "Objection, your Honor. That's totally improper."

With rare exceptions, it's a common courtesy among trial attorneys to forego objections during their opponents' opening statement and closing argument. As Kotkin was discourteous, his objection was not surprising.

"The objection is overruled. Carry on, Mr. Turner."

I suppressed a smile and continued. "So enough about what attorneys think. The evidence," (I emphasized the word) "in this case will show that Allston Walker did not commit this crime. He did not attack Jefferson Devaney. He is absolutely innocent. While there is no question that Mr. Devaney was savagely attacked, there is also no question that Allston Walker was not his attacker.

"The evidence will reveal that on August twenty-fifth of this year at about 8:10 p.m., Jefferson Devaney was reclining on his sofa in his private studio apartment, just behind the front desk. The door to the front desk was left ajar, so he could hear if someone rang the bell."

At this point in my opening statement, about to utter a very important sentence, I noticed that Mr. Schenone, a beefy retired engineer, was asleep. I edged the lectern forward, its wooden legs squeaking across the floor. Problem solved.

"At 8:10 p.m., just before the attack, Jefferson Devaney was asleep"—much like the portly juror, I wanted to add—he was awakened by a knife plunged into his abdomen, and then as you've heard, fought heroically, and saved his own life.

"You will hear the 911 call from Mr. Devaney. The first time he is asked by the dispatcher who stabbed him, Mr. Devaney uttered three words: 'I don't know.'

"The evidence will tell you a little about Allston Walker. The evidence will show that he is not a saint. In his younger days, growing up in west Oakland, he got into some trouble with the law. He's been to state prison, and having met each of you briefly, I can say with confidence that he comes from a different walk of life than yours. You'll hear that he has been convicted of burglarizing cars more than once and has other convictions for minor theft offenses."

Judge Arnadon had already ruled that if Walker testified, the District Attorney could impeach his credibility with the prior convictions on cross-examination. In revealing his past to the jury myself, I hoped to take the starch out of Kotkin's cross examination.

"However, the evidence will clearly show nothing in Allston Walker's past that would even hint that he is a violent man. To the contrary, you will learn that he has never been convicted of a crime of violence."

While I was aware that Walker had been written up in prison for possession of a knife, this didn't qualify as a conviction, so technically, I had told the jury the truth. Thankfully, Kotkin still had not let on that he was aware of the incident.

"You will learn Allston Walker is fifty-eight years old. He grew up in west Oakland, attended McClymonds High School, and served in the Marines for six years before settling back in Oakland, where he worked as a self-employed landscaper and gardener.

"Better yet, you will be able to judge Mr. Walker's credibility for yourself. I will ask you to draw your own conclusions about whether he is telling the truth and whether he is capable of committing this crime.

"You will learn that on August twenty-fifth, Mr. Walker argued with Mr. Devaney about his rent payment. It was a verbal disagreement, but nothing more. The evidence will show that Mr. Walker went to work that day and later retired to his girlfriend's home, where he commonly spends the night. The following day, Mr. Walker returned to the hotel to pay his rent, where he was promptly arrested for a crime he did not commit."

"Ladies and gentlemen, please pay close attention to the evidence. It is extremely important to Allston Walker."

After I had finished, the judge waved us toward the bench. "Gentlemen," he said, covering his microphone. "I have personal business today at 3:30 p.m. Need to shut it down early. Mr. Kotkin, let's have your witnesses ready to go tomorrow morning."

"Indeed, I will."

"Indeed." What a jackass. While I was pretty sure that the judge's personal business involved a tee time at Sequoia Country Club, I was relieved for the respite. After filling Chuck in on custodian Camacho's threat, I found myself driving past my office after court. I went to the driving range, drank a number of beers, then immersed myself in my fantasy baseball team.

CHAPTER 39

Day two of the trial saw Kotkin resplendent in a three-thousand-dollar blue pinstripe suit and gold paisley tie. I had to hand it to him. He could dress. As if I needed another reason to dislike him.

At 9:00 a.m. sharp, the twelve jurors and two alternates filed in from the jury room. Walker and I rose in deference to the jury and faced forward, my client again shadowed by his bailiff. As I stood next to my client, I had the inkling that I had missed something.

Kotkin, to our right at the counsel table, rather than face forward, stood at the end of the table and faced the jurors as they walked past, greeting them with a smarmy smile.

Judge Arnadon took the bench and greeted the jury. "Mr. Kotkin, call your first witness."

"Your Honor, the People call Officer Mark Vanner."

The Officer rose from the second row of the gallery ramrod straight, briefly rubbing the corner of both eyes with thumb and index finger. I hoped that meant he worked a late shift and was short on sleep. He tugged on a sleeve of his ill-fitting sport coat and strode to the stand with purpose. Well-practiced in the courtroom, the officer paused in the well of the court, repeated the oath as read by the clerk, and took his seat in the witness box.

"Officer Vanner, good morning. How are you employed?"

"I am a police officer for the city of Oakland."

"And were you so employed in August?"

"Yes. I was assigned to the patrol division."

"And on that date, at approximately 8:00 p.m., were you detailed to a report of an attempted murder?"

"Yes, I was."

The judge, who appeared asleep, arched an eyebrow toward me. In characterizing the offense as an attempted murder, Kotkin had made an obvious and slightly sleazy misstep. It would be up to the jury to decide if the intent of the attacker had been to kill or merely to hurt a lot, and by referring to the case as an attempted murder, the District Attorney was hoping to help them along with their decision.

I could have objected, and Judge Arnadon had invited me to do so. However, a defense attorney who objects at the drop of a hat appears defensive and afraid of the truth. More importantly, there were not twelve people on earth, let along in the jury box, who would conclude that the attacker did not intend to kill Jefferson Devaney. So, if the jury believed my client was the attacker, the objection would be like re-arranging deck chairs on the Titanic.

"And Officer, did you drive to the Islander Hotel in response to that report of an attempted murder?"

"Objection, Your Honor." Analysis aside, I had my limits.

"Sustained," Judge Arnadon's ruling was immediate. "Ladies and gentlemen, Mr. Kotkin has made the regrettable decision to characterize the alleged offense as an attempted murder on two occasions. As jurors, you will be asked to determine not only whether Mr. Walker committed the acts in question, but also, if he did them, whether those acts constituted an attempted murder. Please disregard the characterization of the crime by Mr. Kotkin as an attempted murder."

Kotkin continued, smug smile still in place. "Officer, was there a description given by dispatch of a suspect in the attack?"

"No sir."

"Did you encounter anyone on the way to the Islander Hotel?"

"Yes, about two blocks away from the hotel, I observed a man running from the scene." A few of the jurors bowed their heads to take notes.

"Did you detain that individual?"

"Yes, briefly, but I determined he was not a suspect and I proceeded to the hotel."

"Please describe the hotel for the jury."

"The entrance to the hotel faces the street. You enter a small lobby. The front desk is to the right. At the end of the counter is a half-door, which allows entry into the area behind the front desk. Behind that, a door leads to a studio apartment."

"Did you observe anyone in the studio apartment?"

"Yes, the victim, later identified as Jefferson Devaney, was found lying just on the other side of the front desk."

"And what was his condition?"

"He was in bad shape. He was bleeding from two significant wounds to his abdomen. He was groaning in pain. His shirt was soaked in blood. He also had numerous lacerations to his face."

"No further questions, Your Honor."

"Mr. Turner, cross examination?" asked Judge Arnadon.

"Good morning officer, my name is Joseph Turner. I have a few questions about the suspect you encountered on the way to the Islander Hotel that night. Where were you when you encountered the suspect running away from the direction of the hotel?"

"He was not a suspect." So much for pleasantries.

"He was running, correct?"

"Yes."

"And when you saw him running, you were involved in a Code 4 response, which means a life is in danger, and every second counts?"

"Yes."

"And you don't interrupt a Code 4 response unless it is very important, correct?"

"Yes."

"Catching a fleeing suspect in a violent crime would qualify as important, right."

"Yes."

"And upon seeing him running, you stopped your patrol vehicle and detained him, correct?"

"Yes."

"And it is not your intention to detain innocent people for no reason, correct?"

"No." The officer almost spat out the answer. His ears were red.

"So, you stopped this individual because you suspected him of committing the crime, correct?"

"I would say he was a person of interest."

"And you were interested in solving the crime, correct?"

"Yes."

"So, Officer, returning to my original question, where were you exactly when you encountered this person of interest running away from the direction of the hotel?"

"In my patrol vehicle," came the snarky reply.

"I realize that Officer," I said pleasantly, trying to take the high road for the jury. "You were about two blocks from the Islander Hotel when you saw the person running?"

"Yes."

"Can you describe him?" I had debated about this inquiry. On one hand, the officer's police report stated that the man running away from the scene was a Black man. But it had also stated that the man was in his early twenties, twenty-five years younger than my client.

"No, I can't."

"So, you don't recall anything about this individual's appearance?"

"No. It's been over a year, so no, I don't recall."

"I understand, Officer. You probably do not recall what he was wearing, either."

"No."

"Do you recall his height or weight?"

"No."

"Is it safe to say, you do not recall anything at all about his appearance?"

"I believe he was a Black male, but other than that, no." I paused briefly as my mind took a detour. Whomever this running man was, it didn't sound like Camacho.

"So, you can't recall if he had blood on his clothing." The officer glared at me with a look that said something similar to, "I want to kill you and all your defense attorney friends," but he was trapped.

"No."

"Officer, whenever there is an eyewitness identification, the eyesight of the witness is important in evaluating the accuracy of the identification, correct?"

"Yes."

"When you first made contact with Mr. Devaney on the floor in the hotel, he was not wearing eyeglasses, correct?"

"Correct."

"The room where this attack on Mr. Devaney took place was small, approximately fifteen by fifteen?"

"I didn't measure it," the officer said, taking every opportunity to be difficult.

"I didn't assume you did. That's why my question asked you to approximate."

"That seems about right," he snapped.

"Did you search the floor for the glasses?"

"No. That would have been the duty of the crime scene technician."

"And crime scene technicians are meticulous in their collection of evidence, correct?"

"Yes."

"They undertake an extensive and very detailed search of the crime scene and process every bit of evidence, don't they?"

"Yes."

"Even processing evidence like drops of blood and hair fibers?"

"Yes," Officer Vanner sighed, looking plaintively at the jury with his best "give me a break" face.

"And if an officer or a crime scene technician were to have seen the glasses in that room, either on the floor or under the couch, or anywhere else in the room, standard procedure would dictate that the evidence would have been logged and documented, right?"

"Yes."

"Officer, are you aware of any glasses being found in that room on the night of the attack on Mr. Devaney?"

"No."

Seven different law enforcement agents and emergency medical personnel had been inside Jefferson Devaney's studio apartment in the hours after the attack. I would ask each one of them the same series of questions, hoping to make it obvious that Mr. Devaney was not wearing his glasses at the time of his assault.

"No further questions, Your Honor."

"Re-direct, Mr. Kotkin?" asked Judge Arnadon.

Kotkin, still wearing the same smile, approached the podium. "Officer Vanner, if you had seen blood on the clothing of the individual who was running from the scene, then would you have simply released him?"

"Obviously not," said the officer, returning the smile.

"Would it refresh your recollection to look at your report to determine that individual's approximate age?"

"Yes." The officer thumbed through his report. "He was in his early twenties."

"No further questions, Your Honor," Kotkin said, oozing smugness as he strolled back to the counsel table.

CHAPTER 40

As the jury filed out for the lunch recess, an elusive thought settled in my mind. He'd told me that he was five feet, eight inches, roughly in line with the five feet, seven inch description of the assailant given by Devaney, dead-on given my assumption of self-inflation.

But as my client and I stood together it was now clear that Walker had no idea how tall he was. I had actually found a man who underestimated his height by a good 3 inches, 4 on the Turner scale. Walker was every bit of six feet tall, a full five inches taller than the person described by Devaney. As most of my time with my client had been spent sitting across from him in the jail, I hadn't noticed.

Kotkin sat at the counsel table and spoke, as he usually did, without really looking at me. "I'll be calling Squires after lunch, then Sergeant Simmons if we get to him."

"What was the first name?" I replied without looking up, trying not to show my panic.

"Langston Squires."

The name meant nothing to me, and now I didn't care if I sounded casual. Whoever Langston Squires was, he was about to testify. "Who the fuck is Langston Squires?" I whispered with vitriol, just loud enough for Kotkin to hear.

"Oh, his name is in the police report," Kotkin calmly replied, attempting to sound slightly surprised.

"Did he make a statement?"

"Not to the police. I interviewed him last week, though. I'm pretty sure I emailed you his statement."

"No, Arnold, you didn't."

Judge Arnadon was still on the bench, and likely overheard our disagreement. "Any matters to take up before we break for lunch?"

"Yes, Your Honor. Mr. Kotkin just revealed that he intends to call a witness I've never heard of. I have no discovery of his pretrial statement."

"Your Honor, the witness is listed in the discovery. I assumed Mr. Turner had his statement. I will give it to him now."

"Is he on your witness list?" the judge asked.

Kotkin already had his witness list in his hand. "Page three, line number 23, witness number 56, Your Honor. Indeed, he is."

The judge shrugged. "Then he can testify."

"Your Honor, I would ask the Court to reconsider." I hated my own whiney tone. "I have no idea what this guy is going to say."

"Mr. Turner, I've made my ruling. The witness is on Mr. Kotkin's witness list, albeit somewhat buried there. You'll have the lunch hour to review his statement. Mr. Kotkin, produce the statement to Mr. Turner forthwith. He should already have it."

"Of course, Your Honor."

I read Squires' statement while I stood in line for a hot dog outside the courthouse. He didn't claim to be an eyewitness to the attack, which was my first fear. However, he claimed to have been present when Walker paid his rent the morning after the attack. According to Squires, Walker was saying things about the attack on Devaney that only the attacker would know.

I was skeptical. It wasn't that I didn't think Walker capable of such stupidity. I just knew he wasn't chatty. Also, the vagueness of the statement was suspicious.

Amanda's name appeared on my phone, and I fumbled it in my excitement.

"Hi there!" I said with a mouthful of hot dog.

"Hey there, attorney stud. Am I interrupting lunch?"

"Not at all. I'm so glad to hear your voice. How are you?"

"I'm doing fine. Isabella and I got on the road early, so we're in San Diego."

"Thanks for letting me know. I feel better with you there."

"So, how did my guy do in court today?"

My guy. I could get used to that. "I was a tour de force, naturally."

"Naturally," she laughed. "Really, do you think it went okay?"

"It went fine, but it's obviously very early."

"Well, I won't keep you. Good luck this afternoon."

"Thanks," I said, pretty sure she could feel my smile through the phone. "It really means a lot that you called."

"Well, I'm thinking about you."

"Me too. Bye."

I breathed deeply, realizing I needed the call more than I knew. Camacho's threat had occupied a corner of my mind since I heard the words eke out the elevator doors. The thought of putting Amanda in danger was unthinkable, and knowing she was safe gave me some peace.

Still, the memory of Camacho's baffling warning lingered in my thoughts as I made my way back to court. It was more than my obvious worry for Amanda. I couldn't put my finger on it, but something about Camacho's choice of words bothered me.

Back in the courtroom after lunch, Kotkin called Squires to the stand. Much as I hated to admit it, Kotkin was calling his witnesses in exactly the order I would have chosen, were I the prosecutor. Lead with the reporting officer to describe the crime scene, follow with motive and circumstantial evidence witnesses before concluding with Devaney himself, to deliver the coup de gras.

It was as good a time as any to sneak in Squires, who promised to be one of the weaker of the prosecution witnesses. His statement had the whiff of someone who wanted credit for solving the crime or perhaps a reward.

Squires' tale would be a tough sell to the jury, but Kotkin couldn't resist. If it went well, the statement could be the delicious frosting atop his eyewitness identification case.

The Black man in his late twenties strutted to the witness stand like a peacock. Sporting a rust orange suit with lapels made for hang gliding, he punctuated every deliberate step with a quick roll to his toe, while keeping his left hand curiously inside his jacket.

After Squires told the jury that he was "an entrepreneur who dabbled in this and that," Kotkin got to the point.

"Do you recall the morning of August twenty-sixth, 2021?"

"Yes, indeed I do. I was conducting some business."

"Do you recall where you were?"

"Matter of fact I was over at the Islander, visiting some associates," replied Squires, who seemed intent on making himself appear as if he were at the Islander Hotel in west Oakland closing an international business deal.

"Did you see anyone in the lobby?"

"Yes, among others, I saw Allston Walker. He came up to me and asked if I knew if they caught the guy who stabbed Devaney." So much for the vague allegations made in his witness statement.

"Those were his words?"

"Yes. That's exactly what he said. I was like, 'How did you know he was stabbed?'"

After the witness identified Walker in Court, Kotkin concluded his testimony, no doubt wanting him off the stand as soon as possible.

As I began my cross examination, I wondered whether Mr. Squires' improved memory could be ascribed to Kotkin's coaching or the witness' increasing desire for the limelight.

"Mr. Squires, good afternoon."

"Good afternoon to you."

"How long have you known Allston Walker?"

"I don't know him well. Just to say hello. Along about three years."

"And what did you say your occupation was?"

"I am a business opportunist, you might say. I dabble in this and that."

"Are they legal enterprises you engage in?"

"Of course."

In fact, Squires' rap sheet indicated his business enterprises included petty theft, disorderly conduct, loitering, and several minor drug offenses. However, as none of the charges were crimes of moral turpitude, the jury wouldn't hear about them.

"So, Mr. Squires, when you arrived at the hotel that morning, Mr. Erickson told you that Mr. Devaney had been attacked the previous day."

"Yes."

"And he also told you about Walker's argument with Mr. Devaney?"

"Yes."

"And so, when Walker showed up in the lobby to pay the remainder of the rent, given your keen intellect and worldly knowledge, I'll bet you already suspected him of attacking Mr. Devaney?"

"You might say so. I do have a keen intellect for these things. Yes, indeed, I am constantly assessing and analyzing situations." Squires had clearly had enough of these one-word answers. Whose show was this, anyway?

"Mr. Squires, you maintain that Allston Walker said to you, 'Did they catch the guy who stabbed Mr. Devaney?'"

"I don't maintain anything," the witness said indignantly. "That's what the man said."

"And you being a civic-minded man, you wanted Walker brought to justice."

"Yes."

"And so, when the police arrived just thirty minutes later, surely you said to them, 'Officer, Allston Walker just asked me if they caught the guy who stabbed Mr. Devaney,' right?"

"No, I didn't believe it was entirely appropriate to speak to the police at that particular time."

As he answered, I retrieved his pre-marked statement from the clerk's desk. "Sir, I'm showing you what's been marked Defense Exhibit A. That's your statement, signed by you?" I asked, handing Squires the statement.

"Yes."

"Mr. Squires, does it say anywhere on your statement that Walker asked if they had caught the guy who stabbed Devaney?"

"No, but he said it," the witness said tersely.

"Does the statement make any reference at all to Mr. Walker saying anything about a stabbing?"

"The statement, don't. No."

"What the statement says is,"—I faced the jury, reading from the document—"'Mr. Walker showed up and said some things that it seemed only he'd know if he'd been guilty.'"

"That's right."

"Sir, Mr. Devaney is a friend of yours, correct?"

"Yes."

"And you wanted to help the police find the person who stabbed him, didn't you?"

"I did do that."

"And when you met with Mr. Kotkin, three weeks ago—the day you signed your witness statement—he must have asked you what, specifically, Mr. Walker had said, right?"

"I don't recall."

"And you didn't attribute any specific statements to Mr. Walker at all, did you?"

"I attributed that in my opinion he was guilty."

"I see. And today, for the first time, you've recalled that Mr. Walker spoke about a stabbing?"

"Not for the first time."

"Well, when did you recall that for the first time?" The witness fidgeted but remained silent. I took a guess.

"You met with Mr. Kotkin today, before court?"

"Yes."

"And this meeting was in Mr. Kotkin's office?"

"Yes."

Kotkin rose, smarmy grin in place. "Your Honor," the prosecutor chuckled, "I really don't see the relevance of..."

"Overruled," interrupted Judge Arnadon. His look was not one of amusement. "You may answer the questions, Mr. Squires."

"We met in his office, yes."

"And it was during this meeting, today, when you were able to recall specifics of a conversation that took place months ago?" I didn't wait for the answer. "Nothing further, Your Honor."

"Mr. Kotkin? Anything further?"

Kotkin rose. "Mr. Squires, have I always told you to tell the truth when you testify?"

Squires, missing the point entirely, replied, "Don't nobody need to tell me to tell the truth. I'm a truthful person."

Judge Arnadon excused the colorful witness, admonished the jury not to discuss the case over the weekend, and ordered all parties to return on Monday.

There was a bounce in my step as I returned to the counsel table to meet Walker's icy stare. "Don't get happy," he whispered to me out of the side of his mouth, as the jury filed past.

My client had put the afternoon's proceeding in perspective in three words. While the cross examination of Squires had gone well, if the jury believed Jefferson Devaney, as Walker might have elaborated, it wouldn't matter a lick.

CHAPTER 41

On the five-minute walk to the Oakland Public Library, Amanda checked in.

—*How was the afternoon session, gorgeous man?*—

—*Uneventful. Currently on my way to visit with a prostitute in a library. Or is it a librarian in a whorehouse? I've forgotten.*—

—*What a life you lead, Joe Turner.*—

I climbed the massive granite steps of the building to be greeted inside by a woman behind the desk who was right out of central casting. The model of silent efficiency, she glided behind the high counter in soft shoes, presented a sign-in clipboard for a conference room, and produced a pen from somewhere near her hair, pulled back tightly from her face.

"For how long do you require the room?" she whispered, her face expressionless under horn-rimmed glasses. Librarians had always intimidated me. They're such quiet, pale masters of their universe.

"Probably thirty minutes?" I said, questioning myself.

She remained silent, but raised both eyebrows dramatically and turned her palms up, just above the counter, saying in her silent library language, "Well, you're the only person who would know."

"Thirty is fine," I whispered obediently.

She produced a key and mouthed the words "number three," nodding her head toward three rooms on the back wall opposite the entrance. I was relieved to find each with a large window.

On my way to the room, I scanned the premises for someone who may be Ms. Belton. Chuck hadn't gotten a description, and it turned out it wasn't necessary.

Speaking of central casting, I thought to myself. She was tall and on the larger side, with shoulder-length peroxided hair I suspected was a wig and enough make-up to make any realistic estimation of her age impossible. A rain coat was cinched tight, wrapping her in black leather, down to thigh-high boots with stiletto heels.

"Ms. Belton?" I said quietly as I approached, not stopping and gesturing toward the conference room. Once inside, I extended my hand. "I'm Joe Turner," I said, shaking a cold hand.

"I'm Sierra," she said in a smoker's raspy voice. "Thanks for meeting me here. I know it's an odd place, but I just need to make sure I'm safe."

"Of course. What's on your mind?" I took a seat and gestured to a chair a few feet away. She sat and set a large leather bag on the floor next to her. She crossed her legs, the stilettos only a few feet away.

"Well..." She paused and looked behind her out into the library. "I'm sorry, I'm just really scared," she said quietly, showing a yellowish smile.

"I completely understand, Ms. Belton. Take your time."

She breathed deeply. "I know I should have spoken up sooner, but I was at the Islander that night, and I saw a man rush out right before the cops and ambulance arrived. I saw Mr. Walker's mugshot a few months ago in the paper after he was arrested. The man I saw that night wasn't Walker. He was a much younger man." I took a legal pad from my satchel and took notes.

"Can you describe the man you saw rush out of the hotel?"

"Well, he was a Black man, or maybe hispanic. About my height. He had kind of a baby face. I'd put him at no more than eighteen or nineteen."

"And where were you when you saw the man?"

"I was in the parking lot headed toward the entrance of the hotel." She paused again, then abruptly stood, as if she had forgotten something. She untied her rain coat and took it off to reveal a low-cut leopard pattern dress that covered far too little of herself.

"Your assistant probably told you, I'm a prostitute." She said the word quickly while staring at the floor, then sat down. I fidgeted in my chair, trying to think of the least offensive thing to say. No use. "Anyway," she continued, "the guy ran right past me in the parking lot."

"Can you describe what he was wearing?"

"The pants, I couldn't say, except they were dark. But he had a black hoodie on with the hood up. It had a small Nike logo on the chest."

"Did you happen to see any blood on him?"

"I definitely saw something." She stared above my head, concentrating. "At the time I didn't know it was blood, and I couldn't see its color, but I did have the impression that he had some substance on the front of his hoodie."

"And you recall it was only a few minutes after he ran out of the hotel that the police and ambulance arrived?"

"Yes. The police arrived first and then the ambulance a few minutes later."

"Do you recall about what time it was?"

"It was around 8:00 p.m. Maybe a little after." I paused to take some notes.

"So, Ms. Belton, you were at the Islander to, uh, meet someone?"

"Yes, it was a trick. It didn't happen, obviously. When the police and ambulance arrived, I left."

"Do you do a lot of your business on the blade?"

She hesitated and shifted in her chair. "I do house calls mainly. I advertise online. I'm a renegade." I hadn't heard the term in years. I was pretty sure it meant that she didn't have a pimp.

"So, Ms. Belton, this information, as you guessed, is extremely important to Mr. Walker's defense. Would you be willing to testify at a trial?"

"Yeah, I can say what I saw. As long as I'm not asked to identify anyone as the guy who did it."

"And I'll need your date of birth for the witness list."

"June 5, 1984."

As I suspected, she hadn't aged well. "The District Attorney will have access to your criminal record. I assume it consists of mostly arrests for solicitation?"

"Yes, exclusively."

"Thanks. Can I get an address?"

"I'd rather just give you my phone number. I don't want my address showing up in any paperwork."

"Okay, that's understandable, but in that case, I'm going to serve you with this subpoena," I explained, while reaching into my jacket pocket to retrieve it. "I'll be in touch to let you know what day you should appear."

"That's fine. I don't suppose there's any compensation available for my testimony?" she asked, standing up to go.

"I'm afraid not. That's not allowed."

"Okay. Just thought I'd ask," she said with a smile of embarrassment. As she was putting on her raincoat, I stole a glance inside her open bag on the floor, where a book rested on top of its contents. I did a double-take and lost my train of thought for a moment.

Through the window, I watched her teeter across the lobby, then waited a minute before returning the key to the librarian's desk, avoiding eye contact with the horn rims.

Inside my car, my mind raced to organize my observations. While the headline was clearly, *Witness Clears Walker*, my gut told me it wasn't that simple. For starters, her recall was almost too good. In my experience, witness memories, even in the best of circumstances, are never perfect.

Usually even the best witnesses end up being wrong about something. Ms. Belton had been right about the time of her observation, the color of the suspect's hoodie and pants, and the order of arrival of the police and ambulance. Even the Nike logo couldn't be disproven by the video. Maybe I just couldn't stand prosperity.

I pulled out of the court parking lot and stopped behind a blue convertible. An unmistakable bleached blonde wig sat behind the wheel. I slid on sunglasses, pulled an A's cap low on my head and decided to tag along for a while. She headed north toward neighboring Berkeley, thankfully sticking to surface streets during rush hour. Although I'd never secretly followed anyone before, I'd seen it a lot on television, and there was enough traffic on the road to remain inconspicuous.

She headed east up into the Berkeley hills, where beautiful homes commanded sweeping views of San Francisco Bay. I slowed a half a block away as she parked on the street next to a multi-level contemporary with lots of glass. Still wearing her boots, she got out of her car and looked up and down the street. I slouched down in my seat. Next, she opened the back door of the car and retrieved a bucket and mop, before hurrying to the front door of the home, disappearing from my view.

Driving home, I was more confused than ever. She had parked on the street so I was fairly certain she didn't live there. Before I saw the mop and bucket, I would have guessed it was one of her high priced "house calls." I had plans to meet Chuck for drinks, and the timing was perfect.

CHAPTER 42

"Of all the gin joints, in all the towns in the world..." Chuck swiveled his barstool toward me as I sat next to him. "How'd it go in the library? Happy ending?"

"Very funny. Lots to tell, my friend."

"Well, let's hear it. And cheers." He slid a pint of brown ale my way.

"Turns out, Ms. Belton, or whoever she is ..." I paused to scan the bar and lowered my voice. "She saw the actual attacker run out of the hotel right before the police arrived. She described him as a man decidedly younger than Walker. He wore a black hoodie, just like the guy in the surveillance video."

"Holy shit, that's fantastic!"

"What, no movie line?"

"I'm floored. This never happens. You know that," he said, grabbing my shoulder.

"I know." I took a long pull on my beer, then sat quietly.

"So why aren't you more excited?"

"Here's the thing, Chuck..."

"I hate it when you say that."

"What?"

"Whenever you say, 'Here's the thing, Chuck,' you inevitably rain on my parade."

"It's just that something about her doesn't sit right."

"Here we go. I knew it. Why can't you just enjoy a lucky break?"

"Just hear me out. I'm actually not sure she's a prostitute."

"Because everyone dreams of being a prostitute and often people lie about it? C'mon, Joe."

"I'm serious. For starters, I'm not sure she knew what the blade was."

"You're not sure? Did she tell you she didn't know what the blade was?"

"No, it's just an impression I got."

"Did she tell you she was a prostitute?"

"Yes."

"Did she dress like a prostitute?"

"Technically, yes, but almost too much like a prostitute."

Chuck smiled and shook his head. "You're way overthinking this, Joe. You can't handle the truth. There's your movie line."

"Okay, how about this: she wore these thigh-high boots and I noticed the price tag was still stuck on the sole."

"Okay, Inspector. Could you also tell her actual occupation by the way one of her gloves was slightly more worn than the other?"

"I'm being serious, Chuck."

"Okay, I know. But you know almost no one walks the streets anymore. They all advertise online. A price tag could stay on for a while."

"Well, how many prostitutes do you know who are reading The Brothers Karamazov?"

"Tolstoy?"

"Solhzenitsyn or Dostoevsky, I think. I tried to read it once."

"Oh, well," he quipped, dripping with sarcasm, "if such a literary giant as you can't get through it, then clearly no prostitute could."

"C'mon, Chuck. I didn't mean it like that. You have to admit, it's a little weird."

"After all," he said, ignoring me, "didn't she ask to meet you in the library? I think there's a movie plot there somewhere."

"I'm not saying she isn't telling the truth. Something's off. That's all."

"I'm just saying if it quacks like a duck...you know the saying. Let me ask this..." He paused, as if to once and for all reveal the truth. "Did she ask you for money?"

"Yes," I sighed, "but...."

"She sounds legit to me," he said, smiling triumphantly.

"I guess," I said with a sigh.

"Look, Joe, I get it. You have good instincts and you may be right. But all I know is, prior to the first ever prostitute descending from heaven, our client was staring down the barrel of a life in prison. And now we got hope. How was court today?" he asked, changing the subject.

"Generally, it was painful."

"Life is pain, Highness. Anyone who tells you any different is trying to sell you something. How bad is it? Trial psychosis hasn't set in yet?"

"Not even a hint of it. Barring a rescue from the prostitute with the love of Russian literature, Walker's fucked."

Chuck belly laughed, and it felt good to see after hours of staring at Walker's sour mug. I'd planned to have a beer with Chuck to ease myself into the weekend. I found that I'd drink less if I started earlier, or at least that's what I told myself. I had taken the train to The Armory, a watering hole near the courthouse, so "a" beer was a fib.

"Investigation updates?"

"I can't find the second paramedic to save myself."

"It's okay. There's no guarantee he'd be helpful anyway."

"You seem awfully negative, even for you."

"Chuck, I'm no slouch in the courtroom, but you remember Devaney. We need a miracle."

"One, you knew that going in. B, you're probably over-reacting. And three, don't sell yourself short, Joe, you're a tremendous slouch."

We ordered burgers and more beer, and discussed other cases while I signed subpoenas. After three or four, he eased himself off his stool.

"When do you want your defense witnesses there?"

"I'll let you know," I said, feeling the effects of the beer for the first time. "Probably a week from Monday. I'll start with Hurricane Hartung and the girl the first morning, then Officer Fredericks in the afternoon. Belton, the bookish hooker is subpoenaed for Tuesday."

Chuck gathered his paperwork and stood. "I will give the haughty hussy, Ms. Belton, a call. Meantime, start kicking ass in court. The opera ain't over 'til the fat lady sings," he said, holding the door open for a group of arriving district attorneys.

"Turner, is your name on that stool?" chided Sean Stein, a senior prosecutor.

"I resemble that remark, Stein," I replied. "It's only 6:00 p.m. Shouldn't you be coaching a witness or hiding defense evidence?"

"It's actually 8:00 p.m., and anyone can prosecute a guilty man," the prosecutor quipped. "It takes true talent to convict the innocent. Pitcher of Trowbridge, guys?" he asked his friends. I didn't understand the fascination with IPAs. They tasted like a bottle of yeast.

I tilted my sixth or eighth frosty pint of brown ale to my lips. Creamy and malty, it reminded me of the chocolate shakes my dad would buy me after Little League games. My face was warm and melty, but it felt good to smile.

After a while, the conversation became difficult to follow, which was fine. I let my mind drift around the group with my eyes, pleasantly placid. I noticed that the bar was full, and wondered how long I'd been there.

I saw my hand reach for the check on the bar, then heard a glass shatter on the floor. I wasn't sure I had done it but assumed so. When I got up to leave, my path to the door seemed to tilt. I tilted with it, and felt my way to the exit.

From there, it was easy. The cool night would help my focus. About fifty paces to the BART station, digging the ticket from my wallet, spilling into the train. It was three stops to the Oakwood station, where I got off to begin the only sketchy part of my journey home. I crossed the street where the lights were brighter. I'd never had an issue on the trip but it was Oakland, after all.

Glancing behind me, I noticed a group follow me across the street. Thoughts flooded my mind as my pace quickened—the recent spike in street muggings, the crappy neighborhood, and my unsteady gait that likely made me an easy target.

Running was obviously out. They appeared younger and I probably couldn't keep my balance anyway. I dug a hand in my front pants pocket, balling a fist around my key ring. But after half a block of uneventful walking, I relaxed, scoffing at my paranoia. I'd be home in ten minutes, ready to pop one last beer and crash on my recliner.

CHAPTER 43

I stirred from what felt like a week-long sleep sometime after 9:00 a.m. Slowly gaining consciousness, I realized I was fully clothed. At least I wasn't on the lawn. Rolling on my left side, the pillow was cool on my cheek. I stretched and felt a sharp pain in my ribs. Good god, I was getting too old for this.

I sat up on the edge of the bed and noticed my pants were ripped and bloodied at the knee. Definitely a fall but I had no recollection. I creaked to a standing position, stepped out of my shoes, and ambled toward my bathroom, wincing as I rubbed my tender face. Cold water helped. Rising from the sink, I shuddered at the sight in the mirror. The left side of my face was red and swollen, my left eye stamped with a shiner that looked like the work of a Hollywood makeup artist. Instinctively, I felt my back pocket of my pants for my wallet. It was there, thank goodness.

I had no memory of the evening but pieced it together from sifting through my pockets. A napkin from The Armory, a receipt and a BART ticket. Then I recalled feeling a distinct uneasiness that must have come before the mugging.

I grabbed an ice pack from the freezer, drank lots of water, made coffee and collapsed on the recliner. Holding the ice to my eyes, I wondered why my wallet wasn't taken. If not a robbery, what was the point?

After a Saturday morning of staring blankly at college football and drinking strong coffee, I emailed the Court and Kotkin, adding one Sierra Belton to the witness list. I spent the rest of the weekend icing my face and immersed in trial preparation.

The trial psychosis referenced by Chuck in the bar last night is a mental affliction that causes lawyers in trial to believe that they will prevail, despite all logical indications to the contrary.

The psychosis preys on human nature's inclination to tell the truth. Because attorneys are not allowed to tell the jury what they actually think about the evidence, they begin to believe their own arguments, no matter how unreasonable.

Also, by the time the case is prepared for trial, the defense attorney has been exposed to an audience very receptive to the defense – the family of the accused, character witnesses who want to believe in their friend's innocence, and the client himself, who is desperate that his attorney believe him.

So, defendant is caught running away from bank carrying the sack of money wearing a shirt soaked with exploding dye? Not to worry, the perpetrator gave him the money, then hugged him. He confessed to the police? No problem. He is constantly confessing to crimes he didn't commit. With Walker's case, I did not have a hint of trial psychosis, which was undoubtedly a bad sign.

For the most part, the trial had gone as expected, which is to say, poorly. Whereas I had successfully cast doubt on Walker's supposed statements to Squires, Devaney's statement to Officer Vanner only minutes after the attack identifying my client as the perpetrator left the home team behind. Belton's potential testimony could be a game changer. If that fell apart, I would probably need a Perry Mason moment with Devaney or else Allston Walker had seen his last daylight.

My phone buzzed in my pocket, and my pulse quickened.

"Hi there, gorgeous man."

"Hi yourself!" I was so happy to hear her voice.

"I hope I'm not interrupting the trial prep. Just thought I'd give you a chance to explain your text about meeting with a prostitute."

"So, you're jealous. I figured."

"Depends on if she was any good, I suppose."

"Well, she was a pro, so, yeah. I'll show you some things."

"Yeah, hilarious, Turner."

"Actually, it turns out she's potentially an important eyewitness who says that Walker is innocent."

"Wow! That's amazing!"

"Yeah, if it works out, it could be good."

"You don't sound very happy."

"It's just that I'm not sure how legit she is. Something doesn't feel right."

"Hmmm. Like what?"

"Well, it felt like she was doing her best to convince me she was a prostitute."

"Like trying too hard? What made you skeptical?"

"Well, she dressed like someone whose Halloween costume was a prostitute."

"I wasn't aware you were such an expert in that department."

"Yeah, I know. Chuck thinks I'm paranoid. But at one point, she made this big production of taking off her coat to show this leopard skin skimpy dress, while announcing, 'I'm a prostitute.'"

"Sounds hot." she said, giggling.

"Not really, no."

"Seriously, though, she probably just felt nervous, meeting with an attorney."

"Yeah, maybe. And then, when I followed her…"

"You followed her! You're kidding? No wonder Chuck thought you were paranoid." Now she sounded actually concerned.

"Well, I didn't mean to, at first."

"Well you can't follow someone by accident."

"I know, but listen." I began trying to suppress a laugh that was building. "So, she pulls up to this really nice house and goes in." I let out the laugh, then stopped for just long enough to deliver the punchline. "She went in with a mop and bucket."

As I continued laughing, she joined in, halting briefly to add, "Maybe the dude had a cleaning fetish."

"Did you say a cleaning fetish?" We were now giggling uncontrollably.

"Yeah, you know," she said seductively, "'Oh you stallion, is that Windex? Use the squeegee, baby. The big one.'"

"Oh baby please," I said, gasping for breaths between laughs, "I need to see you scrub the grout!"

Minutes later, when our laughter had subsided, I said, "Seriously, Chuck says I'm overthinking the prostitute thing. What do you think?"

"Well, it's certainly possible you're overthinking it. I know you're under a lot of pressure. But I also trust your instincts."

"Thanks for listening."

"Good luck in trial and think of me."

"I always do."

CHAPTER 44

August 25, 2021

Devaney reached for a knife that sat on a nearby shelf and sliced his apple again. One of the crazies was yelling outside, and there was no telling how long it would last. He replaced the knife and reached under his glasses to rub his eyes with calloused fingertips.

He heard movement out at the front desk. That'd be Denny now, to stuff the money in a jar in the cupboard above the fridge.

While a car dealer screamed at him on the glary screen, his gaze wandered up to a small window above his sink, where the moonlight shone through black bars on the windows, their shadows casting a cage on his ceiling. Lured in by the promise of easy money and now trapped inside. Trapped inside his tiny cage, inside the colored ghetto, like the possums he used to hunt in Mississippi.

His heavy lids blinked twice in slow motion, his head nodding twice before gray whiskers settled on his chest.

CHAPTER 45

On Monday morning, I arrived at court to find it closed, with hundreds of people milling about the building.

I approached Kokin. "What's this about?"

"Bomb scare. Maybe our guilty verdict will be delayed by a day. Just prolonging the inevitable, wouldn't you say?"

"Whatever, Arnold."

"Hey," he said, trying to sound casual, "if your guy is still planning to testify, then I think I'll save the video evidence for cross examination."

"He's going to testify, but you and I both know the video shows nothing. So, you can stop trying to make me think I've missed something. Give it a rest."

"Trust me. I can't wait to play the video." He shrugged, flashing his smarmy smile as he walked away.

"Careful what you wish for," I called after him. If Sierra Belton testified as I expected, she would be the linchpin of the defense case, and the video of the man in the black hoodie would be important to bolster her credibility. Once Kotkin heard her testimony, I might stroll over to his side of the counsel table and quietly ask him if he still couldn't wait to play the video.

Then again, if prostitute/cleaning woman Sierra Belton was the linchpin of the defense case, I had a feeling we were in deep trouble.

When the trial finally got started, it was 10:00 a.m. Kotkin called a police dispatcher and played Devaney's 911 call for the jury. He knew that if he didn't play the recording, I would, so he was attempting to lessen its impact.

I scanned the jury for reaction when Devaney's voice told the dispatcher he didn't know the name of his attacker. No one took a note or so much as blinked. I was afraid the agony in Devaney's voice drowned out the content.

"The People call Sergeant Thomas Simmons," belted out Kotkin enthusiastically. The officer strode to the stand, his black leather belt creaking like a western saddle with every move. He exuded an intense military bearing that made everyone uncomfortable. It would have made Mussolini uncomfortable.

He was straight lines and right angles, from his laser-like side part to the creases on his uniform that could slice through his shiny leather boots. His answers to Kotkin's questions came in machine gun staccato from behind eyes that seemed to be scanning the courtroom for snipers. I could have sworn that, for an instant, his piercing stare fell on juror number six, and awakened him immediately.

Watching the officer perched on the witness chair like a bird of prey ready to launch, I recalled a study that concluded that the personality types of criminals and police officers are usually similar—aggressive, thrill seekers who thrive on conflict. There is a certain logical appeal to the theory that, apart from morality and circumstance, the same type of person may seek to commit an armed robbery as would choose to wade into a conflict to sort out justice with a gun.

If there was anything to the theory, in another life, Sergeant Simmons would not be a petty thief or a two-bit hustler like Squires. Think hostage situation or postal rampage.

"Officer, you were dispatched to the Islander Hotel in Oakland the day after a stabbing had taken place at that location?"

"Yes."

"For what purpose?"

"The investigating officer had requested that I conduct additional canvassing and take some more photographs of the layout of the hotel."

"And while you were there, were you given access to the hotel registry?"

"I was. I examined it and was given a copy. I preserved it as evidence and sealed it in a manila envelope, affixing the case number and name of the suspect to the envelope, along with my initials and the date."

"Did you bring that evidence with you to court?"

Judge Arnadon, seeing the envelope in the officer's black gloved hands, knew, as did everyone else in the courtroom, that the officer had brought the evidence to court.

"Yes," came the inevitable reply from the witness box. The judge sighed deeply into the microphone.

"Your Honor," continued Kotkin, "I've taken the liberty of having this marked as People's number four and Mr. Turner has seen it. Officer," continued Kotkin, taking great pleasure in his captive audience, and needlessly building the drama, "I'm handing you a pair of scissors. Officer, if you would…"

"Officer, open the envelope, please," Judge Arnadon cut in, much to my delight. The judge continued, "Does it contain the hotel registry?"

"Yes."

"And does it show that Allston Walker resided in room 112 or not?"

"It does."

"That cover it, Mr. Kotkin?"

The prosecutor's shoulders slumped, his high drama squelched. "Yes, Your Honor."

"Fine. Let's break for lunch, ladies and gentlemen. I have a mandatory judge's meeting this afternoon. We'll reconvene at 3:30 p.m."

I grabbed a hot dog and found a bench overlooking Lake Merritt. My eyes wandered to the Lake Chateau Bar and Grill. It would be just a short walk to the patio on the lake where they served ice cold beer in tall, frosty, seductive glasses. I had two and a half hours to kill, after all. So tempting.

I blinked away the image of me drinking in the sun, chastising myself. "You're in trial, Joseph, you fucking lush!" I found another bench that faced away from the bar and forced myself to think about the matter at hand.

I dreaded the afternoon session, which promised to be filled with bloody, sympathetic images of the victim. Rather than showing digital photos of a gory Devaney on the courtroom screen, Kotkin had gone old school, blowing up the photos and mounting them for presentation. We both knew the poster boards would be stored in the courtroom for the remainder of the trial, not necessarily facing the jury, but still a constant reminder of the brutality of the crime.

I had objected to the admission of all three of the gruesome photographs, arguing that they would only serve to inflame the passions of the jury. While I may have been successful in excluding one of the photos, I decided if one of them were in evidence, the damage done by the other two would be negligible. So, once the judge ruled that one of the photos was admitted, I withdrew my objection to the other two.

My plan was to argue to the jury that presenting the giant gory images of Devaney to the jury was a blatant attempt by the prosecution to inspire sympathy for the victim, shifting focus from the actual identity of the perpetrator. Recalling the photos now in my mind, I second-guessed my strategy.

I gazed out across the lake and saw only bloody photos. This time, my dad's face was atop Devaney's ravaged torso. I jerked my head away from the image and felt a flashback coming on but shook it away. Then, in my mind I was back across the lake on the patio my hand on the cool moist glass, beer foam coating my lips.

"Fuck, I need to get out of here." I walked around the lake, trying to focus on Amanda.

CHAPTER 46

I needed a drink more than ever by the time I got back to Department 10. As I sat at the counsel table next to Walker, waiting for the jury, I heard Kotkin's heels coming and pictured his smug expression without looking. "And yet another window closes," he said dramatically, releasing a single page two feet above my laptop, letting it float to rest across my keyboard. "And yes, he's on my witness list."

Fighting the urge to unleash vitriol with every fiber of my being, I closed my eyes and breathed deeply. It was a witness statement of one Dennison Devaney, whose listed address was a room at the Islander. That'd be Denny, Devaney's nephew Walker had described as slow.

Before I could read it, the jury filed in and court was called to order. After Field Marshall Simmons resumed his position on the witness stand, Kotkin asked the officer to describe the crime scene. "I found Officer Vanner tending to the victim in the living quarters behind the front counter. The victim was lying in the doorway. There was a copious amount of blood on the floor and blood splatter on the walls. He appeared to be suffering from multiple stab wounds on his arms, stomach, chest and face. He was bleeding profusely from his chest wound. His clothing was covered in blood."

Kotkin heel-clicked from the podium behind his seat at the counsel table and approached the easel that stood to the right of the witness stand, holding a blown-up photograph of Devaney. The blood-soaked victim was lying on his back. His once white undershirt was crimson. Blood smeared his contorted face.

As Kotkin continued with his presentation of the photos through the officer, the mood in the courtroom grew somber. The second photo depicted a shirtless Devaney on a gurney while still at the crime scene, his sponged torso revealing two distinct stab wounds, red eyes glaring out of his white stomach. Sergeant Simmons recounted how he had assisted paramedics in cutting the clothing from the victim's body so he could be treated.

By the time Kotkin placed the last of the giant photos on the easel, the feelings of sorrow, disgust and anger were palpable, and I was seriously questioning my strategy of not objecting to the final two photos. A few jurors stole glances at Walker, their expressions serious and cold.

The final photo showed Devaney in the ambulance, an oxygen mask accentuating the pain and fear in his eyes. This photo was the most impactful, a familiar image to most adults who have seen their elderly relatives hospitalized. The oxygen mask drove home Jefferson Devaney's utter helplessness. I cursed myself for my idiotic strategy.

His examination complete, Kotkin made his way back to the counsel table, then stopped and turned a final time toward the photo, the jury following his gaze. Relishing the moment, he shook his head in disgust, and walked away. "No further questions, Your Honor."

"Mr. Turner, any re-cross?"

"Yes, thank you." Although I had no interest in discussing the finer details of the photographs—(Exactly how much pain did it appear Mr. Devaney was experiencing in this photo?)—I did want to remind the jury that the ultimate question was not if Devaney had been viciously attacked, but who was responsible.

"Sergeant Simmons, you were informed at the scene that Mr. Devaney had stated that Allston Walker was responsible for his injuries, correct?"

"Yes."

"And you were put in charge of confirming this identification?"

"Yes."

"So, you obtained a photograph of Mr. Walker."

"Yes."

"And did you place Mr. Walker's photo in a photo spread to see if Mr. Devaney could pick out Mr. Walker's photo?"

"I didn't know if I had time for that. I didn't know if Mr. Devaney would live. So, no, I didn't."

"Officer, for the benefit of the jury, a photo spread is a fair procedure designed to test the reliability of an identification wherein an individual's photograph is placed alongside other photographs to see if a witness can choose the suspect's photo, correct?"

"Yes."

"So, instead of this procedure, you obtained a photograph of Mr. Walker and showed that photograph alone to Mr. Devaney, correct?"

"Yes. That was really all I had time for. And Mr. Devaney had already stated that Mr. Walker was responsible."

"And this is how you tested the reliability of his identification."

"That's a fairly common procedure we utilize. Yes."

Next, like all the officers before him, I elicited that Simmons had not seen any glasses on the floor of the apartment.

There was another line of inquiry on my legal pad next to which I had written a question mark. Simmons had stated in his report that Devaney had faded in and out of consciousness on the ride to the hospital. This could impeach his identification, but might also engender more sympathy for Devaney, who may have been on the brink of death. I left it alone.

"No further questions."

"Mr. Kotkin, any re-direct?" asked the judge, fully reclined and staring at the ceiling.

"No, Your Honor."

Sergeant Simmons dismounted the witness stand, and I refrained from tripping him as he walked by.

"Ladies and gentlemen, you are dismissed for the day. You are reminded not to talk about the case. Good evening."

Walker pointed to the witness statement on the counsel table. "Ain't got to worry about Denny. He's a good kid."

"Well, I haven't read his statement yet, Allston," I snapped. "If he IDs you, we should definitely worry about it."

He smiled, as if amused by my salty tone. "Ain't got to worry about Denny," he said shaking his head.

"Awesome," I said, sarcastically.

As I walked out of Department 10, Andy greeted me. "I had to file a motion, so I stopped in and caught the last hour or so."

Once outside the courthouse, clear of jurors, I asked, "How bad?"

"Tremendously bad," my partner replied. "On the bright side, though, at least sentencing isn't this afternoon. Otherwise, they'd give your guy twenty years in the electric chair. And hey, how did all three photos make it into evidence? Didn't you try to exclude them?"

"Andrew J. Kopp."

"Yes?"

"Go fuck yourself."

CHAPTER 47

The evening found me on the recliner with a gin and tonic, about to read what was sure to be the latest bit of bad news, the statement of Devaney's nephew, Denny.

The one-page report was written in the familiar format utilized by the D.A's Office. In the space below the information identifying the witness, a D.A. inspector had handwritten the statement as told by the witness.

On August 25, 2021, around 8:00 p.m., I was walking from the bus stop back to the Islander when I saw an older Black man with a shaved head running away from the hotel. I couldn't see his face.

Denny had signed below the statement in the large, printed script of a fourth grader. So much for Walker's assurances that there was nothing to worry about.

Amanda's name on my phone brightened my evening. "Hi there! Wow, a call. To what do I owe the pleasure?"

"Just wanted to hear that sexy voice."

"Flattery will get you everywhere, babe," I chuckled.

"Are you drinking, Joe?"

"No," I said, pushing my drink away from me on the end table. A few seconds of awkward silence followed.

"Hey, so I've been thinking. I'm really not concerned about that guy Camacho and his threat. I'm sure he just overheard you say my name and knew that it would freak you out."

"Really?"

"Yeah, and like you said, it's not like you're investigating him. As far as he knows, you're heeding his warning, right?"

"You're probably right."

"And in a few days, Walker will testify and then Camacho will know that he has nothing to worry about."

"Okay, so your point is?" I was hoping I'd guessed it.

"So, I want to visit you."

"I was hoping you'd say that. Are you sure you feel okay about it? I promise to protect you from macho Camacho."

She laughed. "I'm sure you will. I hear they call you the Turnernator."

We traded bad puns deep into the night, and I was elated she was coming to visit.

CHAPTER 48

In the morning, after a conference in chambers about jury instructions, Kotkin was at the podium. "The People call Dennison Devaney."

At the back of the courtroom, an assistant with the DA's Office put a hand on the young man's shoulder and gestured up the aisle. Both hands shoved in the pockets of his jeans, he cautiously made his way forward, his head tucked between hunched shoulders as he took in the scene with wide eyes.

Denny looked to be in his early twenties. Tall and sturdy, he wore a blue flannel shirt over a dingy thermal. At the counsel table, he stopped, looking confused as he self-consciously patted down his short blonde hair.

"Mr. Devaney, good morning," came the easy tone of the judge. "Deputy Souza will direct you up to this chair," he said, as if addressing a child.

The clerk rose. "Mr. Devaney, please raise your right hand."

Denny smiled a guileless smile. "Is that the one I write with?" he asked.

The clerk hesitated. "I'll bet it is," the judge said kindly. "Denny, do you plan to tell the truth today?" he asked casually, dispensing with formalities.

"Yes," he said, still smiling.

"Great. Proceed, Mr. Kotkin."

Kotkin got to the point. "Mr. Devaney, you're the nephew of Jeff Devaney, correct?"

"Yes sir."

"Denny, will you please tell us what you observed on August 25, 2021?"

The witness took a deep breath and looked skyward. "Around 8:00 p.m., I was walking from the bus stop back to the Islander when I saw an older Black man with a shaved head running away from the hotel. I couldn't see his face." He spoke in a sing-song cadence, like a child reciting a verse from memory.

"Thank you, Mr. Devaney. I have no further questions."

"Mr. Turner, cross examination?"

On the way to the podium, I looked at Denny's written statement. He had repeated it verbatim. "Hello, Denny," I said pleasantly.

"Hello," he said, returning my tone.

"I understand you like horses."

The witness smiled wide and nodded. "Yessir, I surely do. I love horses."

"So, Denny, could you state again what you saw that night?"

Another deep breath. "Around 8:00 p.m., I was walking from the bus stop back to the Islander when I saw an older Black man with a shaved head running away from the hotel. I couldn't see his face."

"I'm sorry, Denny. I'm not sure I heard all of that. Could you tell us again, nice and loud?"

"Objection, asked and answered," said Kotkin.

"Overruled," said the judge. "Denny, go ahead and tell us again what you saw."

The witness smiled. "Around 8:00 p.m., I was walking from the bus stop back to the Islander when I saw an older Black man with a shaved head running away from the hotel…" He paused to look skyward again.

"And what's the last part?" I asked earnestly. "I couldn't..." I said, prompting him.

"I couldn't see his face," he said with a satisfied smile.

"Excellent. Thank you, Denny," I said walking from the podium to behind Walker at the counsel table. "By the way, do you know this man here?" I asked, putting a hand on my client's shoulder.

Denny's face flashed with recognition. "Oh yeah. That's Allston. Hey," he said, with a timid wave to my client.

"Denny, do you know why Allston is here today. Do you know what all this is about?"

He stared blankly and shook his head. "No sir."

"And this person who was running from the hotel, do you think that could have been Allston?"

Denny was silent, his pleasant face scrunched to a frown. I tried again. "So, when you said that about the older bald man, you weren't describing Allston, here, were you?"

"No," he said, smiling as if my question were absurd.

I walked toward the witness. "You've done a very good job today, Denny. You came in and said what you were supposed to say perfectly, didn't you?"

"I tried to say it perfect but I forgot that last part about not seeing his face," he said sheepishly.

"Thank you, Denny. No further questions."

As the jury filed out for the noon recess, Walker caught my eye with an I-told-you-so smirk. "Okay, you were right," I said. "Nothing to worry about."

CHAPTER 49

The afternoon of day six of the trial brought my client face to face with his accuser. I could not have reasonably hoped that Devaney's physical appearance would change much since the last time I saw him. Still, I was disheartened to see the gray, fragile figure ambling toward the witness stand.

In the less than a month since our meeting in the District Attorney's Office, he had seemingly aged another decade. His pace seemed to say, "I'll get there when I get there." He moved like my grandfather after he threw out his back, with a hint of vertigo, every step feeling for uneven ground in the dark. His face was fixed in pain, like smokers who squint with every drag on a cigarette.

Logically, Mr. Devaney's decrepit nature should not hurt my client's defense. Someone certainly stabbed holes in the poor man, only to be repelled by his superhuman effort. So long as the jury believed that it wasn't Walker, none of that mattered.

The problem, of course, as I explained to myself with time to spare as Devaney made his way up Department 10's center aisle, was that logic in jury trials often ran a close third behind sympathy and tie color. Whereas my diagonal stripes in primary colors would give my client a fighting chance against Kotkin's bright paisley, sympathy was still plodding his way toward the witness stand in the form of a 300-pound gorilla.

I had a feeling I knew how Devaney would be perceived, but just to be clear, I had asked Andy, who asked his wife, an experienced psychologist. "She says Devaney will be viewed as heroic and very sympathetic," he had said, reading his wife's email response. "Most young jurors will identify him as a father or grandfather figure. While they may question his ability to perceive, they'll be very reticent to disbelieve him if he says things like 'I'm sure that's the guy' or 'I'll never forget his face.' Did he say anything like that?" asked my office mate.

"Yes,"

"What did he say?"

"That he's sure that's the guy, and that he'd never forget his face."

"Oh. Bummer."

Devaney's interminable march stopped at the witness stand, where he tilted up to face the two steps like they were Mt. Everest. If it was possible, nine months into his recovery, the man seemed much worse off than he had at the scene of the crime. The entirety of his affect was different shades of gray. From his off-white beard to his storm cloud hair to his pallor of stale oatmeal, he was gray.

As he finally collapsed into the witness chair, a barely audible sigh swept over the courtroom. Kotkin was quick to take up the theme.

"Mr. Devaney, can I get you a cup of water?" Feeling my own unique pain, I rubbed my eyes and whispered, "He's not a fucking invalid" into my palm.

Kotkin's introduction of his star witness was syrupy sweet and lengthy. If Devaney looked like a slow-moving retiree, Kotkin treated him like an arthritic octogenarian with dementia.

"Mr. Devaney, can you hear me okay?" The deputy DA spoke loudly and slowly.

For his part, Devaney was even more charming than I'd remembered. "Yessir, ask away," came the enthusiastic reply, eliciting some smiles from the jury box.

Kotkin's examination covered Devaney's age, career in the military, family life, and part-time job as a caretaker at the Islander.

Whether the product of good coaching by Kotkin or a natural talent, he was every attorney's dream witness. His southern drawl met each question head on, and added just the right amount of detail. He was unfailingly polite, no doubt the product of his southern roots.

Devaney turned to address the jury after every question, his twinkling eyes pausing more often on juror number seven, an elegant retired nurse, who smiled pleasantly back. Speaking slowly with a soothing voice, his impression was that of a favorite grandfather who kept hard candy in his pocket and a joke at the ready.

A southern gentleman rocking on the porch, Devaney told the jury how he'd agreed to the caretaker position at the Islander, despite it taking him away from his loving wife of "38 years this July," three nights a week. My mind laughed at the prostitute theory. As far as the jury knew, Devaney was more likely to show up in the latest rap music video than entertain an impure thought.

It was in the middle of one of Kotkin's questions about his extensive volunteer work at the local rec center that Judge Arnadon put an end to his Senior of the Year Coronation.

"Mr. Kotkin, I'm sure that Mr. Devaney has led an interesting life, but could we move on to testimony more pertinent to this case?"

Clearly with more virtues to extol, Kotkin, with a show of great regret, paged ahead in his legal pad.

CHAPTER 50

August 25, 2021

A distant clatter stirred in a far corner of Jefferson Beauregard Devaney's peaceful doze seconds before he was snapped back to consciousness on the end of a whip. He screamed silently, gasping for air, his hands feeling for the searing pain in his chest.

Just as Devaney's fingers touched the knife, his attacker pulled it out, and as the old man would later put it, "was fixing to get me again." On reflex, Devaney's right hand shot out and met the hand of his attacker six inches from his chest. Without thinking, the old man thrust himself back into the couch, brought his knees to his chest and kicked with all his strength, his socked feet knocking his assailant across the small room.

The attacker, still armed, lunged at Devaney again, who was now standing, and with a sweeping motion, drove the knife deep into his victim's side, perforating his liver. Now losing blood by the pint, Devaney managed to grab the hand that held the knife, bear hug the assailant, and drive them into the back wall of the apartment.

The assailant broke free of Devaney's grasp and jabbed at his face and back while pinned against the wall. Devaney would later say that however excruciating the stabs, he knew that he could not let go and risk another wound to his vital organs. He held on, enduring at least five stab wounds to his back and two slashes to his face before both Devaney and his attacker slipped in the growing pool of blood and fell to the floor, the attacker dropping the knife on the way down.

As his attacker fled through the lobby and into the cool night, Devaney crawled through his pooling blood to the edge of a table, where he pulled himself up to a phone.

CHAPTER 51

"Mr. Devaney, what are your duties at the Islander?"

"I am the caretaker. I collect rent from our extended stay residents. I run the front desk, distribute mail, listen to complaints, sell cigarettes, settle arguments, feed my cat. Li'l bit of everything, I suppose."

"Sir, do you recall August twenty-fifth of last year?"

"Yes, sir, I do."

"Were you working that day?"

"Yes."

"And you mentioned settling arguments. Did you have to settle any arguments that day?"

"No. I was actually involved in an argument myself."

"Is that unusual?"

"Yeah. For most of the regulars, at least. We're a pretty nice community. Most people know each other. We try to get along." Another smile for the retired nurse.

"And with whom did you argue?" I couldn't decide at whom to be mad. Kotkin for saying "with whom," or Devaney, who was laying it on thick.

"I argued with the resident of 112, Allston Walker."

"And do you see Mr. Walker in the courtroom?"

"Yes."

"Sir, please identify him by where he is sitting and an article of clothing he is wearing."

"Sitting on the end of that table next to his lawyer, wearing blue."

"Your Honor, may the record reflect the witness has identified the defendant, Allston Walker?"

"The record will so reflect," said Judge Arnadon.

"What was the nature of the argument?"

"His rent was past due and he received a notice of eviction."

"And this appeared to upset Mr. Walker?"

"Yes, he said he'd been there for a long time and deserved some leeway. I politely explained to him that the notices are generated and sent out based on a computer program, and I wasn't aware of any exceptions made for long-time residents."

"Did Mr. Walker yell at you during this exchange?"

"I wouldn't call it yelling, but his voice was raised."

"And did you two come to a resolution?"

"No. He stomped off."

"Is that the last time you saw Allston Walker that day?"

"No."

"What time did you see him again?"

"About 8:00 p.m."

"And where were you?"

"In my living quarters behind the front desk."

It was 10:30 a.m., and juror number six was nodding off again, so Kotkin told the judge that he was at a natural stopping place for the morning break. The judge cautioned the jury not to discuss the case and ordered the fifteen-minute recess.

After the jury had filed out, the judge addressed Kotkin. "Mr. Kotkin. We're going to complete this trial within the calendar year. Let's move things along."

Suppressing a grin, I made for the hot dog stand outside the courthouse and inhaled a bratwurst with mustard, my standard mid-morning snack. Juror number five, ahead of me in line, dug into the ice chest for a soda, which was prudent but not necessarily good news for the defense.

Back in court, Kotkin casually ambled over to my side of the counsel table while we were alone in the courtroom. Something about his gait made me suspect bad news. He was savoring its delivery.

"So, you may have already noticed, but the surveillance tape is off by one hour. Apparently, the Islander didn't account for daylight savings." He smiled, knowing full well I had no way of knowing of the hotel's mistake.

"Thanks, I saw that," I lied, staring at my laptop, pretending to concentrate on something else, as I digested the potentially devastating news. As soon as the prosecutor sauntered away, I pulled up the surveillance footage. As the video loaded, I cringed at the thought of what I would find. I pictured a blood smeared Walker, sneering menacingly, as he walked out of the Islander. I wondered how long Kotkin had known about the time discrepancy. I cursed myself for not watching all twelve hours of the video.

Soon a still frame of the hotel opened on my screen. I fast forwarded to nineteen zero eight hours, or 7:08 p.m. A deep breath before I clicked play.

I watched for three minutes, but no one came in or out of the door.

Walker entered the courtroom ahead of the jury to find me sitting with both elbows on the table, my forehead resting against both thumbs as I stared at the motionless screen and contemplated the turn of events.

The video confirmed two of my suspicions. First, Kotkin had been messing with me about the importance of the video evidence. The video was almost worthless, failing to capture the suspect on camera. The attacker must have left the lobby through the side door that wasn't monitored by a camera.

Second, Sierra Belton, the self-proclaimed prostitute, was wrong. Her claim about seeing a young man fleeing out the front door of the hotel was flatly disproven by the video. Our eyewitness was gone, and Walker's chances were once again circling the drain.

And what about Ms. Belton? There was strong evidence that she had fabricated her testimony to benefit Walker. Her statement tracked the video's depiction perfectly, except that she hadn't known it was an hour off the correct time. Who was I kidding? Of course she lied! I suspected as much even before the video revelation and was pissed at myself for letting Chuck talk me out of it.

So, how had she seen the video? The burglar, perhaps? The surveillance DVD had been in the file but would there have been time to watch it on a laptop? I thought I recalled the burglar carrying a backpack but wasn't sure.

"You all right?" My client's deep and raspy voice broke my trance.

"Absolutely. What was lunch? A little chateaubriand with a rich Cab? No? Bologna again?"

"Funny." Then he leaned in to whisper. "Hey."

"What's up?"

"Will you please cross examine the shit out of this cracker."

We bumped knuckles. "I will do my best."

CHAPTER 52

When the jury was in place and accounted for, Kotkin, still smirking, heeded the judge's words and resumed his direct examination with purpose.

"Mr. Devaney, do you recall the evening of August 25, 2021 at about 8:10 p.m.?"

"I surely do. I was reclining on my sofa, watching the television when a man barged into my apartment and stabbed me."

"Do you see the man in court who stabbed you?"

"Yes."

"Please point to him and describe what he's wearing."

Devaney raised a steady hand and pointed to Allston Walker. "That's him. Wearing khakis and a dress shirt. Never seen him in those clothes," he said with a smug smile.

The judge did not wait to be asked. "The record will reflect that the witness identified the defendant, Allston Walker."

"Thank you, your Honor. Mr. Devaney, that night, were there lights on in your apartment?"

"I had a reading light on. And there was light from the television. It's a small room. I could see fine."

"When Mr. Walker entered the room, did he make any effort to conceal his face?"

"No."

"Did he wear a mask of any kind, or have a hat pulled down low?"

"No."

"Can you describe how he entered the room?"

"He just barged in through the door as fast as can be. Before I could get up, he was swinging the knife down on me. I didn't have time to get off the sofa."

"So, he tried to stab you while you were still reclining on the sofa?"

"Yes, I was in the process of getting up and he jumped down on me."

"What happened next?"

"I felt that knife go in my chest. Hurt like the dickens. Then he took it out and went to stab me again." By now, the old charmer had the jury's rapt attention, and he was in full story telling mode. "Well, sir," the witness continued, his southern drawl seeming to thicken, "I decided that one of those stabs was enough for me, so when his arm came down another time, somehow I caught his hand and threw him off of me to the side."

"What happened next?"

"We both got to our feet and he came at me again with the knife, slashing at me."

"Did Mr. Walker stab you again?"

"Yes. Several times. In the stomach again, and several times in the arms and once in my thigh."

"After you got to your feet, for how long did the struggle continue?"

"I don't rightly know. Probably two or three minutes."

"And what was happening during that time?"

"He was trying to stab at me. I was trying to hit him. Trying to get the knife from him. Trying not to get stabbed again."

"Did you ever get the knife from him?"

"No."

"How did the attack end?"

"Well, I guess he decided he'd killed me, or maybe he just got tired of stabbing me. Anyway, after one last stab in the gut, he left and I collapsed to the floor. I guess I crawled over and called 911."

"You said, 'I guess.' Do you recall making that call to 911?"

"No. I've been told that I did." Walker and I exchanged looks of disdain. Devaney's answer laid the groundwork for an explanation of his 911 call in which he said he did not know the identity of his attacker. Obviously, he was blacked out and couldn't recall the call at all.

"When Mr. Walker stabbed you while you were lying on the sofa, how close was your face to his face?"

"About 8 inches."

"And when you both were on your feet, and he was slashing at you, how close was your face to Mr. Walker's face?"

"I'd say one or two feet."

"When did you recognize Mr. Walker that night? When did you realize who was attacking you?"

"As soon as he barged into my room."

"Did you know Mr. Walker before the attack that night?"

"Oh, yes. Like I said, he was one of the tenants. I'd seen him around and collected rent from him a dozen or so times."

"So, you knew him and knew his face."

"Oh, yes. Knew him well enough to say hello."

"Any doubt that the man stabbing you was Allston Walker?"

"No," Devaney said, fixing his eyes on Walker, the hint of a smile playing on his lips. He was enjoying the moment. "Absolutely no doubt in my mind."

CHAPTER 53

On Wednesday, a scheduled off day in the trial, I found Chuck in my office, working on subpoenas. "Want to take a ride to the Islander?" I asked.

"Sure, does the hotel have a happy hour I haven't heard about?"

"I need to confront Camacho. If he thinks we know something, he might let something slip." Also, since Amanda was going to visit, I wanted to satisfy myself that she'd be safe.

"And I'm sure he'll be more than happy to share with us."

"I know, but I feel like we should at least try. And let's get going before the sun goes down."

We rode in Chuck's vintage late-seventies jalopy. He said he kept it around because he wouldn't be disappointed if it was stolen, and he had a point. Among its many accolades, Oakland recently had become the auto theft capital of the free world.

As we headed into the setting sun, the bustle of downtown gave way to a residential dystopia. Wrought iron bars bracketed doors and windows of colorful Victorians. Yards were overgrown, the sidewalks littered with garbage. The streets would be quiet for another few hours before the various night hustlers started their day. Chuck parked in front of a corner store across from the Islander and left it open with the windows down. "Might save the windows," he explained.

Whether or not we got to speak to the custodian, Camacho, I was glad to gain the perspective of the place. As was usually the case, my mind's eye had pictured the crime scene and its surroundings larger and more spacious. The security camera that had been pointed at the lobby door had been smashed and now dangled from its position on a flag pole that was no longer in use.

Inside, the lobby was cramped and smelled like an ashtray. Chuck looked at me then shifted his eyes quickly behind the front counter where three rows of mail cubbies lined the back wall. They were labeled with masking tape and a sharpie. One read "Paul Camacho, 116."

As we headed toward a hallway off the lobby, the front door opened behind us.

"Help you guys?" A middle-aged security guard in an ill-fitting baby blue uniform stood with one hand on his belt, the other on a holstered pistol. In case there was lingering doubt as to his occupation, he wore a black baseball cap that read, "ALLIED" in white block letters. I wondered if the Islander had stepped up security since the attack on Devaney.

"Probation officers," Chuck replied without missing a beat, flashing his old probation officer identification that hadn't been valid for over a decade. The guard took his hand off his gun and silently waived us on. More accurately, the Islander had stepped up the appearance of security.

We walked down a dim and narrow hallway with rooms on either side. The faded yellow doors were labeled with violet numbers painted with a stencil and spray gun. A green carpet, strangely spongy underfoot, completed the Mardi gras color scheme which I thought a strange choice for a hotel named the Islander. The farther we walked, the more intense the smell of cigarette smoke.

We stopped after thirty feet at room 116. The bass beat of rap music vibrated from inside so Chuck knocked loudly. After three attempts we heard the slide of the steel deadbolt and the door creaked open six inches, held fast by a thick security chain. Two brown eyes peered up at us through the gap from the level of the doorknob.

"Hello there," said Chuck in a friendly tone, bowing slightly to be closer to the child's height. "Is Paul Camacho home?"

"He ain't here." The voice was a girl's and I assumed it belonged to Camacho's younger sister.

"Do you know if he's here working today at the hotel?"

The eyes darted briefly to her left as if she was going to ask someone inside for advice. "He ain't here," she repeated softly.

"Okay, thanks." Chuck looked at me and shrugged. We headed back to the lobby and out the front door.

Outside the hotel, a group of young males had gathered and were playing dice against the wall of the hotel. Their chatter stopped and I felt their stares as we walked by, acutely aware that we were likely perceived as law enforcement. A prostitute yelled something unintelligible at a passing car. Now that was a prostitute, I thought. As we arrived at Chuck's car, a young man appeared from behind it suddenly.

"Yo, whassup?" he said forcefully, both hands shoved inside the pockets of an overcoat while moving within a foot of us. On the streets, his words were not a pleasant greeting. The rough equivalent was "What's your problem?" or "What the fuck are you doing in my neighborhood?" Both arms were bent at the elbow, his hands pointing at us from inside the pockets.

I didn't recognize him immediately. He peered out from under a black baseball cap pulled down low that obscured his shaved head. As Chuck and I retreated a full step into the street, I saw the custodian's large hoop of keys hanging from his baggy jeans that sagged below his buttocks.

"Mr. Camacho, as you know, my job is to defend…"

"I know that," he said aggressively. "It's disrespectful coming to a man's home uninvited to talk business."

I didn't think the timing was right to point out to Mr. Camacho that technically, since he also worked at the Islander, we were actually at his place of business. The word "disrespectful" had knifed through my ears. Over the years, my job had taught me a thousand seemingly mild slights that were deemed "disrespectful" in Oakland and therefore a justification for lethal retaliation. I fervently hoped I had not learned another.

He was positioned between us and Chuck's car. Behind us, I noticed the chatter of the dice game had subsided and I felt the group from the hotel moving closer to the street. Camacho's hostile tone with the two outsiders was sending signals and I hated where this was going. He was also doing a good impersonation of someone pointing a gun at us from his coat pocket.

Since Camacho's threat, I had fantasized about confronting him. "If you ever lay a hand on Amanda, so help me God...," that sort of thing. I decided on a somewhat more muted approach.

"I'm very sorry, Mr. Camacho," I said with a dry mouth, trying not to stare at the pockets. "We just thought that if we talked this out...."

"Let me put it to you like this," he said, clearly not at all interested in what I had to say. "I'm pretty sure Walker don't know you're here. That being the case, I really don't have nothing to say to you, know what I'm sayin'? If he do know you're here he best check up, know what I'm sayin'?"

Unfortunately, despite his atrocious grammar, I knew exactly what he was sayin'. "Check up" was a shortened version of "Check yourself," which came from the very trite yet extremely descriptive phrase, "Check yourself before you wreck yourself." Paul Camacho had just threatened Walker with death, or at least, serious bodily injury.

"And he know I got peoples," he added, meaning that even though Walker was incarcerated he wouldn't be safe. Camacho had friends in jail and probably prison who could accomplish his goal.

"Walker has no idea we're here," I said hurriedly. "I just saw you in court, and…"

"So y'all get in your raggedy-ass car and get the fuck up out of here."

We were in the car before he finished his sentence and Chuck drove away as quickly as his heap could manage. We both sat breathing hard, digesting the confrontation until safely out of the neighborhood. "What the fuck, Joe! I thought you said he was a nice kid who took care of his sister?"

"That's what Walker told me," I said defensively, my heart still racing.

"Oh, that's what your client who probably killed a man over seventy bucks told you? That makes sense."

"Sorry. Geez, that was scary. I'm pretty sure he had a gun in his jacket."

"Oh, I'm certain he did! And by the way, I'm entirely too old to do any of this actual detective work." He spoke rapidly, clearly rattled by the events. "So in the future, count me out. And what does Walker have on that guy? He must have attacked Devaney, right?"

I had spent a lot of time trying to answer that question. It certainly made sense. Why else would Camacho be so intent on stifling the defense's investigation? On the other hand, there was zero evidence that he had committed the crime. And if Devaney was making an honest mistake, Camacho as the attacker made no sense. He was much younger than Walker and looked nothing like him.

"No idea. Walker's lips are sealed."

"Of course, why name the actual attacker when you can just serve a life sentence instead?"

We rode the rest of the way back to the office in silence. I was exhausted from the adrenaline rush and needed a drink.

As Chuck's giant sedan bounced through the potholes of west Oakland, I had the uneasy feeling that the Walker case itself was traveling its own path and I was merely along for the ride. Between the office burglary, Ms. Belton's strange cameo, and this latest episode, there seemed to be forces at work well beyond my control.

"Not to be overly dramatic, but I was afraid I was going to die back there," I said, climbing out of his car.

"Every man dies," Chuck said enthusiastically, having clearly recovered, "but not every man really lives."

I was sure it was a movie line but didn't have the mental energy.

"Good night, Chuck. Thanks for the help. And I promise, no more actual detective work for you."

CHAPTER 54

On Thursday morning, wearing a dazzling gray suit and red tie, Kotkin resumed his examination of his star witness. "Mr. Devaney, going back to the argument you had with Mr. Walker earlier in the day about the rent payment, did Mr. Walker appear highly agitated?"

"Oh, yeah, he was mad." After a pause, the witness smirked. "Obviously."

"Do you recall what time that argument with Walker took place?"

"I don't recall."

Devaney's answer was another sign of coaching by Kotkin. The witness had told the police that Mr. Walker and he had argued about 7:30 p.m., only about 30 minutes prior to the attack. However, Devaney's sidekick, Mr. Erickson, had told police that he witnessed the argument at 1:30 p.m. in the afternoon. Although not exactly a death blow to the prosecution, the discrepancy still called into question Devaney's memory of the day. It seemed very odd that he would be wrong about the time by such a wide margin.

It had crossed my mind that Devaney had been dreaming about the confrontation with Walker when he was stabbed. If Devaney had been awakened while dozing, his mind could have somehow substituted Walker for the real attacker. It also had crossed my mind that speculating about the content of Devaney's dreams would likely get me laughed out of court.

Anyway, it was good to see Devaney a little shifty on the stand. I was beginning to dislike him.

"Is that day now kind of a blur?"

"Objection, leading," I said, snapped from my thoughts by Kotkin's transparent ploy.

"Sustained," Judge Arnadon ruled immediately. I was now four up in the objection Olympics.

Kotkin paused, then asked to approach the bench.

The judge muted his microphone and leaned toward Kotkin. "Sustained means you lose, Mr. Kotkin."

"Thank you, Judge. I'm aware. May I ask the question in a different way?"

"Let me guess," the judge whispered. "Your witness gave an answer about the time of the argument to the police that was not accurate."

"Yes," I interrupted, trying to hide my glee.

"Mr. Kotkin, step back and move on."

"Mr. Devaney," continued Kotkin as he reached the podium, "I know you have identified Mr. Walker as your attacker. Could you describe what he was wearing that night?"

"Khaki pants, pale-yellow t-shirt and black sneakers."

"Do you recall your attacker's height and weight?"

"Yes. About five feet, nine inches, 175 pounds."

"And that's the same description you gave the police when you were in the hospital?"

"I believe it was, yes."

Kotkin heel-clicked his way to the clerk's desk and retrieved a pre-marked exhibit. "Your Honor, may I approach the witness?"

"Yes, Mr. Kotkin," said Judge Arnadon, exasperated. The judge had made it clear that we did not have to ask to approach the witness, and yet Kotkin had asked at least a dozen times during the trial. Out of the corner of my eye, I saw even Mr. Walker slowly shake his head. I marveled at Kotkin's capacity to piss off every walk of life.

"Mr. Devaney, I'm showing you what has been marked as Prosecution's Exhibit 1. Do you recognize this?"

"Yes," said Devaney, holding the exhibit down to view it through his bifocals. "That's a California driver's license. Name on it is Allston Walker."

"And what is the height and weight listed on the license?"

"Five feet, nine, 165 pounds."

"Mr. Devaney, you've described Mr. Walker during the attack as wearing khaki pants, a pale-yellow T-shirt and black sneakers. Was he wearing the same clothing when you argued about the rent?"

"Yeah, he didn't change. I guess those were his stabbing clothes," Devaney deadpanned, drawing smiles from the jury, and a chuckle from juror number eight, the schoolmarm who was becoming less and less charming.

Devaney's snarky comments aside, the clothing identification was something new from Devaney, but it sounded familiar for some reason. I made a note for cross examination while my client audibly exhaled, shaking his head slowly. He was holding it together, but the trial was wearing on him.

"Mr. Devaney, returning to the attack, after collapsing to the floor, what happened next?"

"My phone was on a chair at my desk. I upended the chair and the phone fell on the floor. I remember having a hell of a time dialing. I smeared blood all over the phone—there was blood everywhere, of course—but I finally managed to dial 911. I was fading fast, so thank God there was a cruiser close by."

"Mr. Devaney, are you aware of the injuries you suffered?" The witness, warming to his role as star witness, looked sideways at Kotkin. "Was I aware of my injuries?" he chuckled. "Yeah, the blood and intense pain tipped me off." Cue the cackling bitch in juror seat number eight.

Kotkin, speaking through a contrived grin, cut through the laughter that was at his expense, "Mr. Devaney, what injuries did you suffer at the hands of your attacker, Mr. Walker?"

The witness took a deep breath and bowed his head, revealing a pate of sparse gray hair and age spots, which made him seem even more vulnerable. The question had taken Devaney back to the night of the attack. He slowly raised his head until his reddened eyes locked on Walker.

Devaney's expression said more than all his previous testimony. Although the witness chair looked down on the counsel table, Devaney's head now tilted back as he stared down at Walker, relishing his position of power. His jaw jutted outward, his small mouth turned up at the corners in a sneering smile. I was sure his fists were clenched, tucked under the witness stand.

Jefferson Devaney had worked for years collecting money from poor people under the threat of eviction. Money that could have been spent on a new pair of boots or a baseball glove for a grandson, or for just once, a night out on the town. For all his charm, he must have known most residents saw him as the enemy, and he'd heard the taunts.

"Fucking cracker, let's see your sorry old ass try and throw my family out. Been in this shithole three years, I'm one month late and you're putting me and my daughter on the street? You heartless, racist, piece of shit."

Beneath Devaney's grandfatherly persona, there was a simmering vengeance seeping through the edges of his fake smile. He'd heard his fill over the years and had never spoken a word in response. It wasn't his money, after all. Just a job. Take the money and keep track of who paid. He'd simply shrugged off the insults and made a note on his ledger.

Later, though, back in his apartment, Devaney would fantasize about a different response. He'd pull a revolver from his waist band and calmly whisper, "What was that, punk?" And he'd hold the gun upright, not like these darkie thugs who turn it sideways. "Who's in charge now?" he'd asked, in his southern drawl. "Now pack up your smelly clothes and get out of my hotel."

The witness' jokes were over now, and the courtroom was deathly silent. "He stabbed me," he began, solemnly. "The first time, I was watching television on the sofa. I remember I was watching *Ms. Pimm's Murder Mysteries*, and I had just about figured out who the killer was." I made a note to have Chuck check what time the program aired.

"He burst through the door and stabbed me in the gut before I could get up. Doc says that one ruptured my stomach lining. While we were up and fighting, he slashed at my face, like a coward." Devaney's unblinking stare never left Walker, and I could feel my client fidgeting next to me.

"Doc Wagner told me there were seventeen separate stab wounds. He stabbed my side, my neck, my back. The last one—I lost a lot of blood and I was getting dizzy—I guess he thought he'd finished me off." A smile played at the corners of Devaney's mouth now, his eyes, still fixed on Walker. *Now, look at who's finishing who off.*

"He had me against the icebox. We'd been slipping all over the floor in my blood, but finally, he got some purchase. He reared back and lunged at me. The knife broke a rib and tore me up pretty good."

Kotkin paused for dramatic effect for the fifteenth time in the trial, this time with good reason. Devaney's haunting smile lent a macabre aura to the courtroom. The prosecutor stood at the podium and let the testimony wash over the jury.

"One last question, Mr. Devaney. Do you have any doubt who attacked you?"

The witness had blinked from his trance. He was back to the venerable, reliable, reasonable Jefferson Devaney. "I have no doubt, sir," he said as if surprised by the question. "The man who attacked me is Allston Walker."

"If you were to put a percentage on your certainty on this answer, what would that be?"

"What's that?" Devaney asked, looking confused.

"How sure are you that the man who stabbed you repeatedly on August 25, 2021 was Allston Walker?"

"Sir, I am one hundred percent certain."

"No further questions."

Judge Arnadon addressed the jury, reminding them not to speak about the case outside the courtroom. "Ladies and Gentleman, it's been a long week. I'm giving you the afternoon off. We'll see you tomorrow morning."

As the jurors solemnly filed out of the courtroom, Walker stared straight ahead, expressionless. We exchanged glances. The testimony had been devastating.

I texted Chuck on my way out of the courtroom.

—*Chuck, what time did Ms. Pimm's Murder Mysteries air on the night of the attack on Devaney?*—

Back at the office, I ate a piece of cold pizza and organized my cross examination. "Piece of cake, partner," Andy said when told of tomorrow's task. "Just convince the jury that he's not the sweet credible gentleman he appears. Instead, just convince them he's a reckless, stubborn, spiteful, near-sighted old man who has made the mistake of his life, all the while being as polite to him as possible."

"Helpful as ever. Thanks."

After reviewing my cross examination outline, I absently flipped through the binder of seventy-two photos, not knowing the reason for my actions. When I saw it, I knew immediately, and my small fist pump surprised me, a nice reminder that my competitive juices still flowed.

There, in a booking photo from Walker's last arrest in 2004 on a public intoxication charge, was the familiar pinched-in mug of my client. He wore a pale-yellow shirt.

It wasn't a smoking gun, but after the bleak day in court, it was something.

CHAPTER 55

I outlined my line of questioning for Devaney, then sat quietly in my deserted office, resting my mind after the ordeal of court. Soon, I felt the bad thoughts gathering forces on my mind's periphery, the familiar surge of nausea.

"This can't happen now, Joe." I said it aloud and scanned the office for a distraction. Late afternoon sunlight shone through window shades, striping an empty beer bottle on my desk. Nothing to focus on. I felt short of breath and had begun to hear the faint hum of the projector when my phone buzzed on my desk.

I shook myself from my thoughts and checked the screen. It was a text from Chuck.

—Ms. Pimm's Murder Mysteries (Episode 24 What You Don't Know Can Kill You) aired on August 25, 2021 from 6:30 p.m. to 7:30 p.m.—
—Thanks! BTW, not to say I told you so, but the so-called prostitute lied.—
—Oh no.—
—Oh yes.—

I blew out a sigh of relief, slid the color photo of Walker out of its clear plastic pocket, gathered my notes and headed for the elevator. It stopped on the second floor where symphony woman boarded. I hadn't seen her since spit-gate.

"You make quite a first impression," she said, extending her hand. "I'm Ashley."

"I'm sorry, you must have me confused with someone else," I deadpanned, shaking her hand. "I'm Joe."

"No, I'm pretty sure it was you," she said smiling, as the elevator arrived. "Right here at the scene of the crime. Isn't that what you call it?"

"Crime scene, technically. But now that you've recognized me, I have no choice but to move away. Probably out of state."

"Oh, don't do that on my account." She was laughing when we got off on my floor.

Of course I can be relaxed and funny when all I care about is Amanda, I thought to myself.

CHAPTER 56

Back in Department 10 on Friday, the judge greeted the jury. "Mr. Turner, cross examination?"

"Good afternoon, Mr. Devaney, my name is Joseph Turner and I represent Allston Walker."

"Afternoon, sir." The greeting was warm and genuine.

"Sir, I'll bet you're an early riser."

"Always have been. Get up at 5:00 a.m."

"So, at the time you were attacked—at about 8:10 p.m., it was past your bedtime?"

"I don't require a lot of sleep," the witness answered, with less warmth.

"The first time you were stabbed, you were on the sofa?"

"The first time Walker stabbed me, yes, that's where I was."

"And the sofa is on the opposite wall from your apartment's door that leads to the lobby, correct?"

"Yes."

"And so, the sofa is about twelve feet from that door."

"Sounds right."

"And you had a knife in your chest before you were able to get off the sofa."

"As I said, he burst through the door and attacked me very quickly. I wasn't expecting it."

"You actually had dozed off a bit prior to being attacked, isn't that right?"

"No, I was awake when Walker attacked me."

"And you said that you were watching *Ms. Pimm's Murder Mysteries* on television, right?"

"Yes, sir."

"Mr. Devaney, you made a recorded statement to the police the day after you were attacked, correct?"

"Yes."

I picked up Devaney's statement and took one step toward this witness. "And sir, in that statement, when asked what television show you were watching at the time of the attack, you said, and I quote, 'I can't recall.' Sir, do you recall making that statement?"

"Yes. I reckon it came to me at some point."

"Mr. Devaney, I notice that you wear glasses. Are those for seeing close-up or far away?"

"For both. They're bifocals. I pretty much always wear them."

"So, you would have been wearing them while you were watching television on the night of the attack?"

"Yes, I was."

"But when you were asked to look at Mr. Walker's photo at the hospital after the attack, you didn't have your glasses on, did you?"

"No, I assume they got knocked off during the tussle."

"I understand your daughter retrieved your glasses for you from your apartment and brought them to you at the hospital."

"Yes."

"And where do you keep your glasses in your apartment when you're sleeping?"

"In my spectacle case, on my desk."

"Is that where your daughter found them?"

"Objection, calls for speculation," said Kotkin.

"Sustained."

"Mr. Devaney, when you were shown Mr. Walker's photo in the hospital, were there other arrest photos along with his?"

"No."

"So, you were not asked to choose a photo of your attacker among a group of photos."

"No. There's was no need for that. I told the police who attacked me." I wasn't sure if I was getting under Devaney's skin, but he was getting under mine.

"Well, the first time someone asked you if you knew who stabbed you, you said you didn't know."

"That 911 call, I was basically unconscious."

"You have described your attacker as five feet, nine inches tall, correct?"

"Yes."

"Mr. Devaney, if you were on the sofa when he stabbed you, how could you possibly get a good read on his height?"

"Don't suppose I was able to," he said calmly, then paused for effect. "But I sure could when we were fighting toe to toe." Devaney wore a self-satisfied grin.

"I see. So, you could tell that he was roughly the same height as you?"

"Yes."

"Mr. Devaney, you testified on direct examination that your attacker wore a pale-yellow T-shirt."

"Yes sir, I did."

"Mr. Devaney, you have been interviewed by a number of police officers who have asked you for a description of your attacker."

"Yes."

"And you didn't tell any one of them that your attacker wore a pale-yellow T-shirt."

"Like I said, some things are coming back to me, I guess."

"Well, today was the first time that you've told anyone that your attacker wore a pale-yellow T-shirt. Did it come back to you today?"

Devaney started to speak, then smiled calmly. "I don't recall when it came to me."

"And you also recall that earlier that day, when you argued with Mr. Walker about the rent, Mr. Walker wore a pale-yellow T-shirt at that time." As I spoke, I moved from the podium to the clerk's desk, where Charlotte affixed a blue letter 'A' to the photo of Walker in pale-yellow.

"Yes, the same as he had on when he attacked me later."

I moved toward the witness, who was even smaller and older up close. "Mr. Devaney, I'm showing you defense exhibit A, a photograph of Allston Walker time stamped September 16, 2004. What color T-shirt is Mr. Walker wearing in this photograph that was taken nearly two decades ago?"

"Yellow."

"Pale-yellow, isn't it?"

"Yeah, I guess that's his color." I didn't hear any chuckles from the jury.

"Mr. Devaney, you saw this photograph at some point in your trial preparation with Mr. Kotkin, didn't you?"

"I can't say, sir. I don't recall."

"Sir, when you testified about your attacker wearing a pale-yellow T-shirt, rather than remembering the attack, you were recalling this photo, taken in 2004, weren't you?"

The witness looked at me hard with pursed lips. "Sir, I recall your client wearing a pale-yellow T-shirt the night he attacked me."

"The source of your memory of a pale-yellow T-shirt is this photograph, correct?"

"No."

"And the source of your identification of Allston Walker as your attacker was an argument you had with him earlier that day, wasn't it?"

"No sir. I told the police he attacked me because he did."

"Were you thinking about your argument with Mr. Walker when you were dozing on the sofa?"

"Objection," blurted out Kotkin. "Assumes facts not in evidence."

"Overruled, Mr. Kotkin. This is cross examination."

"I wasn't dozing off."

"And in your mind, that argument had just taken place, right?"

"I told you I didn't know what time that argument happened."

"Mr. Devaney, in your recorded statement to the police, you were asked what time the argument with Mr. Walker happened, correct?"

"Probably."

"And you're doing your best to tell the truth."

"Yes."

"And, sir, you gave the following answer." I turned to face the jury. "'I argued with Walker about the rent about 7:30 p.m.' And so, in your mind, Mr. Devaney, that argument with Mr. Walker took place less than a half hour before you were attacked."

"I suppose."

"That argument was on your mind just before the attack, wasn't it?"

"No."

"It was on your mind when you identified Allston Walker as your attacker."

"Not at all."

"No further questions."

Judge Arnadon glanced at the clock, which read 4:45 p.m. "Mr. Kotkin, re-direct?"

"Thank you, Your Honor. I have only a few questions." Kotkin walked slowly to the podium, phony smile in place.

"Mr. Devaney." Kotkin paused, as if searching carefully for words, as he poured his star witness a glass of water from the pitcher on the counsel table. I had to hand it to Kotkin. He had a way of communicating with the jury. In this small gesture, he said, "Mr. Devaney, you poor, dear man. Have you survived the rude and obnoxious onslaught from this jerk?"

"Mr. Devaney," began Kotkin again, "do you watch television most nights?"

"Yes."

"And I take it you enjoy *Ms. Pimm's Murder Mysteries*?"

"Yes. Don't mind saying I like that Ms. Pimm, too." Every juror smiled. Hell, I even smiled.

"And Mr. Turner made a big deal of asking you why you didn't recall that before. Have you had time to calmly reflect on this horrific event?"

"Objection, leading."

"Sustained."

Having successfully testified for his witness, Kotkin moved on. "Mr. Devaney, during your waking hours, how often do you wear your glasses?"

"It's very simple," said Devaney, regaining his confidence as he pivoted in his chair to address the jury. "If I'm awake, I'm wearing my spectacles. I have them on until I stop reading at night and click off the light. I put them back on before I get out of bed in the morning."

"Sir, you testified that your attacker was about five feet, nine inches. On cross examination by Mr. Turner" — Kotkin spat out my name like a bad peanut — "you reiterated that he was five feet, nine. Sir, how is it that you were able to accurately estimate your attacker's height?"

"Well, I'm five, nine, myself," said Devaney. "I was standing toe to toe with this guy while he was stabbing me. I remember him clearly as being about my height."

"Finally, Mr. Devaney, you were able to tell the police who attacked you by name?"

"Yes."

"And were you able to tell the police in which room he lived?"

"Yes."

"Do you have a memory today of your attacker stabbing you?"

"Yes."

"And is there any doubt in your mind who stabbed you?"

"None at all. Allston Walker stabbed me."

Kotkin strolled deliberately from the podium back behind the counsel table, clasping his hands in front of him as he nearly bowed to his precious witness. "No further questions."

"Judge Arnadon glanced over his glasses. "Mr. Turner, re-cross?"

"No questions. Thank you."

"Mr. Kotkin, any further witnesses?"

Kotkin did not answer right away. Instead, he rose, no doubt hoping that the judge would do him the courtesy of looking at him.

"Your Honor, the People of the State of California, rest," he said solemnly. I could tell he wanted to bow.

"Ladies and gentlemen," said the judge, now addressing the jury in his venerable and earnest voice, "we have reached the end of the prosecution's case. The defense may now also rest on the state of the evidence, as they have no burden of proof. Or, they may call additional witnesses to refute the prosecution's case. You are dismissed. We'll convene again Monday morning. Have a good weekend."

And with that, Jefferson Beauregard Devaney ambled off the witness stand, past Walker at the counsel table, down the hallway and out into the cool fall air. Was it my imagination, or did his pace quicken as he reached the exit?

CHAPTER 57

Amanda would arrive tomorrow and I couldn't wait to see her. After paying some bills at the office, I treated myself to chicken parm at Café Bellissimo, an Italian restaurant and wine bar a five-minute walk from home that reminded me of a mafia hang-out. Chuck's movie obsession was rubbing off on me. I had a glass of Pinot, then ordered a bottle so I'd drink less. This always seemed like a good strategy but rarely worked out.

In the morning, I awoke feeling dull and thinking of my blunder in allowing the gory photos of Devaney to be paraded before the jury. Deep down, I think I knew this would provoke a flashback. For all the mental anguish, nausea and exhaustion, though, my father's murder was slowly coming into focus.

Potentially, I was an eyewitness. Even if I couldn't recall a face, maybe I had seen something that could catch his killer. Still, my subconscious motives didn't make the episodes any less debilitating. In fact, they were becoming more vivid and intense.

The soundtrack was suddenly loud, the black and white images sharper, jumping at me from the screen.

Still no sequence to the visuals, only snapshots of lunges and groans and savage slashes. My view down the hallway is from the floor, blocked from above by my bed, as the figure moves closer to me, leather boots on the hardwood floors of the hallway.

I try to escape it now. Think of happy times, like sliding down the hallway in my socks, belly-flopping on the couch to watch cartoons. No use.

I hear my dad's voice again. I know it's his but I can't make out what he's saying above the ringing in my ears. The stench is overpowering now. My body spasms in fear and I force my head toward the screen but the projector is on high speed now and the images are flashing too fast for my mind. Finally, the images blur into black and I'm free again. I roll over as the projector clicks slowly to a halt, cooling my sweaty cheek against the pillow.

After I'd recovered, I forced my thoughts to the more current matter of Amanda's visit. I recalled walking home last night and realizing that my house needed cleaning before she arrived. Even after coffee and a shower, there were gaps in my memory of the evening. My house was still a mess, despite the conspicuous presence of my mop on the kitchen floor. I was mildly surprised I owned a mop.

Sensing a frat house smell, I opened all the windows and began collecting beer bottles and wine glasses. It reminded me of college when my roommates and I literally raked beer cans from under our couch before parents' weekend.

I'd used the dining room table as a work station since I moved in and its mahogany finish was a memory. Without time to organize, I slid the mound of paper into three boxes and put them in the garage.

The doorbell rang, and before I had time to worry about a greeting, she was in my arms and on my lips.

"Hey, Counselor," she whispered, before we kissed again.

"Sorry about my coffee breath. Come on in."

"Your house is wonderful. Speaking of taste, how about a tour."

"Sure, I hope it's okay. I intentionally messed the place up a bit for your benefit. It was feeling a little sterile, and I didn't want to intimidate you with my compulsive neatness."

"Nice try. Remember the pizza slice I found in your couch in college?"

"Okay, well, it's cozy. Kitchen, dining room, living room," I said gesturing around but still looking at her. "If it's pizza you're after, I'd check the recliner. What do you think?"

"I think it's a great house in desperate need of a woman's touch." She looked at me and winked. It was quick, but I was pretty sure she winked.

"I was going for new-age crappy."

"You nailed it," she laughed. Her brown eyes scanned the room and seemed to pause on a recycling bin in the kitchen, overflowing with empty bottles.

"Is there a place around to get coffee? I'd love a walk around the neighborhood."

As usual, conversation over coffee was easy. She held my hand on the walk home, and I was embarrassed to see my toothy grin in a shop window. She asked about the Walker trial, and I was impressed with her command of the facts. Really impressed.

"So, how's the real estate business?" I inquired as we walked into the house.

"Business is great, but I'm not thrilled with L.A. I'd like to get back to northern California." She paused and squeezed my hand. "For purely professional reasons, of course."

"Of course." Holy shit, I screamed silently to myself, as we arrived back at my house. This is definitely real.

"Excuse me," she said, checking her phone. She was beaming. "Isabella wants to know if we can have a dance party when I get back. Just the two of us. I know she's my daughter, but that's pretty darn adorable."

"You know, your smile looks a little different when you talk about Isabella."

"Being a single parent is not easy, but she's been really wonderful."

"Would you like a glass of wine? I have a bottle of rosé in the fridge."

"Thanks for remembering. Maybe later. So, you're still drinking now and again?" she asked as casually as she could.

"Recreationally, yes," I smiled.

"Ha! I drank recreationally in college. You were in training for the Olympics." Her smile was truly beautiful.

"Well, I've slowed down a bit since then." Technically, it was probably correct, at least by volume.

"So, did you open all the windows as a ploy to warm me up in your bed?" she asked walking down the hall.

"Well, that and the place smelled like stale beer," I said, following her into my bedroom.

"You silver-tongued charmer."

"I try."

"Take me to bed, Mr. Turner." She closed the door behind us emphatically.

As we lay tangled in my comforter an hour later, she spoke softly and hinted again about moving north. "You know, you may laugh, but I think I could actually help you with your cases."

"I don't doubt it for a second." Still intoxicated with ecstasy, I would have agreed with anything.

"Haven't I been helpful with the Walker case?"

"Apart from the terrible catch phrase contribution, yes you have."

"I'm serious, Joe," she giggled, sitting up in bed. "How's the trial going?"

"It's early, but not great. I was right about the prostitute. She lied."

"So, your instincts were spot on. I had a feeling. I'm falling for a genius." She leaned over and kissed me.

"Have you found the other paramedic yet?"

"Wow, you are deep into this. No, the guy changed jobs and moved out of state. Devaney probably couldn't have spoken to him in the ambulance anyway because of the oxygen mask. I just hate not having all the potential witnesses."

"Is your guy Chuck, um, competent?"

"Despite appearances, yes. Why do you ask?"

"I just remember he was duped by the prostitute."

"Yeah, he didn't meet her in person."

"What about the alibi?"

"It's not airtight. The witnesses need some coaching."

"Then," she said with a sigh, "you should get to work and I promise not to be a distraction. I should visit my mom and stay with her tonight, anyway."

"Are you sure? We could have dinner."

"No, this is a good test for us. We need to be able to allow each other to work."

"Okay, can I see you tomorrow?"

"I think I can probably squeeze you in," she whispered in my ear, then disappeared under the covers.

My laugh turned to a sigh of pleasure and I closed my eyes.

CHAPTER 58

I inhaled through my mouth and stood with my back arched and neck craned high and to the left, seeking air unscented by hair product. As the packed elevator in the courthouse crept upward, I indulged myself with thoughts of Amanda. Her visit Sunday had been perfect — a late lunch in the park, a hike and then mind-blowing sex. Each encounter was becoming less inhibited than the last.

The bump of the arrival of the elevator jostled my mind back to the case and the defense minefield that lay before me. For starters, the Walker defense meant getting my witnesses to court. I planned to present first the high octane, schizophrenic testimony of his girlfriend, Hartung. I hoped that somewhere in her rapid-fire ramblings would emerge my client's alibi, or as she put it, "not really an alibi but more so a premeditation of an alibi that occurred in my absence." The hope was if she went first for the defense, however bad her impression, it wouldn't be lasting.

As I stepped off the elevator on the seventh floor, the foyer echoed with the chatter of attorneys, witnesses, and spectators, all waiting for courtrooms to open. I scanned the room for quick, animated movements and non-stop chatter but found none. Finally, setting my trial box at my feet, my eyes fell to a floppy brown hat atop a woman who sat quietly on a bench within arm's reach. Familiar round blue eyes met my gaze from under the brown bill.

"Good morning, Mr. Turner," said Ms. Hartung quietly, a smile slowly forming on her remarkably tranquil mouth. "Don't worry," she said, rising to pat a reassuring hand on my shoulder, "I'm as calm as can be." She spoke slowly by anyone's standards, almost lethargically, and at eye level I could see that her eyes were dull.

Great, I thought, my alibi witness has swallowed a box of Quaaludes. As if reading my mind, Ms. Hartung said, "Don't worry," for the second time in ten seconds, and patted my arm again, this time to steady herself.

"Stephanie, listen to me," I said. She didn't talk, which I admitted to myself was a welcome change. "You need to wake up and be alert for this. I'm going to get you some coffee. Wait here. Cream and sugar?" She stared, blankly. "Be right back."

While getting coffee, Chuck called with an update. "Hartung should be there, and Julia is on the way."

"Yeah, Hartung's a bit over-medicated. How soon can you get here?"

"Five minutes."

I returned to find said witness reclined against the wall. As she drank her coffee, I briefly considered putting Walker on the stand first and letting Stephanie wake up while he testified. But I had told him he would not testify with his life-long freedom on the line until Thursday. I didn't think, "Surprise, you're on!" would go over well. I urged Ms. Hartung to drink up and smiled at the irony of plying Hurricane Hartung with caffeine.

Chuck arrived to coordinate witnesses and took stock of Ms. Hartung. "Looks like she tried to eat the medicine cabinet. She's higher than a cat's back."

I gathered up my witness and escorted her into the courtroom. As she slouched in the back of the gallery sipping her oversized coffee, I asked Deputy Franz to bring my client into the courtroom.

Walker stole a glance behind him at Ms. Hartung. "Smart putting her on drugs," he deadpanned. I wasn't sure if he was serious.

Ms. Hartung's testimony, although droned in a lazy monotone, was better than I had hoped. Perhaps she merely seemed comatose to those familiar with her normally manic persona. She managed to testify that on the afternoon Devaney was attacked, she brought Walker a snack at his job site.

It was far from an alibi, but it supported what would be Allston's testimony that after arguing with Devaney, far from being consumed by rage, he had gone to work as usual.

Kotkin's cross examination pointed out her obvious bias and confirmed that she was not with Allston at the time of the stabbing. Soon, her glazed smile was floating down the aisle and out the courtroom doors.

Next up was Julia Kendall, the sullen teenager who had arrived with Ms. Hartung and had scarcely looked in my direction. She walked with arms folded to the stand, peering from under long hair that shrouded her face in a jet-black diagonal. I'd seen prisoners being led to jail with more enthusiastic strides. At least there was no danger of her seeming over-anxious to help the defense.

"Ms. Kendall, you are the best friend of Ms. Hartung's daughter, Alana, correct?"

"Yes."

"Can you tell me where you were on August 25, 2021 at about 8:00 p.m.?"

"At my home," came the mumbled reply.

"Did you make any phone calls that evening?"

"Yes, I called Alana."

"Did you place the call to her home or cell phone?"

"I called her cell, but she didn't pick up. So, I called her home."

"Did someone answer the phone?"

"Yes, Mr. Walker answered."

"Objection, lack of foundation." Kotkin's objection was immediate.

"Sustained. Ladies and gentlemen, please disregard the portion of the answer that referred to Mr. Walker."

"Ms. Kendall, who is Mr. Walker?"

"Alana's mom's boyfriend."

"Have you heard his voice before?"

"Yes."

"How many times?"

"A lot. Maybe like 30 times."

"Can you describe his voice?"

"Like, deep and rough."

"The voice you heard when you called Alana's house on the evening of August twenty-fifth, was it a deep, man's voice?"

"Yes."

"Did it also sound rough?"

"Yes."

"And what time did you make that call?"

"Around 8:20 p.m."

Like Ms. Hartung's, Julia's testimony fell well short of an ironclad alibi. Walker may have had time to race to Ms. Hartung's house after the assault and answer the call. Still, it helped. I produced the phone records showing the call was placed at 8:23 p.m. and sat down.

"Good afternoon, Ms. Kendall." Kotkin's creepy sweet tone made the witness squirm in her seat.

"Miss, you can't say for sure if the voice you heard on the phone that night was Mr. Walker's, right?"

"No, but it sounded like him and he stayed there a lot, so I figured it was him."

"You figured. Indeed." Indeed. Truly only the rarest assholes use that word repeatedly.

"Young lady, there were lots of calls from your home to the defendant's, correct?"

"Yes, I guess so."

"Well, you were good friends with this Alana, right?"

"Yes," mumbled the teenager.

"And you two talked on the phone almost every day?"

"Yes."

"You certainly texted every day." Kotkin's saccharine smile was nauseating.

"Yes."

"And I'm guessing it wasn't unusual for the defendant to answer the phone there?"

"No."

"Sometimes he would answer?"

"Yes."

"And sometimes Alana or her mother would answer?"

"Yes." The witness sighed deeply into the microphone, exuding the boredom only a teenager can muster.

"And you don't keep a log of who answers the phone on what day, do you?" I smiled at the line of questioning. Usually, I was above setting traps for my opponent. Another Kotkin exception.

"No."

"But, young lady, for some reason..." Kotkin paused, feigning confusion. "For some reason, now seven months later—countless phone calls later—you remember that when you called way back on August twenty-fifth, it was the defendant who answered the phone?"

"Yes," mumbled the witness.

"And how is that?" I wasn't sure, but I thought I heard regret in Kotkin's voice, even before he had completed the question.

The young girl paused, peering upward under her shroud of hair to meet the prosecutor's eyes. "Because it was my birthday," she said, not mumbling in the least. "We were going to cut the cake and blow out the candles with my family. And we were all waiting for Alana. She arrived while I was on the phone with Mr. Walker."

"Indeed," I whispered to myself.

I felt my client's stare of scorn heating the side of my face. He had read my simple mind and was reminding me that the memory of my petty personal victories would not be worth two cigarettes over the next thirty years in prison. So far, Devaney's testimony had carried the day, and a half-assed alibi was a pebble to the prosecution's tank. I turned, looked him in the eye and nodded, my smug grin gone.

CHAPTER 59

Later that night at the jail, Allston and I went through his direct testimony one last time. He would never be a warm man, but he was making an effort. Predictably, though, my final attempt to persuade him to tell me about Camacho was met with silence.

"So," I said, making conversation while I waited for the jailer to unlock the interview room, "how did you know Denny wouldn't be a problem. His uncle obviously put him up to making his statement, but how did you know he wouldn't identify you?"

Walker grunted. "You know," he said, "it's funny. Everybody has a different brain. Just because someone like Denny don't seem smart in the everyday kind of way don't mean he's stupid. Just different.

"He'd come by my place once in a while. Didn't have any friends. Uncle treated him like shit. I taught him how to play checkers." Walker paused to recall the memory, then continued.

"One day, Denny took me to the track to see his horses. I watched him talking to the horses. Damnest thing I ever saw. Pretty quick, a trainer comes up asking Denny about how their horse looked. Then another. Here they were these professionals, relying on Denny for advice." Walker looked me in the eye and shrugged. "Not stupid. Just different."

"Anyway, he doesn't have a shady bone in his body. I knew he'd tell the truth." My client was proving to be a thoughtful soul. At times like this—when he revealed his sensitive side—I continued to have the distinct impression we'd met before.

As I walked down the interminable hallway on my way out of the jail, every step a snare drum's ricochet off the door at the tunnel's end, I wondered when it was that I had become convinced of Walker's innocence. It was certainly several months after meeting him and hearing his tale. I hoped the jury was quicker to catch on.

Back home I realized that the bizarre case of Sierra Belton was eating at me. Kotkin had mentioned to me that her name and date of birth were fake, all but confirming her attempt to lie for Walker.

Beginning with her weird rendezvous in the Berkeley Hills, nothing about her made sense. Aside from money, what was her motivation to lie? I had shown the video to Walker once before court. It was possible he had put her up to it, but I hated to think so. The video hadn't been obtained by the cops until nearly a month after the crime, so it was possible the video had been leaked to someone at the Islander.

I wondered about Camacho as well. Why had he threatened Amanda? For that matter, what had compelled Devaney to make his nephew testify. More than ever, I felt more like a clueless spectator in this trial.

While I was ninety percent sure that Kotkin had been playing mind games about using the surveillance tape, the ten percent was a pebble in my shoe. What if he'd seen something I'd missed. I hated to admit that Kotkin's tactics had worked, but the only way to ease my mind was to review every minute of the twelve-hour video.

I loaded the video and settled in my recliner, carefully viewing the footage of the Islander's lobby door beginning 30 minutes before the stabbing. No one came in or out of the lobby. Next, I started at the beginning, fast forwarding the footage until someone came in or out of the door, then stopping to make sure it wasn't my client, covered in Devaney's blood and wielding a knife.

I usually dialed down the drinking during a trial but between the trial and the flashbacks, I needed to dull my mind. Besides, there was nothing complicated about the next day's witnesses and this video review was mindless. I fixed myself a tumbler of gin and tonic and resumed my station in the recliner, watching the video.

I woke up in the middle of the night to the chill of my third drink's ice melting on my thigh. I had made it about half way through, which would have to do.

In the morning, a little slow-moving, I called Officer Jeff Fredericks to the stand, the officer who had presided over the searches of Walker's room at the hotel and his vehicle the day after the stabbing.

The examination was straightforward and served its purpose. The jury learned that despite an exhaustive search of his room using ultraviolet light, not a speck of Devaney's blood was found in Allston's room. The day after the stabbing, there were no traces of blood in his car, or on his clothing, shoes or fingernails. Allston also had no cuts on his own hands, often suffered by perpetrators of stabbings.

On my way back to the counsel table, my mind took an abrupt detour to my father's murder. With all those vicious slashes, how had neither of his attackers not cut themselves? I shook away the thought and managed to refocus.

Predictably, on cross examination, Kotkin made clear that Walker was not examined until more than twenty-four hours after the stabbing. Also, Walker's girlfriend's residence, where he now claimed to have been that night, was never searched by the police.

As my next witness approached the stand just before the morning break, I wondered if I could have recognized the dapper and distinguished looking middle-aged man on the street. Chuck's transformation from aging deadhead to law enforcement look-alike never failed to startle me. His hair and beard were trimmed, his Hawaiian shirt, cargo shorts and flip-flops replaced with a dark suit and dress shoes, although I'd be willing to bet he was sockless.

Like the officer before him, my investigator's contribution was helpful, on balance, but just barely. He testified that he drove the six miles from the Islander to Ms. Hartung's house in twenty-two minutes. He described his route, traveling on the same day of the week and time of day as Walker's alibi drive.

The alibi had more holes than Swiss cheese. Most importantly, had Walker raced across town after the stabbing, he may have gotten to Hartung's before the 8:23 p.m. call.

"Mr. Argenal, did you run any red lights on your way to the residence?"

"No."

"Did you exceed the speed limit?"

"I drove the speed limit or slightly above it."

"So, you didn't speed excessively."

"No, not excessively."

"You didn't speed excessively or run red lights because you weren't running from the police, were you?"

"No, Mr. Kotkin, I wasn't running from the police. I was driving as fast as I could within reason."

"And in this case, you were hired by the attorney for Mr. Walker."

"Yes."

"Nothing further." Kotkin finished his questions with a shoulder shrug and a smirk to the jury.

Kotkin agreed to stipulate as true that *Ms. Pimm's Murder Mysteries* ended at 7:30 p.m. "Sure," he had said. "If you think it matters."

CHAPTER 60

After lunch it was time. "The defense calls Allston Walker."

Walker rose and trudged to the witness stand, the eight months of confinement showing with each hinged step. Deputy Franz made a show of protecting the jury from the violent felon. His hand resting on his sidearm, he followed Walker, as if only his presence prevented the defendant from leaping across the courtroom and slashing at the jury with the clerk's letter opener.

"Do you swear to tell the truth, the whole truth and nothing but the truth?"

"I do," came the gravelly response.

While many books have been written and lectures given about the art of cross examination, it is often the defendant's direct examination—the questioning of your own client—that is the most important part of a trial.

No matter how thoroughly I had prepared, the live theatre of the courtroom made direct examination the most stressful part of the trial, especially with clients like Walker. There were no dress rehearsals and one wrong answer could seal his fate. Each question was like rolling a baby stroller into a busy intersection and waiting for a calamity.

After some questions to introduce himself, I requested that his height be measured in front of the jury.

"May we approach, Your Honor?" asked Kotkin.

At the bench, Kotkin whispered, "Your Honor, I object. This is highly unusual."

"Trials are unusual, Mr. Kotkin. But I would have appreciated some notice, Mr. Turner. How do you propose we measure him?"

"I have a height bar right outside the courtroom."

"Okay, bring it in."

As Chuck wheeled in the scale, Judge Arnadon took over. "Mr. Walker, please step over here into the well of the court and be measured." Walker complied, the deputy ready to fill him with lead at the slightest misstep.

Chuck lowered the height bar until it rested on Walker's head. It read seventy-three inches.

"Your Honor," I said as Chuck wheeled away the apparatus, "I'm not sure the jury can see the numbers. I would like to offer a stipulation that Mr. Walker is six feet one inch tall."

"Mr. Kotkin?"

"Fine, Your Honor," said Kotkin, feigning disinterest as he shuffled papers on the counsel table.

If I expected the bright lights of the courtroom to transform Walker into a charming soft touch, I was disappointed. Despite hours of preparation, his answers varied between surly and mean. If anything, the crevices of his pinched face had deepened while in custody, his light brown complexion now tinged with a ghostly yellowish pallor.

But at least his story never wavered. As he had done dozens of times before, he recounted his argument with Devaney, his afternoon at his landscaping job, and his whereabouts at the time of the attack. In the end, it was his demeanor that threatened his downfall.

I had hoped, unrealistically, it turned out, for his plea to the jury to be, "I would never be capable of such a violent act." Instead, it was the same old Allston. His tone was, "I wouldn't try to kill no one for no 70 dollars. And by the way, fuck you all."

Kotkin's cross examination started with flair.

"Where'd you throw your bloody clothing, Mr. Walker?" The witness sat motionless squinting down at Kotkin for what seemed forever. After six or seven seconds, I wondered whether he was actually trying to remember where he had stashed his clothing.

"Didn't have any," came the reply, his expression a half smile, staring at Kotkin like he wanted to kill him.

"So, Mr. Walker, you saw Mr. Devaney testify, correct."

"I was sittin' right here."

"And he told the truth about your argument."

"I argued with him."

"And you would have to agree that someone stabbed him. He didn't make it up, right?"

"Yes."

"And before that day, you knew Mr. Devaney and he knew you."

"We didn't know each other well. I was a tenant and he was the manager."

"He was the man who collected your hard-earned money."

"Yes."

"And you'd lived there for a few years, right?"

"Yes."

"Obviously, you paid a lot of rent to him, month after month."

"That's right."

"And when he told you that you would have to pay a penalty because your rent was only three days late, that made you mad."

"Not mad enough to kill him."

"And after your argument with Mr. Devaney, you went to work."

"Yes."

"And you worked and sweated all day knowing that the money you earned would have to be turned over to Mr. Devaney?"

Walker shrugged.

"You didn't have a choice, did you, Mr. Walker? While you worked, you knew eventually you would have to swallow your pride and pay the man."

"Yes."

"And you thought about that all day, didn't you?"

"I suppose it was on my mind." Kotkin stopped short in mid-heel shuffle, clearly pleasantly surprised by Walker's answer.

"Indeed, Mr. Walker. I'm sure it was on your mind."

"Objection," I said, mainly irritated because Kotkin had said, "Indeed" again. "Counsel is testifying."

"Sustained. Ask questions, Mr. Kotkin."

"Yes, Your Honor, I'm happy to move on. You stabbed him, didn't you, Mr. Walker?" The prosecutor turned his back on the witness and strode toward the jury box, his heel clicks muting Walker's denial.

Kotkin then spun on his heel abruptly and moved closer to the witness. "What'd you do with the knife, Mr. Walker?" Walker was silent. "You do own a knife, though, don't you, Mr. Walker?"

"No."

"Your testimony, Mr. Walker, is that on the date this happened, you didn't own a knife. Not a steak knife or a pocket knife or a hunting knife?"

"Well, I didn't own no knife good for stabbin'." I cringed.

Kotkin paused, letting the answer wash over the jury. "So, Mr. Walker, tell me, what knives, have you found, are good for stabbing?" The prosecutor made air quotes for the last three words.

"Not no kitchen knife."

"Well, what kind of knife, Mr. Walker. You've said what knife is not good for stabbing, please tell the jury your preferred stabbing knife."

"I didn't stab that man."

"Well, you were very mad at him, weren't you?"

"I was a little pushed out of shape."

"Your Honor, at this time I have Prosecution's Exhibit 14, which is a DVD containing surveillance footage, loaded on my laptop. I believe Mr. Turner will stipulate to its authenticity."

At the mention of surveillance tape, my stomach turned. I stood and tried to act casual for the benefit of the jury. "May we approach, Your Honor?"

"Yes. It's about time for our break. Ladies and gentlemen, we'll be in recess for ten minutes. Counsel, c'mon in."

On my way to the judge's chambers, I cursed myself for passing out during last night's video review. What could Kotkin have up his sleeve?

"What's up, Gentlemen?" asked the judge, settling in behind his desk.

"Your Honor," I began, "I'd like to see the video footage Mr. Kotkin plans to show the jury."

"I'm happy to pull up the footage," Kotkin said, beaming as he set up his laptop. "This is just after Walker's argument with Devaney. As the Court has heard, it occurred in the afternoon about 1:30 p.m."

My heart sank. How had I not thought to check that part of the tape? Kotkin paused the footage at the appropriate time. Walker's menacing face appeared in the doorway of the Islander. Not only did he look enraged, but there was a wildness to his expression that was terrifying. The still image was damaging enough, but when Kotkin clicked the play button, Walker flung the heavy door open, narrowly missing a young girl who was entering the hotel.

I gathered my faculties. "Your Honor, I would object that the footage is more prejudicial than probative." The argument was weak and I knew it.

"Nice try, Mr. Turner. The video is very relevant to show your client's state of mind."

"I think showing his face accomplishes that," I countered. "Nearly hitting the young girl with the door is very prejudicial. It was clearly an accident."

"It shows a lack of impulse control, which is very relevant, Your Honor." Kotkin couldn't resist joining an argument that he had already won.

"I've made my ruling," the judge said, ending the debate. "Mr. Turner, you can make your record at the end of the day. And by the way, it's common courtesy for counsel to let each other know exactly what the other has planned in the way of exhibits. You knuckleheads have gone down a different path, and the result is interruptions like this. Let's bring in the jury."

For the rest of the cross examination, Kotkin floated around the courtroom, failing to hide his glee.

"Now, Mr. Walker, when we left you, you were telling me that you were....how did you put it? A little pushed out of shape."

"Yes."

Kotkin connected his laptop to the six-foot square courtroom monitor, and Walker's deranged face immediately filled the screen. It was much worse on the big screen, and some of the jurors seemed to actually recoil in fear.

"Mr. Walker, is this the face you make when you're just a little pushed out of shape?"

"Objection, argumentative." A more accurate statement would have been, "Objection, I'm losing."

"Overruled. You may answer the question, Mr. Walker."

Walker fidgeted in his seat, and stared at the floor as if searching for an escape hatch.

"Do you recall what happened as you exited the hotel that day after arguing with the victim?"

"No."

Kotkin played the footage of Walker violently throwing open the door, causing the girl to jump out of its path.

"You don't even recall that, do you Mr. Walker?"

"No," came the mumbled response.

"You don't recall, Mr. Walker, because you were enraged, weren't you?" The prosecutor didn't wait for a denial. "You were enraged and all you could think about was what you were going to do to Mr. Devaney."

Kotkin, with a look of disgust, turned his back on the witness stand and shook his head as he returned to the counsel table. "No further questions, Your Honor."

Short of eliciting Walker's confession on the stand, Kotkin's cross examination could not have been more successful. By the end, I was certain the jury knew that Walker was eminently capable of the vicious attack.

Judge Arnadon addressed the jury. "Ladies and gentlemen, it's been a long day. We'll resume tomorrow morning at nine o'clock, and you should be able to begin your deliberation by the end of the day. We're adjourned."

I drove home, went for a run and picked up a burrito for dinner. After catching the last quarter of the Warriors game, I collapsed into my recliner with my trial binder and thought about the case.

The jury, I was reasonably sure, was convinced of my client's guilt. In my heart, I knew his half-assed alibi and a few-inch height discrepancy could not trump Devaney's testimony. If his unwavering identification remained unchallenged, it would carry the day.

In closing argument, I would tell the jury that Devaney was mistaken. He had dozed off on the couch while watching television. That's why his glasses had not been found on the floor of the tiny apartment after the struggle, likely put away for the night. Devaney woke up an instant before a knife was plunged into his chest, and his poor vision prevented him from seeing his attacker's face clearly. This is why he initially told the 911 dispatcher that he hadn't known who attacked him.

But while he waited for the police, Devaney had time to reflect on his day. His argument with Walker had upset him, and it may well have been on his mind when he fell asleep. Devaney's subconscious preoccupation with Walker helped explain why he believed he had argued with him only thirty minutes before the attack, when it had actually happened much earlier in the day.

Although I believed in my theory, it was short on facts and long on speculation. I knew in my heart the jury firmly believed Jefferson Devaney. I imagined Kotkin's rebuttal tearing holes in my argument and dozed off with his heel clicks, pointing, and smugness careening through my mind.

CHAPTER 61

Back on my last day at the counsel table, I was grateful for saving Richard Erickson until the end of the defense case. His testimony was not the linchpin of the defense, but at least Walker would not be the last witness the jury would hear before deliberation.

At 8:45 a.m., having spoken briefly to Walker in his cement square, I entered the courtroom to find Chuck standing next to a man in a sparkling white uniform.

"Joe Turner, this is Cameron Peters. You might want to speak with him." There was a gleam in Chuck's eye.

After a firm handshake, I escorted Mr. Peters into a witness room, on the way realizing that Chuck had finally tracked down the ambulance driver who had driven Devaney to the hospital.

In his late twenties, Peters was six feet, one inch, but his perfect posture made him seem taller. He was clean cut and square jawed with boyish good looks, like the spokesperson for milk or orange juice. He reminded me of a police officer straight out of the academy—earnest, forthright, and impossible to cross examine.

The paramedic told me he had moved but had finally gotten a message and returned Chuck's call. "I'm very grateful, Cameron, but we don't have a lot of time. It sounds like you've spoken to Chuck. Do you recall transporting a Mr. Jefferson Devaney to Highland Hospital after a stabbing last year?"

"Sure, remember it well. I rode with the patient on the way to the hospital. He was lucid. He had lost a lot of blood, so I wanted him to remain conscious. I asked him what happened."

Then Paramedic Cameron Peters clearly and concisely recited Devaney's account of the attack. I stood and stared. "Are you sure?" I asked, stupidly, mainly to keep myself from kissing him on the mouth.

"Very sure, sir. This was a call that sticks with you."

I shook myself into attorney mode. "Shit," I said under my breath, searching my trial box frantically for my witness list. I was pretty sure I had included Peters' name, just in case. On the other hand, I recalled being tipsy the night I drafted it, so I wasn't certain.

I opened my laptop and hurriedly drafted a summary of Peter's statement, printed it on the courtroom's printer, and cheerfully handed it to Kotkin. Knowing Judge Arnadon's aversion to surprises, I requested a conference in chambers before the jury arrived. I found a copy of my witness list, and anxiously flipped through it on the way into chambers.

"Your Honor, this is an ambush!" began Kotkin. "I had no notice of this witness before two minutes ago."

"That's a tad dramatic, Mr. Kotkin. It's my understanding that Mr. Turner just met the witness himself. Does he appear on your witness list, Joe?" the judge asked.

I couldn't help myself. "Page two, line number eighteen, witness number nine, Your Honor. Indeed, he does."

"Do you have a summary of his statement, Mr. Kotkin?"

"Yes, but…"

"So, I'll confine his testimony to that statement. Nothing more, Mr. Turner. Let's get this show on the road."

Once the jury had been seated, Judge Arnadon apologized to the jury for the slight delay. "Mr. Turner?"

"Your Honor, the defense calls Richard Erickson." In the morning's excitement, I had nearly forgotten about Erickson. As the spry seventy-year-old made his way to the stand, I caught sight of the haunting life-size photographs of a bloody Jefferson Devaney that the prosecution had paraded in front of the jury and would again in closing argument.

Mr. Erickson confirmed his statement to the police that he witnessed the argument between Devaney and Walker at about 1:30 p.m., some six hours earlier than Devaney's estimation. Also, the witness testified that he was present when Walker came to the hotel the morning after the attack to pay his rent. Erickson told the jury that unlike Squires, he didn't hear Walker ask "Where's the guy who got stabbed?" or anything of the sort.

Kotkin had no cross examination, still busy poring over my summary of the paramedic's statement, in search of an avenue of attack.

"The defense calls Cameron Peters."

CHAPTER 62

He was the perfect witness—slight military bearing, sure of himself, and deadly earnest. The jury sat captivated as the bright young paramedic recounted Devaney's explanation of the crime as they rode to the hospital.

"He told me that a young man knocked on his door wanting to use his office phone," Peters told the jury. "Mr. Devaney explained to him that because the guy wasn't a resident of the hotel, he couldn't let him use the phone. The two argued and the kid left. Mr. Devaney told me that later, while he was dozing on his couch, the same kid came back and stabbed him."

I was silent for several seconds, allowing the bombshell testimony to fully resonate with the jury. "Mr. Peters, was this a memorable event for you in your line of work?"

"It was very memorable. The attack on Mr. Devaney made quite an impression on me. He was savagely stabbed, and I wanted to help him."

"During the ambulance ride, was Mr. Devaney conscious?"

"Yes. It is very important for someone on the verge of shock to remain conscious. I spoke with him for the purpose of keeping him conscious. He remained with me throughout most of the ride to the hospital. He went into shock as we arrived at the hospital."

As the paramedic concluded his answer, I saw Kotkin in my peripheral vision maneuvering one of the blown-up photographs of Devaney in preparation for his cross examination. My heart sank, anticipating his line of questioning, but I pressed on.

"Mr. Peters, how certain are you about what you heard Mr. Devaney say on the way to the hospital."

"One hundred percent certain, sir."

"No further questions."

Kotkin rose quickly from his seat. "Mr. Peters, you were able to converse with Mr. Devaney clearly during the ride to the hospital?"

"Yes."

"No trouble hearing him?"

"No, sir."

"Mr. Devaney spoke to you in a normal tone of voice? He wasn't shouting, was he?"

"No, sir. He was speaking normally."

"And he obviously had been seen and treated by a paramedic prior to being loaded into the ambulance."

"Yes, sir."

Kotkin retrieved the blown-up photograph and smiled broadly facing the jury. "Mr. Peters, while Mr. Devaney was in the ambulance, at the time you say he made this statement to you…" He paused so long that he had to begin his question again. "Isn't it true that Mr. Devaney wore an oxygen mask in the ambulance?" Kotkin revealed the photo to the jury with a flourish. It depicted Devaney lying in the ambulance with the mask covering his nose and mouth.

"Yes, sir, he did have on a mask." My heart skipped a beat. I was hoping that he had removed the mask.

"Well, then Mr. Peters. Isn't it true that given the oxygen mask, you could not have possibly heard what Mr. Devaney told you during that ride?"

The witness smiled calmly. "Actually, I could hear him perfectly. These newer masks are designed so that you can hear through them." The witness pointed to the photo. "This mask worn by Mr. Devaney was one of the new Oxy-mask 2000s. It's designed specifically for ambulance rides where we're still gathering information that could be crucial to the treatment of the patient."

Kotkin smiled to keep up appearances. But it was a smile of failure; the smile professional athletes flash when they make a horrendous gaffe, like dropping an easy touchdown pass or letting a grounder go through their legs. "No further questions."

"Mr. Turner?"

"No, Your Honor." I rose, unable to suppress my own smile. "The defense rests."

CHAPTER 63

Before the lunch break, I met with Allston, who looked as worried as ever, and with good reason. Although Peters had given us a fighting chance, the jury would remain eager to bring someone to justice for Devaney, still the most charming witness in the trial.

The afternoon session began with Kotkin's closing argument. As much as I hated to admit it, his closing was solid, playing to his case's strength. After reviewing the evidence and summarizing the law, the prosecutor moved from behind the podium and took off his glasses, centering himself in front of the jury box.

"This case is not complicated," he said. "Jefferson Devaney stood toe to toe with the man you see in court, the same man he had argued with earlier in the day. He didn't get just a glimpse of Allston Walker or catch a fleeting profile. He saw his face in a fully lit room. He saw Walker's face as he plunged the knife into his chest. He saw Walker's face as he wrestled with him, sliding around in his own blood. He saw him and recognized him, just as you would recognize someone you knew—your neighbor or co-worker. And he remained conscious on the phone. And he said to the police, 'Allston Walker stabbed me.'"

Kotkin had spoken for fifty-five minutes before he heel-clicked from the podium, centering himself in front of the jury, within arm's reach of the rail. He ended, as I knew he would, with

Walker's crazed face on the big screen. "This, ladies and gentlemen," he said in a hushed tone, "is the face of a killer."

"Mr. Turner, closing argument?" Judge Arnadon spoke before Kotkin had reached his seat.

"It is natural to want to provide justice to Jefferson Devaney," I began. "He is a charming man who heroically survived a vicious attack. But we have to remind ourselves that this case is not Jefferson Devaney versus Allston Walker.

It's not about who we like more or who is the better public speaker or who engenders the most sympathy. It's about whether we can say, beyond a reasonable doubt, that Allston Vayne Walker, a gardener from west Oakland, committed this crime." The last word caught in my throat, as the puzzle piece slipped into place and the courtroom began to spin. "Vayne!" The name pinged off my skull like a wrench on concrete. It was my last coherent thought before my knees buckled and the courtroom lights went out.

CHAPTER 64

By the time I'd fully regained my faculties, the judge had dismissed the jury for the day and summoned a paramedic, who took my vitals as I sat on the courtroom floor, leaning against the court reporter's desk. I was mortified and still dumbfounded by my realization.

Eventually, I convinced everyone that I was fine and was released with a promise to rest. I drove home on autopilot, and now sat in my recliner, alone with my thoughts.

I hadn't heard my client's middle name since the outset of the trial when the judge read the criminal complaint to the jury. On all other police records, he went by the middle initial "V." The name, Vayne, seemed familiar for some reason. Wrapped up in the excitement of the trial, I hadn't recognized it as Amanda's middle name.

"Fuck me," I said audibly, then heard myself repeat the words of Amanda. "He's a gardener my mom knows," she had written about Walker. Then I saw her mother again, fit and tan, at home with her flowers. She used to have a gardener, "but now would never dream of hiring one," she'd told me. No wonder Amanda had been so curious about the case. I shook my head, recalling my strange sense of familiarity with Walker's mannerisms—the feeling like we'd met before. Another mystery solved. Even in college, Amanda had never mentioned her father, and now it all made sense.

After a time, I walked to the kitchen for a beer and took out my notes on tomorrow's closing argument where I would argue for the freedom of my client, Amanda's father.

CHAPTER 65

I awoke early and walked to court before it opened, thinking about Amanda on the way. My first instinct was to call her. How, in God's name could she have kept this from me? Not to mention, why? I mean, I could understand not wanting to reveal her dad to be a felon but I would have understood.

I slouched to a park bench and sipped coffee, staring vacantly at a racing shell gliding across the lake. I felt like I'd been hit in the face with one of its oars. My mind scrambled for perspective. Was I overreacting? It didn't seem like a small deception. Not "I had a drunken fling" but more like "I have a secret family in Oregon."

"And by the way," I heard myself whisper, "her dad's life is in my hands." And that was what mattered now. Irrespective of my smoldering tire fire of a love life, Allston Walker was my client and he needed me.

So, I breathed in the cool fall air and focused. Squeezing the issue of my client's identity from my mind for now, I dispassionately reviewed my closing argument during a walk around Lake Merritt.

Returning to the courtroom and my familiar seat at the counsel table, I felt strangely calm. Women and relationships were an exhausting exercise in confusing frustration. This, I could do. Resuming my closing argument, after an awkward apology for the previous day's drama, I reviewed the evidence for the jury and asked them to consider the prosecution's theory.

"On one hand, the prosecution would have you believe Allston Walker was allegedly able to participate in the bloodiest of struggles, leaving no trace of physical evidence behind—not a smudge of blood in his car, a drop on his shoe or a cut on his hand. Immediately after the attack, he was able to race across town, risking being stopped while allegedly still covered in blood, in order to answer the phone, securing his alibi.

"Then after the intricate planning and meticulous attention to detail—cleaning every microbe of blood from his clothing—he allegedly returned to the crime scene in the morning and asked about, quote, the guy who got stabbed? So, which is it? Is Mr. Walker a criminal genius or a bumbling idiot?

"The prosecution must acknowledge that Allston Walker is 58 years old and has never committed a violent crime. But, according to Mr. Kotkin, this man committed a vicious attack because of a petty dispute about 70 dollars. And not an attack where he flew off the handle and went crazy on the spot. The prosecution would have you believe that because of this minor argument, Mr. Walker set about calmly planning Mr. Devaney's death hours later. It just does not add up."

After covering my theory about Devaney's dream-induced misidentification, I reviewed the testimony of Paramedic Cameron Peters, which fit perfectly with the victim's mistake about which television show he had last watched. Clearly, the initial encounter with the attacker had been erased from his memory.

Not only was Peters' credibility unassailable, the crime of passion made much more sense if committed mere minutes after the perceived slight about the use of a phone. Devaney's knife was a weapon of convenience for the assailant. Surely a planned attack would not have relied on its presence. I left the connection between the actual culprit and the man running away from the hotel for the jury to make. After just over an hour, I sat down, exhausted.

Kotkin rose for his rebuttal argument. "Mr. Turner's argument reminds me of the story about an old man looking down at a stream so clear you could see to the bottom. The man called his grandson over to look at how beautiful the stream was. The boy came splashing over, stirring up the mud, and turning the stream brown. 'It's not clear at all,' said the boy. 'It's all murky. I can't see the bottom.' The grandfather looked at the boy and said, 'Just wait. Give it time. Let it settle.'

"Ladies and gentlemen, let it settle," Kotkin quietly told the jury. "Mr. Turner has done a good job of stirring it up, trying to obscure the truth which is crystal clear. He's stirred it up with talk of a few inches difference in height, Mr. Devaney's half-conscious ramblings, and what program was on television.

"But take a moment, let it settle, and think about what's really important. Because nothing can change the simple, undeniable fact that Allston Walker attacked Jefferson Devaney, and Mr. Devaney saw him do it."

As Kotkin continued, I tuned it out, only listening for objectionable argument. Mostly, I thought bad thoughts.

I thought about whether Walker was guilty. I thought about the shank he had possessed while in prison, and pictured his pinched face grotesquely contorting as he manically slashed with a knife.

I thought about Officer Percy's police report which described Devaney as fading in and out of consciousness even before the ambulance ride. Had he suddenly become more lucid in the ambulance, or had the paramedic heard the ramblings of a medication-induced dream?

I thought about the paramedic report that said Devaney had been intubated while on the way to the hospital, something Kotkin had missed. Could he have spoken with a hole in his throat?

I wondered if I was the only one in the courtroom to see a fleeting glimpse of Devaney as bullied and vengeful, and then wondered if I had imagined it. I wished I had asked Peters if

Devaney had used the term "African American" or a different term to describe the man who stabbed him.

I was consumed by daydreams and questioned my judgment. I thought about that artist's sketch in my mom's binder glaring back at me and tried to recall whether it looked like my client in the least.

I thought about what I would have done if I had found out that Walker had been out of custody at the time of my dad's murder. Would I have put the paramedic on the stand, or might I have conveniently considered his tale too unreliable? After all, it had been several months, and was it believable he could hear through an oxygen mask?

I imagined deciding to bury the paramedic, and then later learning that the lab had gotten the blood typing wrong. I wondered what Dad would do and wished he was around to talk about my cases.

I thought these thoughts until the judge had concluded the jury instructions, and the jury had filed out to decide Walker's fate on this earth.

CHAPTER 66

Before I had gathered my files, the jury informed the Court that it planned to go home and start their deliberation in the morning. The juror note was signed by juror number three, Mr. Epps, the software salesman who had served on a civil jury once before.

"I was hoping he'd be the foreperson," said Kotkin to no one in particular. An ass to the end.

I checked my phone on my way out of court and found a text from my client's daughter.

—How's it going?—

In the privacy of my car, I considered my answer. There, as the undefeated hero in my own private fantasy world, I often give the perfect comeback to a judge's critique, spouting courtroom invective that would have me disbarred.

"How's it going?" I belted out, pulling out of the court parking lot. "How's it going, Amanda? Or should I say Amanda Vayne Kensey? Well, for starters, your mother fucked the gardener! I mean, what the fuck, Amanda! Were you ever going to bother to tell me I was representing your dad, who by the way"—I was yelling now—"is doing an awesome imitation of a stone-cold killer!"

"Oh, and you'll get a kick out of this, Ms. Mother's Former Gardener's Daughter whatever the fuck! In a funny little aside," I said, chuckling sarcastically, "until recently, I thought my client—that is, your giant turd of a dad,"—I yelled, "may have actually killed my own father!"

I turned up my hard rock mix tape and started thinking about what I would drink when I got home.

Halfway through my second gin and tonic, I returned her text.

—Hi Amanda VAYNE. It's been eventful, as you might imagine.—

That'll show her, I thought to myself, disgusted with my spinelessness.

—Joe, I never knew him. My mom didn't even tell me he was her gardener until about a year ago. We reconnected then. I'm not even sure I want a relationship with him... but he is my dad. I'm sorry for not telling you. I hope you can forgive my dishonesty. Besides, I thought it would be a good excuse to reconnect. Please do your best for him.—

—Because nothing says let's reconnect like attempted murder??? And I always do my best.—

As I relaxed on the recliner, thoughts of Amanda made me think of Walker. There had always been something familiar about my client's manner, and now I saw a lot of Amanda in him -- his dry wit, the way he cocked his head to one side when he asked a question, and his ability to cut to the chase.

As I knew they would, thoughts of Walker and the trial led me to my dad. I remembered his thick hand tousling my hair as I sat on his knee, his deep voice soothing my mind, asking about the ball game. I missed him the most after trials, when I knew we would have had so much to talk about.

And then the projector was on again, now the images more defined than before. He was slipping down to the blood-slicked floor, just like Devaney. I saw him rise, only to flail helplessly amidst flashes of the knife.

I heard his voice for the first time, recognizing its tenor in syncopated heaves and chokes of agony. The camera zoomed in and his face emerged from the static, its image shaky but clear. As he sank near the bottom of the screen under the onslaught, his eyes widened, scanning the room in terror. The image was jarring; the strong confident face I knew, now panicked with the fear of death.

His eyes fell directly on mine. He didn't call out, but his pleading look screamed at me in silence. The film paused, my father's face frozen on the screen and burned into my memory, begging me for help.

I saw him go down again, sinking from view one final time, slipping below the screen. Then I heard him yell my name over and over in plaintive wails, calling for help that never came. The projector fluttered to an end as I cowered under the bed, frozen with fear.

I jerked my head to the side, out of my trance and out of breath. My hand quivered, rattling the ice in my glass as I raised it for a drink. My vision blurred with tears as I felt for the glass with salty lips. I gulped down my drink, but knew it was no use.

I had been so desperate to know what I had done, what mistake I had made that led to his death. Just to know how I had failed him, so I could say, "Sorry, Dad," no matter how stupidly inadequate. So maybe someday I could move on.

But this was too much.

"You should have known, Joseph, you fucking coward," I whispered, convulsing into a pillow. "It's what you didn't do."

CHAPTER 67

My vast experience had taught me that the jury would be out anywhere from fifteen minutes to two weeks. Lots of lawyers pass the time while their jury deliberates by rehashing the trial, complaining to other defense attorneys about the prosecutor or the judge, second guessing their decisions, predicting what the jury must be thinking and who among them would be elected foreperson.

Not I. After the trial preparation, the pretrial anxiety and the trial itself, I want to think about anything but the trial. I gave my cell phone number to Charlotte and promised to stay within shouting distance.

As I headed through the massive oaken doors, downstairs and past the metal detector, the cool air and bright sun jolted my senses that had lain dormant for two weeks under the tepid florescence of Department 10. I walked briskly east, leaning against a stiff breeze on a perfect fall day, the odors of the street assaulting my nose. I gazed at the sky as fast-moving clouds changed their shapes, the late afternoon sun casting a vibrant glow ahead.

If a few weeks of indoor living could make me feel like my senses were on steroids, what must it feel like for someone walking out of prison after twenty years? So much for not thinking about the case.

After a walk around Lake Merritt, I visited Allston in the holding cell on the top floor of the courthouse, its metal bars and enormous locks from a bygone era. Our chat was short, mainly because I couldn't answer any of his questions. I had no idea how the trial had gone or how long the jury would be out, and had no clue what to make of the foreperson. I certainly couldn't tell what their verdict would be and didn't want to even offer my best guess.

"So, you really don't know shit, do you?" Allston deadpanned with a twinkle in his eye. He had proven to be full of surprises.

Judge Arnadon had requested that the attorneys stay within ten minutes of the courtroom while the jury deliberated, which for me, meant my office. On Tuesday morning, I began the task of catching up with tending to all my clients not named Allston Walker.

Two days passed without so much as a question from the jury. Then a third. I checked on Walker again, who had been moved upstairs to the courthouse's top floor. A deputy ushered me to a chilly, twelve by twelve cell. Light blue paint peeled in long shreds from the cement walls and ceiling. On one side, the wall jutted into the room at knee level to form a bench. A stainless-steel toilet sat starkly in the middle of the room. An exposed light bulb hung on a chain from the twelve-foot ceiling. High on one wall, an opaque window sealed the room from the outside world.

There cannot be a more stressful situation than that of a criminal defendant awaiting a verdict in a case where the punishment is life in prison or death. Walker was holding up better than most, which is to say I didn't smell vomit.

He sat on the cement bench, hands on his knees, rubbing his hands together, staring at the floor. He didn't look up when I came in.

"How are you doing?" I asked, immediately realizing the stupidity of my question. He looked up with a poker face and silently shook his head.

"It's really cold in here. I can ask for a blanket if you want."

"I'm good."

I sat down next to him, mimicking his position. We sat quietly for a full two minutes before I stood. "Well, you probably want to be alone, Allston. I just wondered how you were holding up." As I reached for the call buzzer, he looked up, then hesitated before he spoke.

"You probably got court to get to," he said, staring at the floor again.

"No, I'm free for a bit." I sat down next to him again.

After several more minutes, his familiar gravelly voice broke the silence. "You see the paint peeling down in strips off the walls in here?"

"Yes."

"You know how many strips there are?" he asked, still staring at the floor.

"No, but I'll bet you do."

"Damn right, I do. I know how many are hanging from the ceiling, how many from each wall. I know how many cracks there are in the floor, too."

"I imagine anything to take your mind off the jury."

He nodded, and we sat quietly for another five minutes. I was beginning to feel the pace of doing time in custody for the first time. The old saw was true. The incarcerated truly have nothing but time.

"You know," he finally said, "listening to that caretaker say it was me who stabbed him. He's a cracker for sure, but it seemed like he really believed it. Got me wondering how that could be."

"Yeah?"

He paused, forming his thoughts. "When I was a kid, coming up in Oakland, I wasn't very good at my schoolwork. Got lots of D's and F's. I remember once in the third grade, one of my little friends got their hands on the answers for a test in math. A bunch of my friends got caught, you know, because they got perfect scores. I got away with it, probably because I missed a few on purpose.

"Anyway, I got my test back..." He paused and stared into space, smiling, remembering the event. "I'll never forget it. On the top of the test, it had a red A- with a gold star next to it. One of them gold star stickers."

"The teacher told me she was proud of me. My mom was happy. Anyway, before you know it, I started walking around with my chest out, proud of that test. I started believing that I'd earned that gold star. It was just easier to believe it."

I sat there for a while quietly, making sure he was finished. Impressed by his insight, I enjoyed listening to him. I could see him telling stories on a porch like my relatives in Arkansas and hoped he'd get the chance.

"Is it a good sign if it takes longer?" he asked, after a time.

"No one knows, Allston," I said, answering a version of the same question every trial attorney knows well.

He clutched his bologna sandwich and shook his head for several minutes.

"So, what's up with the Camacho kid?" I asked. "You can tell me now." I was pretty sure he knew something and I wanted to take his mind off the jury.

He smiled. "Nothing really." We were alone in the cell, but he still looked around and leaned in, continuing in a low voice. "Probably nothing. It's just that a while back there was a rumor that Devaney tried something with Camacho's younger sister." He paused, as if anticipating my question. "But I ain't no snitch. I got a daughter out there to think about."

I sat there, digesting his answer, the word "daughter" ringing in my ears.

The young custodian's motive alone would have made him a suspect. Certainly, it could have cast more doubt on Walker's guilt. Camacho's court visit had been an obvious warning that Walker keep quiet. And the streets didn't care that Camacho's motive alone wouldn't put him at risk for prosecution. If Walker pointed the finger, he'd be labeled a snitch and his concern for his daughter would be justified. His daughter, Amanda.

In one sense, I was glad to be hearing about this for the first time after the trial. Ethical representation would have required encouraging Walker to testify and putting Amanda in danger—not something I would have done. It was the second potential conflict of interest I was happy to avoid.

Walker's revelation about Camacho also made me mad at myself. My instincts had told me that Camacho, at the very least, knew something about the attack. I should have had Chuck turn over more rocks.

"Also, it was just a rumor." Walker had seen my wheels turning. "Young man's got a youngster to take care of. I'm in here for no reason," he said shaking his head. "Say he ends up in here and I'm the reason. I don't want that on me."

I could have told him that Camacho's motive would not be enough to prosecute or that he should have been honest with his attorney, but I held my tongue. If we were about to hear a guilty verdict, a lecture on what he should have done differently didn't seem right.

"I understand," I said quietly.

It occurred to me that Walker's news about Camacho still didn't explain how Camacho had known about Amanda — her existence, her name, or of our relationship. Also, something about the threat itself still didn't make sense. I supposed that would remain a mystery.

We both sat there for several seconds before the silence was broken by the faint sound of three buzzes from the jury room. He looked up, furtively, fear in his eyes.

I nodded. "Three buzzes. That's a verdict. Hang in there."

CHAPTER 68

It was time for the highest drama of the trial. In moments, the clerk would stand and say, "We, the jury, in the above-entitled case, find the defendant…"—at this point, time usually stands still for several seconds before the clerk says either guilty or not guilty. Then, the defendant either hugs his counsel and mouths the words "thank you" to the jury or is handcuffed while mouthing slightly different words.

I was escorted from the cell into the courtroom, followed by my client. Remarkably, Kotkin was already there, chatting nervously with the court reporter and a handful of other district attorneys. I always thought it was morbid for them to show up and cheer a guilty verdict, but it did make the rare acquittals all the more enjoyable.

Judge Arnadon breezed in, pulling on his robe as he ascended the bench. The jury filed in. "Juror number three, Mr. Epps, I understand you have been designated as the foreperson of the jury."

"Yes."

"Very well. Have you reached a verdict?"

"Yes, Your Honor, we have."

"Then please hand the verdict to the bailiff." The bailiff delivered the forms to the judge without looking at them. There were two forms, one read guilty and one, not guilty. One was signed and the other was not. Judge Arnadon's face was inscrutable as he reviewed the forms and then handed one to his clerk.

"Will the defendant please rise," asked the judge. Allston and I rose, our shoulders touching. "Madam Clerk, please read the verdict into the record."

Charlotte cleared her throat. "We, the jury, in the above-entitled case, find the defendant, Allston Vayne Walker, accused of Attempted Murder, not guilty."

Allston sank into his chair, and I could see relief wash over him. His taut forearms were limp on the counsel table, his head rolling on his neck in a circle, his darting bird eyes now gazing around the courtroom, as if seeing it in color for the first time. His face changed, too, before my eyes. The pinched face opened slightly, the crevices on the sketch pad blurred.

As Judge Arnadon thanked the jurors for their service, Allston returned to his notebook, as if determined to hand transcribe every line of the trial. As he had explained to me, just in case he was ever accused of stabbing Devaney again, he wanted "to document this shit." Finally, he looked up at the jurors as they began to file out, and nodded slightly, a solemn thank you.

"Mr. Walker, you will be given a ride back to Santa Rita to collect your belongings. You are a free man."

Walker closed his eyes and nodded again, a smile forming on the corners of his mouth. We shook hands. "Thank you, Joe." It was the only time he'd called me by my first name, any name, really. Then he was led through the side door of the courtroom, and I never laid eyes on him again.

I decided to walk back to the office. I could take the train home after a few celebratory shots with Andy and Chuck and retrieve my car tomorrow. But I arrived to find the office empty. Chuck and Andy had sent texts. Chuck's, "Freedom!" so predictable. Boxes and files covered my desk, the logjam of my practice on hold for a month. But they could wait.

I grabbed a six-pack from the office kitchen and collapsed into my chair. As I unloaded my briefcase on my desk, I picked up a single yellow sheet, folded once. Written in my client's unmistakable script was one word. "Perfect."

I smiled, anticipating my text to Amanda. No, not a text. I'd call to give her the news. I'd finally take action, too. I pictured her smile and couldn't wait to see it again.

But first I knew there was something I had to do, no matter how painful. Over the years, I had observed that children are often the perfect witness to a traumatic event. Without the life experience to sense imminent danger, a child often remains calm in times of crisis, their perception of events, remarkably clear. I needed to remember, now, for my father.

I shut my window and now the office was silent except for the hum of the overhead fan. My body tensed at the thought of another flashback but I owed it to my dad. I didn't expect to recognize his killer or even see his face. But if there was a clue there somewhere in that home movie of horror, I needed to see it. And I knew there was more to see.

What I couldn't figure out is why my mind now seemed to be blocking it out. I had allowed myself to see my father's agonizing death. Surely, there was nothing more horrible than that.

I waited a few minutes, bracing myself for the ordeal but nothing happened. I wondered if the demons had to catch me unawares for maximum effect, smiling at the irony. I guess that's the thing about gut-wrenching, vomit-inducing memories: they're never around when you need them.

Usually, when I need to think of a name or movie title that escapes me, I think about something completely different, and it pops into my head. It's as if I have to stop looking down the wrong brain path in order to discover the right one.

I noticed the fan overhead had grown louder. Then I realized it wasn't the fan, but the whir of the projector. While I had been thinking about why I couldn't summon them, my memories had been quietly marshalling forces, and their invasion was sudden.

I am under my bed where my mother hid me before I heard her heels on the hardwood, running to the phone in my parents' bedroom to call for help. My dad's death groans are now faint. He's calling my name. Not a plea for help, but a warning as the heavy boots grow louder in the hallway. Then I see the worn black leather step onto the carpet of my bedroom. The boots pause and pivot not three feet away. Then leather and long hair block my view from under the bed and my dark hideout is fogged with the horrible stench.

Now, I know what's coming. I remember.

My own scream splits my ears as steel flashes under the bed. I scramble in retreat, clawing back against the wires of the metal bed frame, just out of reach of the knife. A grotesque grunt and the knife pierces the darkness again, slashing inches from my face. Quivering, I press myself against the wall. Another grunt and the knife pings against the bed frame. Then I see the boots again. The stench is on its feet and the boots clomp out of the room, running back down the hallway as sirens wail in the distance.

When the flashback was over, I found myself curled tightly on the floor under my desk, sweating and gasping for air. After several minutes, I was calm enough to take in the memory. Slowly, my body unclenched as recognition brought comfort. I sat up and wiped tears of relief from my eyes. My father hadn't called my name so his twelve-year old son could wade into harm's way. It seemed so obvious now. He called my name because he feared for my life. His killer was coming for the witnesses.

But the episode had taught me more. I suppose part of me realized it even during the flashback itself, but I'd been preoccupied with staying alive. That, and I wanted to see it through, once and for all.

Ever since I read that binder in my mom's house, the evidence of my father's murder had been committed to memory. I had dissected its contents and mapped it out in my mind, desperate to find something useful.

The blood smears left on my Raiders bedspread had always seemed out of place. I remembered crawling out from under the bed and into my mother's arms, and her holding me there on the floor next to the bed, but not on top of it. And while she might have had some traces of my dad's blood on her hands, the copious smears depicted in the photos were more consistent with someone grabbing the bedspread. Someone grabbing it with a bleeding hand, while slashing at me under the bed.

I reached for my phone and messaged Matt.

—We need to run DNA on the blood found on my Raiders bedspread. I'll explain later.—

CHAPTER 69

My phone vibrated in my hand, Chuck's name on its screen.

"Hey."

"Inconceivable! Well done, Counselor!"

"I owe it all to that unbelievably perfect paramedic."

"I stayed for his testimony. He was awesome. How in the hell did you find him, anyway? I tracked him to Nevada but finally gave up."

I paused, processing Chuck's question. "What?"

"I said, how did you find the paramedic? I had given him up for dead."

"Chuck, I didn't find him. He told me he returned your call…" My words slowed and trailed to vapor as the realization slowly washed over me. I desperately searched for another explanation. Maybe one of Chuck's old subpoenas had made its way to him. Perhaps Chuck had misunderstood my question.

"What do you mean he returned my call? I never talked to the guy. I'm not tracking, Joe. I spoke to him for the first time in court."

"Come on, tell me you found the paramedic, Chuck." I was frantically grasping at straws, knowing the truth but not admitting it to myself.

I collapsed back into my chair and cursed myself, the phone falling to the floor. I stared into space, piecing together the last few months. The email out of the blue, the concealment of Walker's identity as her father, our fevered courtship. And then the paramedic had magically appeared.

"Amanda Vayne fucking Kensey," I whispered to myself. How had I been so utterly blind? I was so good at reading people, so practiced at being lied to, such an expert in seeing the angles. I laughed out loud at my incompetence.

And now it was so absurdly obvious. Just as she had hoped, I had mistaken her inquiries about the case as genuine interest in me. Naturally, she had tried to keep her relationship with Walker a secret, in order to shield her from suspicion by any right-thinking attorney.

But even after it had been revealed, I remained as gullible as ever. What was it she had written? She thought asking me to represent her father accused of attempted murder was a good excuse to reconnect? And this made sense to me?

And she had asked for the police reports and immersed herself in them. How many family members of an accused had ever done so? Not to mention that, objectively, she was completely out of my league.

"Wow, Joe," I mocked myself. "She is genuinely interested in your work. She must really have a thing for you."

If that had not been enough to arouse the suspicions of the most dim-witted, there was the giant red flag that now flapped in my face. Amanda had asked exactly one question about the specifics of the trial. Not about her father's testimony or the victim's. Her only question about the trial, asked after sex: Had we found the paramedic? And when she found out we hadn't, she made her move.

While deceiving me was child's play, the gambit itself had been orchestrated with precision. It had been the last day of trial, so Kotkin hadn't time to verify the identity of the paramedic or check his rap sheet. Not that he necessarily would have checked. He was a uniformed paramedic after all, and no doubt had a fake I.D., just in case.

My mind raced with thoughts of ethical obligations. I was an officer of the court and a fraud had been perpetrated. I was pretty sure, anyway, but was I sure enough? How could I be sure of anything now? The thought of a call to Kotkin made me wince.

And what of one Allston Walker? Had I been wrong about him, too? I recalled mentioning the potential problem of the oxygen mask to Amanda, and the paramedic had been prepared. I felt a surge of nausea.

I looked at my phone and imagined another call, this one ranting and filled with satisfying invective. How, in God's name, can you live with yourself, Amanda? Did you ever believe any of your own bullshit? Was the paramedic your derelict brother or an actor or someone else you manipulated? But these words would be hollow and pointless because I knew she didn't care.

I popped open a beer on the ledge of my desk and reclined, tilting my head back, feeling its cool relief. I chugged the beer and slid open the bottom drawer of my desk. The flask was usually reserved for toasting trial victories. I fumbled with its cap, my new reality careening about my skull. The agony of my dad's suffering was real and the Amanda I believed was falling in love with me never even existed. "Cheers, Jackass," then a gulp that singed my throat, and another.

I picked up my phone again and dialed Amanda's number. The call went straight to voicemail and when I heard her low, throaty voice it seemed now to mock me.

"Fuck it," I said, smashing the phone face down on my desk. There was nothing else to say.

Cradling the flask, I reclined again and put my feet up on the desk. I took another long, burning swig. As the whiskey slowly numbed my mind, I stared up at the ceiling fan, its soothing rhythm short breaths on my heavy lids.

CHAPTER 70

I woke up in my recliner with no memory of my trip home. I stared at the ceiling as the pain of Amanda's deception filled my consciousness. My first instinct was to keep drinking. I kept the Bloody Mary mix on hand and plenty of vodka. On the way to the fridge I caught sight of my face in the oven door and paused. My sunken eyes looked at me sadly. I looked awful. I opted for water and put on a pot of coffee.

After a long, hot shower, I fished jeans and a sweatshirt out of my clean laundry pile and sipped coffee on the recliner, gathering my scattered thoughts. For starters, in the sober light of day, I admitted that Amanda's gambit, however reckless, was in some ways understandable. Dads were important and hers was about to be taken away.

On the other hand, did I really know the paramedic had been a fake? Maybe I was jumping to conclusions. After all, I didn't have proof that would stand up in court.

But deep down I knew.

I also knew full well what my dad would tell me if he were alive: The verdict could not stand because it had not been a fair trial. I heard his voice clearly, as I sat on his knee. "You lied to your mother about eating the cookies, Joseph. What do you think is fair punishment?" Matt Eisner had called him the fairest man he knew for a reason. I recalled hearing how, as a young Deputy District

Attorney he had threatened to resign over a decision to prosecute a developmentally disabled young man as a sex offender.

While I may or may not have been a coward in the last moments of my dad's life, I could still honor him in death. The verdict could not stand, at least not now. I would tell the D.A.'s Office what I knew and they could take whatever action was necessary.

I looked down at the Walker file boxes against the wall and thought of my ornery friend breathing fresh air now. "He is innocent." I surprised myself by saying it aloud. I wasn't sure why I knew it, but I smiled at my best answer. Walker just didn't seem like a guy who would kill a man for no seventy dollars. And I wanted to prove it, for both our sakes.

After a bowl of cereal, I hoisted the boxes on my table and began thumbing through the pages of police reports and photos, hoping to see something differently. After three hours, I needed some air. I walked the four blocks to Elan, my favorite coffee place, where I had taken Amanda. When we walked around holding hands that day, I didn't know if I'd ever been happier in the company of another.

I was still thinking of her when I returned to my laptop. It was in hibernation mode, so I turned on the power and keyed in my passcode, Duke—the name of my childhood dog. Then I recalled the night I spent at her mother's home, when I found her looking at the surveillance footage in the middle of the night.

That night, I suppose on some level, I knew that she hadn't just found my laptop running and had a look. Somewhere in my consciousness, I knew she would have had to turn the computer on, enter the passcode, then lie to me about it. She knew me well, so she may have figured out the code. Either that or she stood behind me once when I logged in. Deep down, I'd probably known all this was true, like Walker had known he had cheated on that test. It was just easier not to believe it.

Of course, once she'd seen the surveillance tape, she could tell Ms. Belton what to say. For me, this deception seemed even worse than the paramedic. Even though she hadn't pulled it off, she'd lied to me directly about it.

I remembered our first long talk about the case, when I had floated the theory about Devaney seeing a prostitute and told her the Islander was on the "blade." Now, I wondered how early on she'd begun formulating her plan. And what was it she had said about my skepticism of Ms. Belton? "You may well be overthinking it, but you should trust your instincts." She hadn't wanted to give herself away by vouching for her.

Of course, she'd been behind the office burglary. I felt like I was still there—on all fours in my office with a face full of dirt.

I was silly for believing that she would suddenly fall for me after years of rejection in college. I closed my eyes and pictured her face once more. I'd been serious when I told her that her smile looked different when she spoke of her daughter. Maybe that smile had been the only genuine one I'd seen.

CHAPTER 71

I told myself to stop whining and focus, and resumed my review of every aspect of the Walker case. After two hours, I called Chuck at home to break up the monotony. It went to voicemail, but then he answered talking over the greeting message.

"Hey, Joe, how you holding up?" No movie line or southern saying today.

"You know, Chuck, almost no one still uses a landline, let alone a tape machine."

"Just us old guys." Chuck's answer made me think of Devaney, the old guy I'd been looking at in the crime scene photos. Then, a light went on.

"Holy crap, Chuck! Can you text me the number of the Islander? Got to go."

I walked back to the table with purpose, trying to recall Devaney's trial testimony. I opened the photo binder again and leafed through it to a wide-angle photograph of the crime scene. Devaney had testified that he knocked his phone off a chair and called 911. At the time, I was too worried about his graphic description of the blood-smeared phone to notice. That, and probably too hung-over, I admitted.

When I'd first seen the photo of the old rotary phone, its bloody handle hanging down to the floor from an end table, I had assumed that Devaney used the phone to call 911. But if Devaney had used his cell phone, who had used the land line? The attacker or at the very least, a witness to the crime. Given the bloody handle, my money was on the former.

Chuck texted with the Islander Hotel's phone number, and I found the 911 documents confirming that the call had been made from a different number, presumably Devaney's cell phone. Next, I checked the evidence log. The land line phone had been tagged and seized as evidence, but not processed for fingerprints. The cops had assumed Devaney had used the phone to call 911 as well, so hadn't bothered.

My mind raced with questions, and it felt good. Why had there been only one 911 call if someone had picked up the rotary phone? Surely, no one would bother to make a social call after the attack? And why had the attacker bothered with a call for help at all? Could it be that my crazy love tryst theory was right after all? If so, Chuck and Andy would never hear the end of it. I put on a collared shirt and drove to the D.A.'s Office, calling Matt on the way.

"It's great news," the Deputy D.A. said, after I explained my bedspread theory. "I expedited the lab tests yesterday, but the results won't be in for another hour. Why do we need to meet? I'm pretty swamped."

"Will take five minutes. I'll explain when I get there. Thanks."

Without an appointment to see Matt, I had time to assess my predicament in the waiting room. I needed to have the blood on Devaney's land line phone analyzed. I couldn't ask the D.A.'s Office to do the DNA test without revealing the reason for my request. I wanted to avoid opening that can of worms if at all possible, as it might involve Walker's re-incarceration and maybe even Amanda's prosecution. Matt had been my dad's best friend, but if I told him the truth now, he'd be forced to play it by the book.

On the other hand, if I could prove Walker's innocence and validate his acquittal, then I could justify taking my little secret to the grave. The problem was, the phone was under lock and key inside the cage—the District Attorney's cavernous evidence locker that stored all trial evidence.

"Let me get this straight, Joseph," Matt said calmly after hearing my plan. "You want me to risk my career without telling me why? Has your ponytail cut off the circulation to your brain?"

"You won't be involved, Matt. Just get me inside the cage, and you can accidentally lose track of me in there."

"I'll have to sign you out, Dumbass."

"Oh, well..." I hadn't thought of that. "Matt, you know I wouldn't ask if it wasn't important."

"Not good enough. Seriously, what's going on? Are you okay? You've obviously been thinking about your dad's case. And I assume this little excursion is about the Walker trial?"

"Sorry, Matt. I can't tell you. I just..."

"Then I can't help you," he cut in, palms up.

"Okay, thanks anyway." I walked dejectedly out of his office, already thinking of a Plan B.

CHAPTER 72

Back in my car, my cell phone rang. It was Amanda, so I let it go to voicemail. I wasn't ready and likely never would be. Anyway, one debacle at a time.

Now another call. Good God, Amanda. But this time it was Matt.

"The lab just called. The bedspread blood wasn't your dad's."

"Yes!" I mouthed to myself, pumping my fist. "That's great news, Matt."

"Damn right it is. I'll run it through the database. We're going to catch'em, Joey."

By the year 2000, most of the nation was collecting the DNA of every person convicted of a crime. While there was no guarantee that one of my dad's killers would be in the system, we both knew the odds were good.

"On that other thing, Joe, I can get you in and give you a key to get out. You can leave once it shuts down for the night, but that's it. And I don't want to know shit about this."

"Thanks so much, Matt. It's important, otherwise I…"

"Yeah, yeah. Otherwise, you wouldn't ask. You said that already. We should do this today. Burnsy is on duty and he likes to nap. He won't notice if I leave without you and you can hide in there until he closes up. Meet me at four and wear a hoodie," he said, and the line went dead.

At home, I called Forensic Allies, a private lab I used for DNA tests. Walker's DNA was available for comparison in the county database. Once the lab had the telephone, the comparison would take four to five hours. If there wasn't a match, then SOMDI, and I could strongly suggest that Matt run the DNA profile through the national database to try and catch the other mother. If Walker's DNA was on the phone, then another acronym came to mind. FUBAR. Fucked Up Beyond All Recognition.

The cage is a massive free-standing structure made of cyclone fencing, housed inside a warehouse that sits on two city blocks next to the Oakland Police Station. Once inside, Matt and I were enveloped by uncomfortably warm, stale air. Just outside the cage, a corpulent officer in a sweat-stained shirt reclined behind a desk, his cap tilted forward on his head.

"Burnsy!" Matt greeted him as we approached at a brisk walk. My heart pounded and suddenly everything was very real.

"Hello, uh, Matt," The officer seemed startled, and sat up in his chair, getting his bearings.

Matt quickened his pace and I kept up. "Don't get up big guy, we'll sign ourselves in."

"Oh okay, thanks, Matt," he answered, eyeing me briefly, then settling back and wiping his face with a white handkerchief. "It's miserable in here. The heater's stuck on high, and Maintenance is off until morning."

Matt flipped open a binder on the desk and signed us in, then led me quickly to the cage door, where he thumbed through a laminated ledger that hung from the door on a lanyard.

Next, he unlocked an enormous padlock on the cage door, and we were in, my heart pounding in my ears as I stepped inside the cage. We walked down one of two main hallways, past endless numbered aisles, each with shelves from the cement floor to the twelve-foot ceiling of cyclone fencing. "What the fuck are you doing, Joe?" I asked myself, and screamed the answer in my mind,

"Ruining your career!" The fencing seemed to foreshadow my impending incarceration. I felt queasy.

We walked for at least five minutes in the same direction, and I was sweating profusely. Finally, I followed Matt to the right, down aisle 357, stopping thirty feet down the aisle where a black, stenciled number 21 was painted on the floor. I almost told Matt I would just follow him out, but knew I couldn't stop now.

In the middle of the aisle, a metal ladder on wheels reached to the top shelf. On the left, six boxes sat on the bottom shelf, each marked, "Walker, Allston."

"Here you go, Joe. I don't want to know what you have planned." Matt's tone was hushed and serious.

I was almost too nervous to speak. "Thanks. Really, thank you."

"Okay, listen. Burnsy is supposed to stay until seven, but he usually knocks off around five. You'll know when he turns off the lights. I'll sign us out. He'll be dozing. Here's the key to the padlock," he said, extending his hand. The small silver key slipped through my sweaty fingers, its clink on the cement floor echoing throughout the warehouse.

"Jesus, Joey. Are you okay?"

"Yeah. Sorry," I said picking up the key. "I've just never, you know…"

"Committed a felony? Yeah, me neither. As you heard, sound travels, so keep it quiet until he closes it down. Burnsy's supposed to walk the aisles before he leaves, but he never does. The only camera in here is by the gate, so put your hood up when you leave. Once you're out of the cage, you're home free. The warehouse isn't locked from the inside. My cell phone will be on. Let me know when you're out."

My mouth was too dry to speak, so I nodded. I listened to his footsteps travel back down the hallway until they disappeared, then heard the faint yet ominous clang of the door locking me inside.

CHAPTER 73

I wanted to find the phone right away, rather than waiting until Burnsy left and rooting around in the dark with my cell phone flashlight. Besides, I needed activity to keep my mind at bay. The last thing I needed was a flashback.

After shedding my hoodie, I carefully lifted the Walker boxes off the bottom shelf, avoiding contact with the ladder, and one by one sifted through their contents. There was the blood-stained clothing, the knife wrapped in bubble wrap, and Devaney's "that's him" note.

It felt strange to be alone with the objects. I thought about the stabbing and all the attack set in motion—Amanda, my father's memory, the trial. Now, all that was left were random scraps of evidence, packed away in aisle 357 amid thousands of generic boxes in the middle of a giant warehouse.

I found it in the third box I opened. The blood-smeared phone was packed tight inside a shoebox, wrapped in heavy plastic. I carefully placed the shoe box on the floor, replaced the larger boxes on the shelf, and sat down in the aisle.

At 5:30 p.m., my ass hurt and I was drenched in sweat. "Okay Burnsy," I whispered to myself. "Time to go home." Silently, I leaned back, eased myself back onto the floor, the cement cooling my moist back. I tried to relax and cursed my stupidity for trying to pull this off.

I had been picturing the sedentary officer snoozing behind the desk, so the soft echo of footsteps didn't register right away. I sat up in a panic and listened. He was coming my way. To my right and left were walls of boxes with no gaps for hiding, and I couldn't run down the aisle without the noise announcing my presence.

"What the hell! Officer Fat Ass chooses tonight to walk the aisles?" I felt nauseous as the footsteps grew louder. He was walking down the main walkway and would be thirty feet away, looking down my aisle in moments. I could hear his labored breathing now, puffing with each step.

Looking down the aisle toward the footsteps, I noticed that some of the boxes protruded into the aisle by what seemed like a few inches. Not enough to conceal me, but it was my only chance. I faced the box wall and stretched up to grab the highest shelf I could reach, jamming my sweaty fingers between cardboard and metal, flattening myself against the shelves. I held my breath as he trudged past, my toes dangling, just above the edge of the bottom shelf.

A few steps past my aisle, the footsteps stopped, but I could still hear his heavy breathing. Had he seen me? What was he doing? I remained frozen. I didn't dare risk a noisy dismount from my awkward position, but my shoulders were burning now and my out-of-shape core was quivering with fatigue. Then the footsteps resumed. I exhaled slowly as the steps grew gradually distant, only to stop again after about thirty seconds.

Then it occurred to me, while I was hanging there is pain, cursing my abandonment of my fitness routine after the first pathetic night of sit-ups. The obese officer wasn't patrolling. He was exercising and stopping to rest periodically. That's why he hadn't seen me. The footsteps began again.

I couldn't hold my grip much longer. As a single drop of perspiration trickled down the center of my back, I felt my fingers begin to slip. My dangling toes frantically reached for purchase but I misjudged the distance to the shelf, falling backwards to the warehouse floor. My fall was silent, until my shoulder nudged the ladder. The clatter of metal pierced the warehouse silence.

Again, Burnsy's footsteps stopped. I closed my eyes and froze, my teeth clenched, bracing for the worst. Maybe he hadn't heard it. He couldn't be sure, anyway. Surely there were occasional warehouse noises. And then it came.

"Hey! Who's there?"

CHAPTER 74

"Shit," I exhaled silently. I rose silently to my feet and picked up the shoebox and hoodie, ready to run like I stole something, which seemed appropriate. My mind flooded with horrible thoughts. I was pretty sure I could outrun Burnsy but the prospect of a sprint for freedom now seemed like a horrible plan. Wouldn't he just radio for backup? Surely, he wouldn't shoot me, but he certainly would use his taser if he got close enough.

Several seconds passed. Then, the sweet sounds of the big man's plodding footsteps again echoed throughout the warehouse, growing more distant with each step. I collapsed in relief, and considered my two options. Both were sub-optimal. I could wait for Burnsy to complete his exercise, risking being found out if his route crossed my path again, or I could make a run for the exit once he was out of sight.

Without further analysis, I found myself slipping off my shoes and tiptoeing down toward the main aisle. I peered down toward Burnsy just in time to see him disappear around a corner, maybe three hundred yards away.

I turned and sprinted toward the cage's exit, wondering if the officer had a taser, wondering if he carried a radio on his walk, and mostly wondering what in God's name I was doing burglarizing the police in my socks. After about twenty seconds at a full sprint, I stopped, doubled over at the knees and gasping for air. There was no sign of Burnsy behind me but I knew he'd be making his way back toward the exit by now, down the other main aisle of the warehouse.

I took off again, my lungs burning. The cage door seemed at least another three football fields away, so I paced myself, whispering, "Please don't shoot, please don't shoot" in rhythmic breaths. The hallway was endless and I felt like I was running the wrong way on an airport moving walkway.

A hundred yards from the exit, I stopped to pull on the hoodie, yanking it over my sweat-drenched back. I cinched the hood tight, fished Matt's key out of my pocket, and was off again. "Don't drop the key, don't drop the key." Sweat blurred my vision and my side ached, reminding me of fourth grade gym class. Why was I thinking about gym class? God my legs hurt. Focus, Joe!

Finally there, I set down the shoe box, dropped my shoes and collapsed against the cage door, clinging to the fencing with both hands, gasping for air. As my lungs heaved, I was overcome by a wave of nausea, and retched as I hung from the cage, my vomit splattering the cement.

I wiped my mouth and listened. Burnsy's faint steps were there again. He'd be rounding a corner not twenty feet away at some point. My sprint had bought me some time, but not more than a few minutes. Controlling my breathing with a shaky hand, I slid Matt's key into the massive padlock.

And nothing happened.

The key wouldn't turn. I felt my face heat up as I struggled with the lock. I took the key out and breathed deeply. Don't panic, Joe. I put the key in again, and tried to turn it right, then left to no effect. I looked at the corner. The footsteps were plainly audible now. He had to be less than fifty yards away.

Should I go hide again? I felt light-headed. Was this it? My career could be over. I pictured myself doing the perp walk, indicted for burglary. Everyone would assume I'd been tampering with evidence, which technically I was.

Shit, Joe! Think! Now I could hear his heavy breathing again. The steps paused again, then resumed, his final push to the finish. I texted Matt.

—*Key won't work!*—

His response was immediate.

—*Jiggle it.*—

I nearly laughed. I knew I would later if it opened. But now I could feel Burnsy very close, bearing down on me with each heavy stride and labored breath. I slid the key in again and jiggled it ever so slightly. The key smoothly turned to the right, the padlock clicked open and I was free. I dropped to my knees and frantically wiped up my vomit with the sleeves of my hoodie, picked up the shoe box, then quietly locked the gate behind me.

Outside the cage, clutching the shoebox in one hand and my shoes in the other, I ran for the green exit sign without looking back, my legs threatening to seize up with every stride. Outside, I peeled off the hoodie. A cool breeze against my soaked shirt gave me new life for a sprint to my car. I carefully placed the shoe box inside.

"Hey!" The harsh voice came from behind me in the street and made me jump out of my skin. I turned to see Matt, leaning out the window of his jeep. "Thought you might need the cavalry," he laughed.

I exhaled and shook my head, unable to speak.

The D.A. looked at me standing there, soaked in sweat, cradling my shoes and holding the disgusting sweatshirt at arms' length. "Counselor, you'd better keep your day job, because apparently you have no aptitude for crime." He was laughing as he drove away.

CHAPTER 75

High on adrenaline, I stayed up late, devoured a pizza and fell asleep filling out an online order for the lab. I was there when they opened at 9:00 a.m. to drop off the phone.

After coffee and an entertaining debriefing with Matt, I went to the gym to renew my membership and kill time while I waited for the call from the lab. My entire body hurt, so I would start the actual exercise another day. Baby steps.

The call officially confirming Allston Walker's innocence came at 4:15 p.m. The fingerprints on the rotary phone were not Walker's, nor Devaney's. To find the real attacker, the prints were being run through the national database at the request of Deputy District Attorney Matt Eisner. Matt had received an "anonymous tip" and had processed the phone for prints through the Alameda County Crime Lab.

I called Chuck with the good news and recounted my role in what would have been the slowest chase scene in cinematic history.

"Here's looking at you, kid."

"Thanks, Chuck."

Back home, while organizing some files, Amanda called again. I couldn't avoid it forever.

"Hi."

"Hi, Joe. I know how you must feel, but... he's my dad."

"I know. And I know I didn't exactly inspire a lot of confidence as his lawyer."

"No, that wasn't it."

"Well, that was part of it, Amanda. I drank my way through the trial. I was a mess, obviously. It was your dad, I get it. And without your…your move, well, it didn't look good."

"I still care about you."

I had thought a lot about my response. I guess that meant I knew she cared. Part of me wanted to think that she had used me from the beginning. She knew I'd always had a thing for her, so I'd be easy to manipulate. Believing in a grand Machiavellian plan to seduce me, only to treat my heart like a piñata would make it easy to say goodbye. But deep down, I was pretty sure she had acted out of desperation to save her father, something I wished I could have done for mine.

The problem was the foundation of our entire renewed relationship was built on her deception. Everything I had learned about her—the indescribable nuances that made me fall for her, the intimate shared feelings—all of it was now tainted by a tinge of doubt. To say nothing of the bigger questions. Did she really grow up without her dad around like me or was that part of the narrative she had sold me? Were our senses of humor truly the perfect match or were some of her laughs forced?

I forced myself to view our past through a clear and focused lens. The images were sharp, no longer distorted by shadows or shades of rose. "How did my guy do in court?" she had asked, and I recalled my delight in her words. She was, I supposed, sincere in her interest but "her guy" had been her dad. I had never been her guy and I felt silly for allowing myself to believe it.

God knows I was already insecure enough in the bedroom. Whereas once my mind replayed our lovemaking with joy and pleasure, now it critiqued my performance and questioned the results with jaded skepticism.

It wasn't that I didn't have feelings for Amanda. I just wasn't sure I knew her.

"I think I care about you, too. But..." I breathed deeply. "There's just been a lot, Amanda. I'm not sure I know you very well."

"Yeah, I know. I've been so dishonest." Several seconds of silence followed, while I remembered her texting those exact words once before, after I'd found out that Walker was her father.

"I'm still trying to figure out exactly what was real and what wasn't. I mean, the fake prostitute. That was your doing, right? Your first attempt at winning the case?"

A deep sigh gave me the answer I knew was coming.

"Our jokes about the cleaning fetish...." My voice trailed off. "I had such a good time with you, and I feel like it was all fake."

"Please don't say that."

I could have gone on but listing all her subtle deceptions would've been pointless. I didn't even want to know them all, but it didn't matter. They just kept seeping into my consciousness. Like now, when I finally realized what had been bothering me about the wording of Camacho's threat. "You all best back off or get hurt. You and Amanda," he had said. He could have just made it clear that Amanda was in danger if I didn't back off. Instead, he had specifically told her to back off as well.

I assumed Amanda's father had told her about the Camacho rumor, and she had poked around behind my back—maybe asked some tenants about his motive to commit the crime.

I thought of her fake shock when I told her of the threat on the phone. I didn't recall her exact words, but remembered her laying it on thick. *He said what? I'm not understanding this! Who is he?* Something to that effect. But I did recall the end of our conversation with crystal clarity. *I wish I was in your arms*, she had told me.

"I don't know what to say, I guess, Amanda."

"Well, I don't want to give up." Her voice changed its pitch, and I knew she was fighting tears.

"Stubborn, just like your dad."

"Well, for one thing, you really need a decorator." We both laughed, desperate for a break in the sadness. "And Joe, you probably don't believe me, but he's innocent."

And there it was. I didn't know the real Amanda, and she'd just proven that she didn't know me either. "I know he's innocent, Amanda." I swallowed hard and felt my voice starting to crack. "He told me the truth."

"Goodbye, Joe."

I collapsed into the recliner, blinking away tears. After a time, though, I thought of Allston Walker, now free from jail, maybe enjoying some warm apple pie. I thought of Kotkin's face when the verdict was read and relived the moment in my mind.

This time, I imagined approaching Kotkin as the jury filed out of the courtroom and extended a hand. "Do you like apples?" I asked.

"Yes," he said quizzically, shaking my hand.

"Well, how do you like them apples?" I asked triumphantly.

I recalled the comically absurd rescue of the fingerprint evidence, smiling at my pathetic footrace for freedom.

Then I pictured my dad, telling me bedtime stories about the courtroom as I snuggled in my Raiders bedspread. I thought he might be proud of me.

Not that day, but eventually, I thought of the girl upstairs who smelled like lime and imagined another witty line when I saw her again.

CHAPTER 76

It was 11:15 p.m. and Loren Mello was texting with her girlfriend, sipping coffee, occasionally glancing up at her computer screen. So far, for the graduate student at Cal, the promised exciting internship at the Alameda County Crime Lab had proven a cure for insomnia. Rather than using her forensic expertise to solve cold cases, she was entering data into Codis, the national DNA Database maintained by the FBI, and waiting for a "cold hit."

The data entry was tedious enough but at least she was doing something. As she had explained to her friends, her job consisted of staring at the pale blue screen with the spinning blue circle in the middle until it stopped spinning, then entering another DNA profile and watching the ball spin some more. During her six-hour shift, she repeated the mind-numbing process forty to fifty times.

The intern didn't notice the change in her screen right away. She was more than halfway through her late-night shift and the caffeine was wearing off. When it registered, she sat up suddenly, blinked twice and re-read the message, which appeared in bold type.

"URGENT. SAMPLE IDENTIFIED. MULTIPLE-ALLELE MATCH."

CHAPTER 77

The young man's DNA had been in the system for four years, ever since he'd severely beaten a football player who had picked on a friend from his special-education class. Diagnosed with borderline personality disorder and autism as a child, he took medication to manage his mood swings.

Oakland Police detectives found him at the Golden Gate Fields racetrack, his pockets stuffed with betting slips, cash and carrots. The interrogation, if you can call it that, was brief.

"I could tell Beau was hurt." The young man spoke slowly, in a monotone southern drawl, without a hint of deceit. "He's got a longer race name, but I call him Beau."

"How'd you know, Denny? How'd you know the horse was hurt?"

"Cause he t…" He stopped to smile. "Y'all are gonna say I'm crazy, but them horses talk to me." He looked down and bit his bottom lip. "That Beau was a good horse," he said, nodding to himself, then looking up with moist eyes. "My favoritest one."

"Anyway, Beau didn't want to run, but they ran him, 'course. I didn't want to bet on him on account of I knew he'd try real hard to win if I did. Beau always knew when I wanted him to win. I didn't want to bet on him but Uncle Jeff made me. Said he needed a big win."

"This is your uncle, Jefferson Devaney?" the detective asked, pushing the tape recorder closer to his suspect.

Denny paused, staring off into space, then sighed. "I guess they say he broke both his front legs, so they had to, you know, put him down."

"And did that make you upset?"

"Yeah, cuz, ya know, Beau being my favoritest horse and all."

"What happened when you got home, Denny?"

"Well, Uncle Jeff wanted his money stuffed in his jar, but I didn't have no money cuz I forgot to cash the slips that day. I guess, on account of being sad about Beau."

"Okay. So, what happened at your Uncle Jeff's place?"

"It was my fault for not cashing those slips," he said earnestly. "Anyway, he yelled at me, and I..." The young man looked down.

"Did you get angry, Denny?"

"Yeah. I just felt like if Uncle Jeff didn't make me bet, then Beau wouldn't a hurt hisself trying to win for me." He wiped his tear-streaked face with his shirtsleeve. "I saw a knife there so I just started stabbin' Uncle Jeff. Then I felt bad. Tried to call for help, but..." He paused again and smiled sheepishly across the table. "But I couldn't think. Sometimes I just don't think right."

"Thank you, Denny." The detective's tone was compassionate. "We're going to get you something to eat and drink. And Denny, do you take any medications? They'll be asking me at the j..." He stopped in mid-sentence.

"I used to but I don't anymore on account of Uncle Jeff don't like me to take 'em. Says I can't pick his horses if I'm drugged up." Denny spoke up again as the detective reached the door. "Um, you know, Uncle Jeff said it was okay. Said he forgives me and all, so long as, you know, I keep picking his horses for him."

"Okay, Denny, we'll have to sort this out."

"Cuz, I should be getting back to the horses," he said quietly. "They'll be missin' me."

ABOUT THE AUTHOR

T.L. Bequette is a criminal defense attorney-turned author from Lafayette, California. His debut novel, *Good Lookin'*, the first of the Joe Turner series, was hailed by Kirkus reviews as "a rigorous, thoroughly engrossing mystery from a writer with immense potential." As an attorney, Mr. Bequette has tried more than thirty murder trials, mostly defending young men in Oakland. He holds degrees from The University of the Pacific and Georgetown Law School and serves annually on faculty of the Stanford Law School Trial Advocacy Clinic. The third in the series of Joe Turner Mysteries is in the works.

NOTE FROM THE AUTHOR

Word-of-mouth is crucial for any author to succeed. If you enjoyed *Blood Perfect*, please leave a review online—anywhere you are able. Even if it's just a sentence or two. It would make all the difference and would be very much appreciated.

Thanks!
T.L. Bequette

We hope you enjoyed reading this title from:

BLACK ROSE writing™

www.blackrosewriting.com

Subscribe to our mailing list – *The Rosevine* – and receive **FREE** books, daily deals, and stay current with news about upcoming releases and our hottest authors.
Scan the QR code below to sign up.

Already a subscriber? Please accept a sincere thank you for being a fan of Black Rose Writing authors.

View other Black Rose Writing titles at www.blackrosewriting.com/books and use promo code **PRINT** to receive a **20% discount** when purchasing.

We hope you enjoyed reading this title from

BLACK ROSE
writing

www.blackrosewriting.com

Subscribe to our mailing list – The Rosevine – and receive FREE books, daily deals, and stay current with news about upcoming releases and our hottest authors.

Scan the QR code below to sign up.

Already a subscriber? Please accept a sincere thank you for being a fan of Black Rose Writing authors.

WITHDRAWN

View other Black Rose Writing titles at www.blackrosewriting.com/books and use promo code PRINT to receive a 20% discount when purchasing.